DEVIL
SENT THE
RAIN

Also by Lisa Turner

A Little Death in Dixie
The Gone Dead Train

DEVIL SENT THE RAIN

A Mystery

LISA TURNER

wm

WILLIAM MORROW

An Imprint of HarperCollins*Publishers*

HarperCollins books may be purchased for educational, business, or sales promotional use. For information please e-mail the Special Markets Department at SPsales@harpercollins.com.

FIRST EDITION

Designed by Diahann Sturge

Library of Congress Cataloging-in-Publication Data has been applied for.

ISBN 978-0-06-213621-3

16 17 18 19 20   RRD   10 9 8 7 6 5 4 3 2 1

For Rob Sangster, the "Travelin' Man"

DEVIL
SENT THE
RAIN

Prologue

The radio was playing "Blue Skies" when the gun went off.

She'd been the one driving. They talked about the good times ahead, the wedding, the baby. A fresh start. Then the conversation turned sad. She tuned the radio to an oldies station.

Let's not talk about Finn, she said. Not tonight.

"Blue Skies" came on, her favorite version with Willie Nelson singing the Irving Berlin classic, the perfect song for a cold and rainy November night.

If the baby was a girl, she'd name her Skye.

She was only twenty-nine, but her obstetrician had warned this could be a high-risk pregnancy. She might not carry the baby to term if she didn't stop taking the drugs. No more alcohol. No more stress, the doctor said. Take a sabbatical from your law practice until the baby comes.

Pregnant. It's the word that changes everything. Her life had gone from disaster to wedding bells, from hot mess to lollipop dreams in a matter of days. Her mother used to say, "Caroline, you have a talent for picking the wrong men."

Not this time, Mom.

Rain misted the Camaro's windshield. She flipped on the

wipers and pulled the sweater close about her shoulders, glad to have it, a last-minute offering to keep away the chill. It was blue, a sentimental color, perfect for a wedding. She'd left her coat at home not wanting to crush the delicate lace on the sleeves of her dress. French nuns had made the lace a hundred years ago for her great grandmother's wedding dress. So beautiful and it might bring a touch of luck.

She turned up the music and glanced over at the passenger side expecting a smile to come to her through the shadows. Instead she was met with the barrel of a gun. The face behind the gun—the one she truly loved—was unrecognizable.

"Turn here."

The voice sounded strange, impersonal. Stunned, she did as she was told, the car's headlights sliding along the white board fence in the darkness.

"Pull over."

"Why?" she asked, her own voice thin as a child's.

"I said *pull over.*"

Gravel popped beneath the tires as they dropped off the pavement. Something about the sound made her know that if she stopped the car she was dead.

"No!" Her hand came off the wheel and knocked the gun away. The car lit with a flash and a deafening bang. Her ears rang. Her foot jammed down on the accelerator. The Camaro leapt forward and smashed into a farm gate then flew into the field and hit with a jolt. The car's rear end fishtailed in the mud. Dark figures with scarlet eyes and glistening nostrils lumbered past the headlights. The engine raced. The car nose-dived and slammed to a stop. She pushed back off the steering wheel and made a grab for the gun, fighting and twisting the barrel. The gun flashed again. The bullet struck with the force of a punch to the face. She sank into darkness. Paralyzing silence.

She lost time.

She felt a warm hand on her arm, fingers stroking her lace sleeve. The sweater lifted from her shoulders. Something heavy fell in her lap. She opened her eyes.

But you loved me. Why did you do this?

Her cheek burned. Something warm and wet ran from her nose. The passenger door clicked open. The light was too bright.

Please don't leave. The baby.

The door shut. The light cut off. She closed her eyes. Rain peppered the roof. Willie Nelson sang as she drifted in the dark.

Blue skies, smiling at me. Nothing but blue skies do I see . . .

Chapter 1

The Ford F-150 pickup rocked along in the dark, spinning up loose gravel on the park's access road. The old truck, loaned to him by his brother-in-law, had busted struts and seats soaked in defoliants and nicotine. The brakes were shot. Through the hole in the floorboard he could see the asphalt flying by, but he had no complaints. He was headed to work early, 4:00 am, fingernails clipped and his hair slicked back. Roscoe Hanson was lean and clean. The ladies love a clean man, especially a man with tattoos. He had his eye on a young thing working the line, the one with the big tits and soft mouth. She made sure to bump his butt when she passed on her way to the sink.

The truck's headlights streamed across the white board fence. Cold night air rolled through the cab window intoxicating his thoughts. The white line dropped off at the farm gate and picked up again. Ten seconds down the road his brain clicked in. He pumped the brakes and backed onto the shoulder to shine his high beams. The aluminum gate was bent in the middle and hanging open, the kind of damage done by a swerving car.

The herd of bison in that field was the park's biggest attraction. He didn't understand why people lined their cars on the road to watch a bunch of fancy damned buffalo at feeding time, but they did. Securing those bison might mean a reward. He leaned across the seat and opened the glove box for the flashlight.

As he climbed out of the truck, the night around him was black as carbon from the rainstorm that had just passed. He sensed the dark forms ranging through the pasture, disturbed and restless, their padded hooves heavy on the wet grass. No way to know if any of them had escaped to the road. Hit one of them monsters and you'd be road jelly. When he got to the restaurant, he'd call the Shelby Farms office and leave a message saying how he'd kept their animals from crashing into cars on Walnut Grove.

He used the flashlight to scrounge baling wire from the truck bed. He was wiring the gate shut when a bison somewhere deep in the field must have moved because a slice of red taillight was suddenly visible in the dark. *Sumbitch.* The car that had smashed the gate was out there. Either the driver walked out and left the gate open, or he was passed out drunk behind the wheel. Give the guy a hand and he might come across with a couple of twenties.

He unwired the gate, searching the dark for the bison. No matter. Ain't nothing out there but a herd of cows called by a different name.

The muck in the field slimed his boots as he made his way to the back of a red 1968 Chevy Camaro Z/28. A gotdamned hot car. The engine was running, exhaust puffing from the tailpipe. He shone the beam over the vanity plate. SPARROW. The flashlight dimmed. He shook it and fanned the light across the car's interior. A woman was in the driver's seat. She was alone.

"Hey, you. In the car. You all right?" He rapped on the trunk with his knuckles and walked around to the driver's side. The woman had her head turned away from the window, her blond hair covering the side of her face. He tapped the glass with the rim of the flashlight and shone the light inside.

"Hey."

She didn't respond.

He trailed the light over her white dress and down the long skirt she'd piled onto the center console. The beam caught the sparkle of a small handbag in her lap. He got it. This was a bride, a runaway bride. Before the guy could get her out of the dress she'd stolen his car and run the damned thing into the field. Hot damn this was rich. He opened the door. The interior light came on.

"Wake up, lady."

Passed out. Drunk like he'd figured. Weddings will do that. In-laws start fistfights in the parking lot. The groom goes out back of the hall with his buddies and gets ripped then makes a fool of himself on the dance floor. Can't blame a gal for running off. He touched her hand and snatched back from it. She was cold as lard. Then he saw the blood on the front of her dress.

Jesus God, she was dead. Been dead awhile. He took a step back, unwilling to be caught with a dead woman when he was four months out on parole and getting his act up and running again. His gaze went to the handbag with little crystals sparkling in the dome light. Hell, she didn't need it so why not? He grabbed it, opened it. Inside was the usual crap and—Wow!—a silver money clip, its jaws wide around a stack of bills. He stuffed the money in his pocket, wiped his prints off the frame of the bag and flipped it across the woman to the passenger side. Smart move coming here. Time to get out.

He was backing away when a pounding sound made him swing around and raise the flashlight. The beam struck the eye of a bull charging at him like a battering ram. *Shit!* He scrambled to put the car between him and the bull and made it as far as the front tire when he knew the bull had him. The massive head hooked upward and sent him flying, his body slamming onto the Camaro's hood. The bull backed off and bellowed, swung his head, and charged again, ramming the fender so hard the car shuddered. He climbed to his hands and knees. Pain jolted through his shoulder as he flung himself onto the roof. He grabbed his arm. His hand came away bloody.

The bull stood six feet from the Camaro, shaking his horns and shifting side to side. No phone. No traffic. But there would be. There would be cops.

He was fucked.

Chapter 2

Detective Billy Able fumbled in the dark for his mobile phone vibrating on the nightstand. He checked the screen. Dispatch. A 5:33 am call out.

"Able," he answered, his voice rough with sleep. He felt for the water glass on the nightstand and took a swallow.

"Morning, Detective. A park ranger out at Shelby Farms got himself a dead female in a car. EMS made their run. Perimeter's set."

"What's the location?"

"Farm Road at Walnut Grove."

Billy visualized the spot where the access road met the busy thoroughfare. Not a high crime area. "Which side of the road?"

"Not the road. The pasture."

He sat up. "Where they keep the bison?"

"You got it."

He swung his legs over the side of the bed. "Call Malone. Have her meet me there."

"By the way, that ranger was pretty shook up," the dispatcher said. "He kept going on about a wedding dress."

Billy hung up and listened for the sound of rain that had pounded the deck outside his porthole all night long. Rain had blown through the city off and on for most of November. The weatherman blamed late tropical storms spinning up from the gulf, but this rain had felt more like retribution than the effects of high and low pressures.

Awake now, he headed for the bathroom to scrub the back of his neck with a soapy washcloth and give himself a quick shave. A wedding dress. What the hell was that about? First reports were generally unreliable. Probably the ranger's first dead body.

Bush-league casework used to drive him crazy when he was coming up in the squad as a hotshot detective wearing shades and thrift store suits. His cocky attitude had worked as long as his partner was the most seasoned cop on the squad. Then his partner offed himself and everything went to hell. But you can't dwell on that kind of loss. It only makes you cynical.

Coming out of the bathroom he dressed in a heavy cotton shirt, a fleece vest, and a waterproof Memphis Police Department jacket. He slipped his SIG P250 compact .40 caliber into a concealed holster and patted his badge wallet in his pocket. At thirty-three, he was less of a hothead and more passionate about the work. The job was the thing. He'd given himself over to it.

He drank two cups of black coffee and ate cheese toast standing over the sink then sat on the sofa to pull on his field boots. Across the room a brand-new Samsung flat screen waited inside the box. He'd planned to install it tomorrow so he could come home and watch the UofM Tigers basketball game on a big screen. From the sound of the call out, that wasn't going to happen.

Scooping his keys out of a metal bowl on the counter, he glanced around the living area of his home, a self-propelled barge that had been converted to a rental and docked on the Mississippi River in downtown Memphis. Five years ago a friend had purchased the barge at auction and moved it to a slip in the slack water near the Hernando de Soto Bridge known to Memphians as the new bridge. The friend had the barge refitted as a bar and grill and turned it over to his son to manage. The place went bust inside of two years as bars are known to do. His friend installed a shower and turned the small office into a bedroom. The place was great for a guy who worked downtown and who liked to watch the river traffic and the sunset on the water. Billy had signed a three-year lease.

Outside in the pre-dawn darkness he turned to lock his door, his breath coming out in puffs beneath the overhead light. The deck felt slick beneath his boots. Rain, rain, rain. The bison field would be trampled to a muddy mess. At the bottom of the ramp, pools of water surrounded his city-issued Dodge Charger parked next to his personal car. He got in and started the engine, trying to recall if anyone had ever been murdered in the park. No, not since he'd been on the squad. Possibly a jogger had a heart attack, but that was it. He texted his partner to confirm she was familiar with the scene's location. Frankie Malone wasn't a Memphis girl, and Shelby Farms was at the outer boundary of their jurisdiction.

She texted back "K." He dropped the transmission into drive and rolled up the steep cobblestone landing.

The sky was lightening to a morose gray as he took the Walnut Grove exit to the 4500-acre park. For decades the park had been known as the Shelby County Penal Farm, where low-risk offenders had done their time by farming the acreage for their food and selling the overage for profit. Now Shelby Farms was one of the largest urban parks in the nation.

At the Farm Road traffic light, an officer waved him past the black-and-white-striped barrier to park at the head of the line of the service vehicles. He noticed an EMT in the back of the ambulance wrapping a man's arm with gauze. The man was seated and staring out at the road, his face narrow with sunken cheeks and hair combed back off his forehead.

In the field to Billy's left, he saw the bison had crowded themselves against the far fence line. Two females moaned. The bull paced in front of them and shook his massive head, wanting an excuse to charge. The activity on the road and the smell of blood must be putting the herd on edge. They were a well-fed, amiable lot, willing to remain behind a fence they could easily smash through, but they were also capable of attacking a man on foot. Could be the reason for the man's bandaged arm.

Directly ahead his partner was standing in the road in the flat light of dawn, speaking with a tall guy dressed in a uniform and wearing a Smokey the Bear hat.

The ranger towered over Frankie's five-foot-five frame, but her intensity was what drew Billy's eye. He had requested her as a partner upon his return to the department after a nine-month leave. She'd been new to the squad, but what she lacked in experience she'd made up with drive, intelligence, and a talent for exhaustive research.

Her gaze flicked in his direction. She held up a finger to say "hold on" while the ranger recited his notes.

Billy got out of his car and leaned against the fender to take in the scene beginning with the red Camaro several hundred feet out in the field. He was looking at the rear end of the car, the front of it tilted down in the field's natural trough. The driver's door was hanging open, and white fabric spilled over the door frame. That must be the dress the ranger had been going on about.

He walked the road, taking in the damaged farm gate and the

truck parked beside it with rusted-out doors and its back bumper wired on. Officers had already blocked off skid marks on the side of the road with orange cones. He squatted down to inspect the marks. The Camaro had been traveling north, pulled off onto the shoulder, and then accelerated, leaving remnants of rubber scrubbed off on the rises and falls of the asphalt. The driver must have lost control, smacked into the gate, and fishtailed in the mud until the car had come to a stop in the low-lying trough running through the center of the field.

Too soon to draw conclusions.

He stood at the sound of shod hooves on the road, two men arriving on horseback to move the herd so they could get out to the Camaro. Frankie was finishing with the park ranger, who handed her a package. They clasped hands and parted.

She walked toward Billy dressed in her Memphis Police Department waterproof jacket that she'd had tailored to fit her petite frame. Under the jacket she wore a turtleneck sweater and dark slacks stuffed inside a pair of Wellington boots. The boots were blue and covered with yellow baby ducks.

"We have a white female deceased behind the wheel," she said as she came up to him. "Single gunshot wound to the right cheek. No exit wound. EMTs found the driver's side door open and the victim DRT, 'dead right there.' They ran a strip to confirm absence of heart activity. The bull took a run at them. We'll have to wait for the herd to be moved before we can evaluate the scene."

"Good morning," he said. "Love the boots."

"Don't make fun. They work."

She was the damnedest creature. He'd never met anyone so set on following the rules until she decided to break them.

Frankie liked to keep fit. She wore her mink-brown hair cut short and minimal makeup, the kind of woman who didn't need to check herself in every mirror she passed. Standing this close, he could smell her lavender shampoo, which meant she'd showered before making the scene. Her ability to appear wide-awake with her motor constantly running unnerved him.

"Are you thinking suicide?" he asked.

"The vic is dressed in a wedding gown, so yeah, suicide crossed my mind."

He laughed. She blinked, unaware she'd said something revealing.

"Do we have a suspect?" He indicated the man seated in the back of the ambulance.

"Roscoe Hanson. That's his truck next to the gate. He says he was on his way to work when he noticed the gate was open and stopped to close it. The bull attacked when he entered the field to check the driver. The ranger found him on top of the vehicle hollering his head off. He'll need stitches. The EMTs have patched him up, so we can chat with him before he's transported to the MED."

She handed over the package made of folded newspaper. "It's a money clip the ranger found near the car. He figures Hanson took it off the victim and tossed it once he was trapped."

Billy studied the sterling clip that secured several one-hundred-dollar bills. "Have an officer drag Hanson's ass over here."

Roscoe Hanson was a wiry specimen around five foot seven with the cagey walk of a man with a progressive criminal record. He had on cowboy boots with stacked heels meant to add two inches to his height and his jeans jacket draped over his shoulders. A splotch of blood had soaked through the gauze on his bandaged right arm.

Billy nodded at the pickup as Hanson approached. "We should lock you up for that piece of shit you're driving."

Hanson raised his bandaged arm. "Fine by me. The city's going to buy me a new ride. Nerve damage, post-traumatic stress. Good for a hundred thou easy."

"I hear all that. Tell me about the woman in the Camaro."

"I don't know a damned thing."

He knew Hanson's type—a repeater who is wise to the system and knows how to work it.

"Where were you last night?"

Hanson smiled. "Out. With buddies."

"You got a job?"

"The Cracker Barrel. I'm a fry cook."

"These people you were hanging out with," he said. "I want names, numbers, and where to find them."

Hanson's eyes shifted.

"Where you living?" he asked.

"I got a trailer, back of my sister's property."

Billy held up the money clip between two fingers. "Want to explain this?"

Hanson scratched the side of his nose. "Never seen it before."

"I say we'll find your prints on this clip and the gun when we find it. You might as well cooperate. Things will go easier."

"I never touched that money, and I sure as hell didn't shoot that woman."

The bull bellowed as the horsemen circled the herd. Hanson's head jerked in that direction. "That bastard nearly tore off my arm."

"Okay, stay with me," Billy said, using a conciliatory tone. A switch in approach sometimes worked. "Here's how I see it. You found the lady passed out and started to help yourself to her purse. She came to, she pulled a gun. The two of you struggled. Bang."

"No sir. I stopped to close the gate and saw taillights in the field. She was dead when I found her."

Frankie walked up. "I ran Hanson's sheet. Two times down. Moved from carjacking to home invasion. He stuck a gun in a drug dealer's face and threatened his pregnant wife. Pulled eight years. Gated out of Turney Center four months ago."

Billy sucked his teeth. "Roscoe, your sheet makes me think, 'Out of prison and this dude gets himself a gun. He's capable of doing a lot of damage quickly.'"

"Now hold on," Roscoe said.

"You broke parole, so you're heading back to—" He turned to Frankie. "Where did you say?"

"Turney. Down the road from Bucksnort, Tennessee. Maximum security."

Billy shook his head. "Too bad. You won't make bond, so we'll keep you locked up till we find a way to charge you with murder. At the very least, you're going back in the program at Turney Center to serve out your sentence."

"I *ain't* fired *no* gun." Roscoe shoved his palms forward. "Run the swabs. Line me up a lawyer. I said all I'm gonna say."

Frankie gave Billy an eye roll. They were done with Roscoe for now.

"You follow through on the residue swabs and run the plates," he said to her. "I'm going in for a look at the body."

Frankie nodded, but he caught the twitch at the side of her

mouth. She hated to be ordered around, the same way he'd felt when his old partner had made a point of belittling him.

"Please and thank you, ma'am," he added.

Her mouth curved up, and she clamped a hand on Hanson's shoulder. "Come on, Roscoe. Let's find out how dirty your hands are."

Chapter 3

The horsemen move the herd along the fence and toward the gate. Billy circled left to stay out of their way and trudged through the bison flop and soured mud, dropping markers as he went for the CSU crew to follow. Footprints left by the ranger and first responders had mucked up the ground on all sides of the car. Casting impressions was going to be a hell of a job.

First thing he noticed as he approached the Camaro was the vanity plate on the back. SPARROW. Odd choice for a muscle car. Must be a story there.

The driver's side door was open, the victim seated behind the wheel, her left arm hanging at her side. He noted the purple discoloration of her fingertips and the lack of an engagement or wedding ring on her finger. Her body was angled toward the car's interior, her head falling forward causing a curtain of blond hair to obscure her face. Leaning inside the car, he saw her right hand laying palm up on the console. Her little finger was bruised, possibly broken. Looked like she'd put up a fight.

The voluminous train of the dress filled the driver's foot well and overflowed onto the console. The victim had pushed it to one side to access the gearshift. The transmission had remained in Drive. Her foot depressing the brake pedal and frozen there in death was the reason Hanson had seen the taillights burning.

A wedding gown and no rings. Did Hanson take the rings or had the victim fought with the groom and removed them? Or had she been on her way to be married when she died? He radioed Frankie to have Hanson frisked for the rings before being transported from the scene.

He walked around the back of the car and put on latex gloves before opening the passenger side door. An evening bag lay on the floor. Frankie could inspect its contents and search the car for a weapon. She was good at that. She never overlooked the details.

He leaned in, aware of the faint, fetid odor of death. Last night's low temperature had slowed the degradation of the body, but that would change as the day warmed. The Camaro would never be free of the smell. He scanned the back seat and looked up to see the small rip in the black fabric headliner above the driver's seat. Possibly a bullet hole. He snapped a photo with his mobile.

Moving on, he rested his hand on the edge of the seat and leaned in farther for a look at the victim. Beneath the veil of blond hair, he saw where a bullet had entered below her right cheekbone and most likely found a path through the sinuses to the brain. Blood had leaked from her nostrils and dripped onto the front of the dress. Suicides usually aim for the temple, or they eat the barrel. This wound didn't appear to be self-inflicted.

He snapped more photos. Despite the dress covering her torso, arms and legs, he could tell the body was already losing muscle shape. The muscles in her jaw had loosened, dropping her mouth open. Lividity appeared only in her reddish earlobes, her fingertips, and the back of her wrist that rested on the console, but full rigor had begun to set in. Life had abandoned this body several hours ago.

"What happened here, sweetheart?" he murmured and reached across to move the hair draped over her face. Powder tattoo marks speckled her cheek around the wound. The reddish-brown color indicated she'd been alive when she was shot, and the gun had been fired from about a foot away. It takes a particular kind of viciousness to shoot someone in the face at that close range. He looked past the damaged cheek and focused on her features already distorted by gravity—eyelids drooping, bowed mouth drawn down, a tiny beauty mark in the right corner.

Recognition struck. He stumbled back from the car, swearing. The victim was Caroline Lee. No, maybe not. The deterioration was significant. This woman may only look like her. He forced himself to lean back in and saw on her right wrist a small scar, a scrape from a barbed wire fence. He remembered the day it happened.

It was Caroline.

She'd called a few days ago to let him know she was now the attorney of record for his uncle's will. Before hanging up she'd said, "Good to hear your voice again, Billy."

He stood beside the car and wiped away tears. The vanity plate made sense to him now. Sparrow. Her dad used to call her that name. He looked around the vacant field, his breath streaming out in the cold. He wondered if she'd suffered—waiting alone in the dark for help to come.

He heard the farm gate on the road scrape across gravel as it swung open. Frankie was just starting up the path he'd marked. They would inspect the body together, pick over the scene, open a file, and compile evidence. They would draw conclusions about suspects and write affidavits for warrants. All by the book, all impersonal. Suddenly the business of murder sickened him.

The ground beneath him seemed to tilt as he walked around the back of the car to intercept Frankie, feeling the need to come between her and Caroline. Rage was building in his gut.

"Why the hell are you wearing those ridiculous boots?" he barked as she walked up.

She looked at him hard. "Why do you care?"

"They're an insult to the victim."

Her lips parted. "What in God's name is wrong with you?"

He lifted his chin at her mobile, struggling for control. "Forget it. Did you find anything?"

Her gaze stayed with him a couple of beats longer than it had to. "Our victim is Caroline Lee, age twenty-nine. She works as an estate attorney at the Lee Law Firm, daughter of Saunders and Rosalyn Lee. That's as blueblood as you get in this city, right? The car's registered in her name. Kind of unusual for a society babe to drive a muscle car."

He nodded. A hawk was riding the air currents high above the pasture across the road. It folded its wings and dove behind the tree break.

He wondered if he could hold on.

Frankie continued. "Her name came up in the *Commercial Appeal*'s wedding announcement archives. She was to marry a Dr. Raj Sharma five weeks ago." She frowned, staring at him. "Billy? Are you listening? You should see your face."

He had to tell her. She had a right to know. "The Lees have a home in Mississippi. The family used to come by my uncle's diner. Saunders Lee was my uncle's attorney. Caroline Lee called a few days ago to tell me she was closing out his will."

He searched the sky for the hawk. Instead he saw Caroline's face close to his, her arms wrapped around his bare neck, her body glued to his. "One, two, three," she would whisper, and they'd spring from the tree limb that stretched over the lake at the back of her father's property.

They would hit the water as one.

He realized Frankie was studying him.

"You really think we should work this case?" she asked.

"I haven't seen the Lees in years. I'm not a part of my uncle's will. I'll inform Middlebrook, but I don't expect a problem."

The hawk lifted in the air from behind the tree break. Something squirmed in its beak.

His rage returned. He imagined Caroline fighting for her life, the bullet striking, her body shutting down.

His blood pulsed, pushing out the words. "If I get my hands on the son of a bitch who did this, I'll kill him."

Chapter 4

Frankie watched her partner fumble in his jacket for a pen. He opened his memo book, wrote a few words, crossed them out and wrote again. His hand was shaking. The media was going to zero in on this scene, and Billy was in no shape to have a microphone stuck in his face.

"The watch commander is here," she said. "I've contacted Deputy Chief Middlebrook's office. The chief is doing a grip-and-grin at a Chamber of Commerce breakfast at the Racquet Club. He'll be here soon as he learns the victim is Saunders Lee's daughter."

Billy blinked a few times as if coming back to himself. "Right. There's a handbag in the front seat. Check around the car's interior for a weapon and ejected casings. I'll search the trunk."

She walked around the car and squatted beside the opened passenger's side door. Tiny crystals sparkled on the handbag resting on the floor inside. She put on gloves and pulled a folded piece of paper from her pocket to spread on the mat where she dumped the handbag's contents—driver's license, tube of lipstick, a smartphone, and at the bottom of the bag a pearl-handled derringer. She bent and sniffed the barrel. Not recently fired.

Placing a knee on the seat, she leaned in and used her phone to snap close-ups of the gunshot wound and bruised hand. She backed off for a couple of wide-angle shots then checked the photos. The ruined face and bloody gown made the shots look like a Wes Craven movie poster. Billy obviously cared about this woman. No wonder he was so upset.

She stepped away for a breath of fresh air, for some reason feeling a connection with this woman. They were close to the same age, both of them at the beginning of their careers. Lives of innocent people can be snatched away in an instant. That's probably what happened here. She walked around to the driver's side door. The dress looked like a Pat Kerr original, a Memphis designer who has an international reputation for creating wedding gowns from heirloom lace. Kneeling to bunch the skirt, she peered at the floorboard beneath the victim's feet. No weapon there.

Stepping back she noticed the side zipper on the dress was halfway down. Did the victim leave the zipper undone to make getting in and out of the car easier or had she put on weight in the weeks since the final fitting?

She walked to where Billy was staring inside the open trunk, his hands in his pockets. His color was better. He seemed to have calmed down. Inside the trunk was a small Louis Vuitton suitcase with its lid up. A pink negligee lay on top. Frankie could smell the perfume.

"The trunk is empty except for this bag," he said.

"There's a derringer in her handbag. It hasn't been fired."

He nodded.

"You don't seem surprised the victim was carrying."

"Mississippi women carry pistols, even grandmothers. A .32 goes in the purse, a .357 under the car seat."

"What are these women afraid of?" she asked.

"Not a damned thing. You grow up in the country, you're comfortable with guns."

She studied the negligee. "Looks like she packed for a honeymoon, yet she was supposed to have been married five weeks ago."

"And no rings," he said.

"No rings. Got any ideas?"

"First scenario. She was married sometime on Monday. The couple had a fight. She took off. She was texting or maybe she was drunk. She lost control of the car and ended up in the field. She called the guy to come get her. He parked on the road, walked in, and shot her. He walked out and drove away."

"That doesn't explain the bullet hole above her head."

"Second idea. She had a passenger. They pulled over, had an argument. He pulled a gun and they struggled. That's your bullet in the headliner. She hit the gas, ran into the gate, and drove into the field. He killed her with the second shot."

"Try this one," she said. "The zipper on the dress is undone. Someone came to her house, forced her to put on the dress, abducted, and killed her."

"That's possible. And there's Hanson, but I have a hunch he didn't do it."

"Why's that?"

"He's so damned sure of himself. He's talking about collecting damages from the city, not beating a murder charge. He ripped off the money clip, got trapped on the roof, and realized the clip would send him back to Turney. He wiped his prints and tossed it."

She marveled at how Billy relied on gut feeling to solve cases. Logic was her thing. They made a great team, except that she'd begun to feel cramped in her position as his understudy.

The chop of helicopter blades broke the air as Channel Five Traffic Scan flew south over the stalled traffic on Walnut Grove. It banked north and turned.

She looked at the line of cruisers and service vehicles on the road. "The pilot knows something's up. He's going to do a flyover. They'll want footage for the morning broadcast."

Billy pulled a rag from the trunk and tucked it around the license plate as the chopper approached. "The media will foam at the mouth soon as they know the victim is a Lee. We need a tent. And I want to notify her parents before they see her car on TV."

Chapter 5

own at the road, Billy requested that officers be dispatched to Caroline's home to secure it as a possible secondary crime scene. Anyone with access could go in and destroy evidence, including the killer. He advised CSU to requisition a tent and asked the watch commander to take over the scene until Chief Middlebrook arrived, so they could locate the family and make the death notification.

They took his car. He drove on the shoulder to bypass the traffic, the black Charger's LED lights flashing in the front grill and back deck. Frankie found the Lees' address, their home located in the Shady Grove area nearby. He hoped to make the notification before the Lees left for morning appointments at their law office.

At the light in front of the hospital, he turned left and drove quiet streets that wound through some of the most expensive properties in the city. Enclaves surrounded by stone walls served as sanctuaries for the Delta plantation society who, bonded by birth and wealth, took their privileges for granted. The Lees lived inside the walls of Shaking Tree, the most exclusive neighborhood in the area.

Saunders Lee and his wife Rosalyn managed the family's

venerable Memphis law firm, and maintained Airlee Plantation, Saunders Lee's ancestral home in Mississippi. The plantation's big house needed constant tending as did the grounds, formal gardens, and the greenhouses maintained year-round to provide fresh cut flowers.

Billy had met the family as a teenager when, on Saturday afternoons, Saunders Lee would stop by the diner, Kane's Kanteen, bringing along his young daughter Caroline, his son Martin, and their various cousins. While the kids ate at the picnic table outside, Mr. Lee and Billy's uncle Kane would sit at the front window table and discuss Mississippi politics.

Although Kane had dropped out of school in the ninth grade, he was a sharp observer of human nature. Having an educated man, a plantation owner like Mr. Lee, ask his opinion about the state senate race meant the world to Kane. After about an hour, the men would stand and shake hands as if having reached an agreement. Kane would then move to Mr. Lee's chair and smoke a cigarette while studying the traffic out the window.

His uncle always held Saunders Lee in high regard. So had Billy. He still did. Mr. Lee represented the best part of the old South culture—honor, civility, and integrity.

He pulled up to the security kiosk at Shaking Tree and asked the guard to ring the Lees' number. The housekeeper answered and would only say that Mr. and Mrs. Lee weren't home.

"I'm calling the law office," Frankie said as he was backing out. She listened for a moment. "It's a recording."

"Their offices are about ten minutes from here on Poplar Ave.," he said, and sped down the shaded road that millennia ago had been dense hardwood forests. Multi-million dollar properties stood where trees measuring five feet in diameter once grew. In minutes he pulled into the parking lot of the

two-story Victorian house the Lees had rescued from demoli-
tion a few years ago. Two cars, a late model Jaguar and an Alfa
Romeo 4C convertible, were parked on the lot.

Frankie ran the plates. "The Jag is registered to Rosalyn
Taylor Lee, the convertible to Martin Lee."

"That's Caroline's older brother."

They hurried down the walk past hollies that sheltered the
white, clapboard building's front porch from traffic noise. Formal
brass carriage lamps flanked the glass door through which they
saw a spacious foyer and staircase. The door was locked. The only
lights on were in offices down a hallway that led to the back of
the building.

"I'll call again," she said.

He shook his head and pounded the door with his fist.

"Calm down, Billy."

"Attorneys keep TVs in their offices. I don't want the Lees
to look up and see Caroline's car surrounded by emergency vehicles."

A young man in a dark suit stepped out of a hallway to the
right. He pointed at his watch, waved them away, and disappeared down the hall.

"What a jerk," Frankie said.

"That's Martin."

He'd known Martin Lee as a stuck-up little kid who quit
coming to the diner on Saturdays with his family after he'd been
given a T-Bird convertible for his sixteenth birthday. Martin would
show up by himself, order a takeout cheeseburger, and then count
the quarters and dimes Billy had given him as change. Even at that
age, Martin had loved money and hated like crazy to part with it.

Billy was ready to pound the door again when Rosalyn Lee
walked through the foyer, her head down over a file she was car-

rying. She had to be in her fifties now, still trim and stylish in a red suit. He tapped his badge wallet on the door then pressed his shield to the glass.

Rosalyn closed the file and looked annoyed as she came to the door. He could see Caroline in her face, the same classic features.

"May I help you?" she asked through the glass.

"Detective Billy Able, MPD. This is Detective Malone. We're here on police business."

She unlocked the door and took his ID. A question crossed her face as she glanced up, but she handed it back and opened the door for them to step inside. His uncle had introduced them years ago when they'd catered a fund-raising barbeque for a political candidate on Airlee's back terrace. She wouldn't remember him of course. At that time, he'd been the help.

"What seems to be the problem?" she asked.

"We need a word with you and your husband," he said. "Is there someplace we can talk in private?"

"Saunders isn't here. He's ill." She gestured to a long hallway leading off the foyer. "My son is waiting in my office. This way."

At the end of the hall, double doors opened into what had been the morning room of the original home. The office was spacious with floor-to-ceiling windows extending the length of the south and eastern walls letting in the morning light.

To the left, wingback chairs stood on either side of a fireplace with a mahogany mantel intricately carved with a scene of huntsmen and hounds in full cry. A young black woman in a maid's uniform stood at a tea table beside the fireplace and was pouring coffee from a sterling pot. The coffee was for Martin Lee, who was seated in one of the chairs. He came to his feet, his irritation at their intrusion showing.

Martin hadn't changed much from the boy Billy remembered. His face was that of a man who'd experienced few difficulties in life. Knowing Martin, there'd been difficulties, but he'd refused to acknowledge them.

Rosalyn dismissed the maid and introduced her son, who didn't offer to shake hands. She walked to her desk, the sound of morning traffic filtering through the windows.

"Now what's this about?" she asked.

Billy clasped his hands in front of him. He'd delivered many death notifications in his career. This might be the most difficult. "I'm sorry to inform you, your daughter Caroline has died."

Chapter 6

Rosalyn took a step back. "What makes you think it's my daughter?"

Good question. Last year the department had two well-publicized incidences of death notifications made to the wrong families. "I know your daughter. I made the ID at the scene."

Her chin lifted, and she eased back against her desk, arms crossed in defiance.

Martin came to stand at his mother's side. "Where did it happen?" he asked, his tone more aggressive than concerned.

"At Shelby Farms," Frankie said. "A park ranger discovered her car early this morning."

"Shelby Farms? Why would she—" Rosalyn stopped. Her gaze went to her son, and something passed between them. "Was it suicide?"

"No, ma'am," he said. "The medical examiner will make the final determination, but it appears she was murdered."

Rosalyn paled. Finally a reaction. He allowed a few seconds for the reality to set in before he spoke again. "We're sorry for your loss, ma'am. I know this is a hard time, but we have a few questions."

"Not now," Martin said, cutting him off.

Rosalyn ignored him. "What do you need?"

"A release giving us permission to search your daughter's house," Frankie said.

"Absolutely not," Martin barked.

Rosalyn placed a hand on his arm. "I have her key and the alarm code. You'll need a photo of Caroline for identification. My assistant will print copies for you."

"We'll want to speak with your daughter's friends and the people she confides in," Frankie said.

Rosalyn stopped to consider. "There's her cousin Zelda. She clerks in our file room."

"When does she come in?"

"Late. Sometimes not at all." Rosalyn shrugged. "She's a dancer, a choreographer. She needed a paycheck. Family, you know? I'll have my assistant find her."

Billy heard female voices in the foyer. A distant phone rang. The business day was starting. This would be a hard one for Rosalyn Lee. What he was about to say would make it even harder.

"Your daughter was wearing a wedding gown when she died. What can you tell us about that?"

"You must be mistaken."

"No, ma'am," Frankie said. "Antique lace, a train. It's a wedding gown."

Rosalyn turned to pluck a tissue from the box on the desk. When she turned back, Billy glimpsed something he hadn't expected. He'd seen hysteria at these notifications, chest pains, swinging fists. He'd never seen guile on the face of a victim's mother.

"I can't explain the dress, but I can tell you she called off a wedding five weeks ago. Dr. Raj Sharma was her fiancé. You should speak with him."

"He's been harassing Caroline," Martin put in. "Showing up at her house at all hours and here at the office. That's stalking."

"I warned her," Rosalyn said. "Dr. Sharma is Indian, not even American-born. It's hard enough to stay married to a man from your own culture. Then the babies come. People can be so cruel to racially mixed children."

Frankie glanced at Billy. Rosalyn picked up on it.

"I know that sounds racist," she said, "but I'm an estate attorney. I've seen families go to war over mixed marriages. Children are always the casualties." She moved around the desk, wrote on a pad, and handed the paper to Frankie. "Dr. Sharma is a neurosurgeon. This is his assistant's number at the Bathe Clinic."

Billy had already pictured the scenario Rosalyn was hinting at. Caroline called off the wedding. Sharma was humiliated. He pursued her until he pressured her into marrying him. He talked her into eloping instead of risking a public ceremony. She agreed but wanted to wear the dress. Instead of happily-ever-after he killed her. Revenge cuts deep. This murder stank of it.

Frankie took Sharma's number from Rosalyn and went into the hall to call the doctor's office.

"I'll need to speak with your attorneys and staff," Billy said to Rosalyn. "How many are there?"

"Eight support staff, six attorneys." She blinked. "Five without Caroline. My husband no longer practices. One attorney is out of town."

"I'd like to speak with everyone available." He looked at Martin. "Are you with the firm?"

"I'm president and senior trust officer of Airlee Bank. It's family owned. My office is two blocks down the street." He checked his watch. "Mother, I need to make some calls."

"I have to ask both of you not to discuss the details I've given you with anyone except for your husband, of course, Mrs. Lee," he said. "If you feel you need to make a statement to the press, please ask a liaison from our public information office to arrange it."

"We're not idiots," Martin snapped. "We'll require your discretion as well."

Billy ignored him and spoke directly to Rosalyn. "I've attempted to shield your daughter's identity from the media until the department makes an official statement, but there's always a chance of leaks. Be prepared to hear her name on the news sometime today."

Martin grunted and made a show of kissing his mother's cheek. He slammed the door behind him as he left.

"My son is angry," she said.

"I'm angry, too."

She cut her eyes at him but didn't pursue it.

"I'll need to see your daughter's appointment calendar for the last three months, her client list, and the files in her office. Don't touch anything else. Lock her office door right away. We'll be back later."

Rosalyn's eyes hardened. "This firm has a fiduciary responsibility to protect the privacy of Caroline's clients."

Her resistance didn't surprise him. The best approach with an attorney is to assume the sale. "I understand your concern, but what I've requested may lead to her killer. Please have the client list and the files delivered to me by noon. Be sure nothing in the records is deleted or altered. Our IT people will spot any change." He wasn't sure if that was possible, but it sounded good.

"I'll send her appointment schedule and client list," she said, unmoved.

This was one tough woman standing there in her red suit with her perfect hair. She'd just received the worst possible news, the death of her daughter, and yet she was all business. At this early stage of the investigation, a judicial magistrate would refuse their request for a search warrant. Stalemate.

"I'll get back to you on the files." His hand came up. "And I must tell you how truly sorry I am for your loss. Your daughter was a fine person."

Rosalyn's expression remained unreadable, as glazed as skim ice on a pond.

"Thank you, Detective. Please close the door behind you."

Frankie was at the end of the hall on her mobile and scribbling notes. As he walked toward her, a door between them opened. Martin leaned out. "Detective. May I have a word?"

The guy had already pissed him off, but he might have something important to say. They stepped into a small conference room.

Martin flashed an ingratiating smile. "I remember your involvement in the Sid Garrett investigation. That footage of you and Sid on the train tracks went viral."

"What's your point?"

"You and your pretty partner attract media attention."

"And?"

"Just this. I want my sister's privacy protected. With your notoriety that may be impossible. If you feel you can't handle the case with discretion, I'll ask my friend the mayor to step in."

Martin folded his arms across his chest. The backs of his hands were white and smooth as a baby's bottom. The son of a bitch thought he could say anything he pleased.

He gave Martin a fake smile. "By the way, Mr. Lee. Where were you last night?"

"At home. Why?"

"Got any idea who killed your sister?"

Realization grew on Martin's face. It reddened. "I believe that's your job."

"You're damned right it's my job, so stop bullshitting me about the mayor. You're interested in protecting your business not your sister's privacy."

"Our clients expect us to focus on their problems, not our own," Martin said, and started for the door. He turned back. "If you want my alibi for last night, call my house. My girlfriend lives with me." He stormed out, bumping into Frankie, who had been waiting outside the door.

Billy stepped into the hall and caught her predatory stare as she tracked Martin's retreat. Billy motioned her to join him in the conference room.

"What's going on?" she asked.

"The creep is worried his sister's murder will hurt the firm's image. He threatened to call his buddy the mayor if we don't handle the case the way he wants."

She laughed. "And you let him live?"

Billy had been around city politics longer than Frankie. Jeff Davis was the mayor's new appointee as director of the MPD. If Martin had the pull with the mayor that he claimed, Director Davis might bird-dog the case. That would be a royal pain.

"Did you locate Dr. Sharma?" he asked.

"He's prepping for surgery at Baptist Hospital. He won't be available for ten to twelve hours."

Billy gave that some thought. "Tell you what . . . You do the walk-through at Caroline's house. Call if you find anything. I'll question the staff." He nodded toward the foyer, indicating the women who'd gathered at the foot of the stairs. Two of them glanced in their direction, looking wide-eyed and shaken.

"God love her," a gray-haired woman wailed. Another broke into throaty sobs.

"Oh, brother," he said. "One of them saw Caroline's car on the newscast. You do the interviews. I'll check the house."

"Not on your life. You're better with the ladies." She lowered her voice. "By the way, what's with Mrs. Lee? We told her that her daughter had been murdered, and she barely flinched. We work murders all the time. We don't see that kind of disregard."

"It looks like indifference, but it's not. Rosalyn Lee is Mississippi old school. She was raised to tough it out in public. If she decides Sharma murdered her daughter, we'll find his hide nailed to a fence post."

Chapter 7

E ven with her office door closed, Rosalyn could hear Glenda's shuddery voice wailing "God love her" followed by sobs. More than anything she detested emotional displays, and there was more to come. She had to take hold to protect her law firm.

First step was to get control of the staff before they could spin off into hysterics. Her office manager Glenda was the key. She marched out of her office, brushing past Able and that young woman he'd brought with him. Glenda must have heard her coming because she turned around, tears wetting her face, her arms coming up to give her a hug. Rosalyn hated hugs. Glenda picked up on her get-hold-of-yourself look, dropped her arms, and shushed the group.

"Ladies," Rosalyn said. "This is Detective Able and . . ."

"Detective Malone," Able said.

"They have informed me that Caroline died last night. We'll learn the details later. For now I need you to pull yourselves together. Glenda, cancel my appointments. I've forwarded a photo of Caroline to you. Make copies for the detectives, as many as they need. Everyone else go to the break room. Detective Able will speak with each of you. Otherwise you're not to discuss this sad event with anyone. No one, understand? Not your family, not clients. I'll prepare a statement for you to work from when the time is appropriate."

She turned on her heel, thought better of it, and came back. "This is a terrible shock, but our clients depend on us to look after their interests. It's what Caroline would have wanted."

Back in her office, Rosalyn poured coffee from the silver service and drank the entire cup while standing there. Her daughter was dead, murdered. Everyone would be watching to see how she handled this crisis—their clients, business associates, and especially her enemies. Those bitches at the club who pretended to be her friends would be eager to fawn over the grieving mother, expecting tears. Jackie Kennedy never publicly broke down over Jack. She wouldn't cry about Caroline either. Setting the tone was her responsibility. She didn't just represent the firm; she *was* the firm. She wouldn't let gossip tarnish the Lee Law Firm's reputation or her own.

She glanced down at her suit, the red Armani of all things. Lavonia at the house could bring over the black Dior. No, the navy was more appropriate. The right costume would carry her through. Lavonia didn't need to know about Caroline yet. She had no more tolerance for tears.

She poured more coffee and went to her desk, already composing in her mind the notification of Caroline's death to the firm's attorneys, a statement they could refer to when calling their clients. She wrote quickly, emphasizing key phrases—deeply saddened, anticipating a just resolution. Set the tone, something easy that everyone would stick to. Next, she told Glenda to call Martin's assistant at the bank. She would meet with him in the bank's conference room in an hour to prepare a plan. The firm and the bank must present a united front.

She looked up Caroline's client list, which was much larger than she'd realized. The most important clients she knew personally. She would call them herself. The rest she would leave for her other attorneys to contact with assurances of a smooth transition. The Lee Law Firm represented multi-million-dollar trusts spanning two and three generations. She had no intention of losing those fee-paying clients.

Would the timing of her calls seem coldhearted? She continued to write. No, not if she asked to be remembered in their prayers.

She clicked the TV remote. On the local NBC news channel, a BREAKING NEWS banner ran below the video, footage of Caroline's Camaro shot from overhead. The driver's side door was open. Thank God the camera angle revealed only a trail of white dress spilling over the doorsill.

The camera zoomed in on Able and his partner standing at the car's open trunk. Able looked up, frowning. She hadn't recognized him at the door this morning until she'd read his ID. Billy was taller than his father and more muscular, but the resemblance was especially clear seeing his face on the TV screen.

Years ago, she'd been aware of the summer romance between Caroline and Jackson Able's son. She'd said nothing, knowing that it would be a brief fling for her daughter on the poor side of town. She'd done the same thing when she was young.

She ran the footage back to Able's upturned face and froze the image. He had his daddy's Irish good looks and those eyes. So angry. He must have known it was Caroline in the car. She turned from the screen. Jackson Able had once said his name, derived from Gaelic, meant "able to defend." Having Jackson's son investigate Caroline's murder might work to their advantage.

Or it might work against them. Too soon to know. She would discuss it with Martin at the meeting.

At her computer, she pulled up the photo of Caroline she'd forwarded to Glenda, a candid shot taken seven weeks earlier at the final fitting of the wedding gown. The dress had been stunning on Caroline—a tight silhouette with a mermaid train. The designer had incorporated lace on the sleeves and bodice from Great-Granny Lee's bridal gown.

She hadn't realized how thin Caroline looked in the photo or the shadows under her eyes. An aura of depression showed through her smile.

You see, she thought. I warned you about choosing the wrong man. You wouldn't listen.

Able had wanted access to the files in Caroline's office, giving the excuse that a client among them might be the murderer. Ridiculous. Caroline had taken over the majority of her father's client list, all good families, not the type who murder people. She opened her center drawer and took out the key to Caroline's office. She would remove the files now. Able couldn't demand to see what he didn't know was there. She would do it herself and not leave it for that idiot Zelda.

But first she took out a hand mirror, smoothed her hair, and checked her lipstick. At times like this, appearance was everything.

Chapter 8

The front door key wouldn't work. Frankie pulled the door tight and tried again. She pushed hard, jiggled it. The two officers standing next to their vehicle on the street were watching her with their arms crossed. A third cop with hands like mitts and a slab of flesh for a nose stood on the porch directly behind her. The three officers had secured the outside of the victim's Cape-style house. Now it was time for her to do her job. But she couldn't get the damned door open. The victim must have changed the lock and not given her mother the new key, possibly on purpose.

The cop behind her belched, emitting an odor like tuna fish.

"Need a hand with that lock, Detective?" he said, crowding in. He had pockets of fat beneath his eyes and an inner tube of flab circling his waist.

"No thanks. Would you step back please?"

Some of the uniformed officers believed she'd been promoted to homicide because of the attention she received after the Sid Garrett case. To hell with them. Six years of patrolling the streets of Key West and Memphis and she'd dealt with drunks, petty criminals, crazy people, and plenty of regular Joe tourists she had arrested for aggravated ignorance. She'd earned the promotion to homicide with her top fitness report and nearly perfect test scores. That, plus Billy's recommendation, had landed her a spot on the squad.

So, she wasn't about to let this damned house key throw her.

She took out a bump key, a blank with the pins filed down to the lowest point. Positioning the key in the lock, she simultaneously turned and whacked it with the back of the hard plastic brush she carried for these occasions. The door opened. She stepped in and entered the alarm code.

The officer with tuna breath was now standing in the driveway, munching a Snickers Bar. She decided to nickname him Snackbar. It lightened her mood.

"We're in," she called, and stepped inside.

The house smelled of green apples and cedar. Nothing appeared out of order in the living room, a space lit by sunlight filtering through French doors. She could see that the front hall led to a large tidy kitchen. A study opened on the right of the entry with a desk, a laptop, and a wall of built-in bookcases. Several shipping boxes had been stacked on a card table and on the floor by a corner window. She saw no evidence of a struggle or that the place had been tossed.

Snackbar followed her in crinkling the candy wrapper as he shoved it in his pocket. At least he hadn't dropped it on the driveway.

"Check the laundry room, back entry, and garage," she said. "I'll take the rest of the house."

He grunted and lumbered down the hall.

"Don't touch anything," she called after him.

She drew her SIG for the walk-through of the two guest bedrooms, two bathrooms, and into the master at the back of the house. She checked bathtubs, showers, closets, and under the beds as she went. The entire place was show-house neat, not a book out of place or a piece of clothing on the floor.

Snackbar was waiting for her in the entry. "All clear. It's a damned clean house except for the litter box in the laundry room."

"Did you see the cat?"

"Nope. Must be hiding."

"Please wait on the porch. And let me know when the investigators show up to knock on doors. Detective Able will bring a photo of the victim."

She pulled out her mobile and used the video recorder to pan across the study, stopping at the desk for a quick look through a stack of folders. Inside were household receipts and paperwork from the wedding. These would go with her to the Criminal Justice Complex. Because the victim was an attorney, the laptop would have special encryption that would take the computer techs a couple of days to hack.

A coat tossed on the desk chair caught her eye. So far it was the only thing she'd seen out of place in the house.

She went to the bookcase and videoed family photos, most of them snapshots of the victim as a child. One was of five kids in their Sunday clothes grouped on the lawn in front of a grand house and holding Easter baskets. She recognized a young Martin Lee by his dark hair and glasses. There was little Caroline in her pink smocked dress, holding her basket in front of her with both hands. A taller sturdy kid grinned at the camera, his arm draped over the shoulders of a young boy who was squinting against the sun. Standing a little away from the group was an awkward-looking girl with frizzy hair and gawky legs.

Frankie moved on to a recent shot of the victim wearing a black bikini and sitting by a pool in the shade of a striped umbrella with a frosted drink on the table beside her and a cigarette in her hand. She held herself with the cool confidence of a Ralph Lauren model, blond hair swept back from her face. Her eyes appeared to be following someone outside the shot with a hint of smolder in her gaze. Frankie glanced around, not seeing a single photo of the victim with her Indian fiancé. Had she been angry about the breakup and ripped up his pictures out of spite?

Moving to the shipping boxes on the card table, she poked around in the bubble pack, uncovering sterling serving pieces and crystal stemware. A folder labeled Wedding Gifts Returned contained a list of two hundred names and addresses, most of them lined out in red. The boxes on the table must be the gifts left to return.

Down the hall, the kitchen was like those HGTV makeover shows—granite countertops, a farm sink, a Sub-Zero fridge, custom cabinetry, a six-burner gas stove, and two ovens stacked in the wall so the cook didn't have to throw out her back lifting a twenty-five-pound turkey. No smudges on the stainless steel appliances, no crumbs on the counter.

Frankie's duplex had a forty-year-old kitchen with ripped linoleum and an electric stove with only two working burners. She had to prop the oven door closed with the back of a chair. She loved to cook, so yeah, she envied the victim her kitchen. But she didn't envy the part about being dead.

She opened the fridge expecting to see skinny people food. Instead, she found four bottles of Cordon Rouge Brut and six bottles of Piper-Heidsieck Champagne lying on the bottom shelf. The only food was four containers of zero fat Greek yogurt, an apple, and a solitary head of iceberg lettuce in the vegetable bin.

"For God's sakes," she mumbled, and removed the lettuce, snapping off the plastic bottom to pull out a wad of hundreds.

Every burglar who can bump a lock or pop out a pane of glass knows about these fake lettuce safes. Better to leave five twenties in plain sight for a snatch-and-run rather than have scumbags tear up your house looking for cash. In the freezer, another favorite hiding place, she found eight containers of gelato, all nearly empty. The victim was either eating every meal out or binging on gelato and champagne. One cabinet contained forty-eight cans of cat food. At least the cat was well fed.

She'd been through the entire house and was videoing the living room when Billy came in.

"How's it going?" he asked.

"She kept this place like a showroom. How did you do with the ladies?"

"Lots of tears. Nothing of consequence except Caroline's assistant said that Caroline and her cousin Zelda had an argument behind closed doors on Monday. The assistant assumed it was a family matter. The cousin is the artsy type. Drama is a staple in her repertoire. Definitely something to follow up."

They went outside to meet with the ten uniformed and plain-clothes investigators who would conduct the neighborhood canvass. Frankie distributed Caroline's photo and briefed them on the kind of information they were after. Had anyone seen the victim on Monday evening? Was someone with her? Had they noticed a strange car in her driveway or parked on the street? Any unusual sounds or an argument? Had the victim expressed concern for her safety?

Those were the direct questions. Then there were the rumors and innuendos a good investigator can cajole out of the neighbors. That sort of information won't hold up in court, but it can point in the right direction.

The photo Billy brought for the canvass showed a very different person from the confident woman Frankie had seen posing under the beach umbrella. This Caroline was frail-looking with hollows around her collarbones and a forced smile. Frankie wondered if her weight loss had been due to wedding jitters or the stress of having her mother ride her about marrying an Indian national.

She held up the photo for Billy. "I'll bet she starved herself for the wedding. She called it off and regained the weight by eating gelato and drinking champagne. Probably the reason she couldn't zip the dress."

"Good eye. What else?"

"Follow me."

Chapter 9

Caroline's bedroom reminded Billy of the second-story boudoir of a New Orleans lady friend he had occasion to visit on trips to that city. This room had the same shadowed, sweet atmosphere with billowy silk draperies and a crystal chandelier over the king-sized bed. The antique lamps on the nightstands must have cost more than he made in three months.

A three-by-five-foot painting by acclaimed artist Tom Donahue hung on the wall across from the bed, a portrait of Caroline seated next to her father, her head resting on his shoulder. She wore a demure dress with long sleeves, her golden hair brushed straight and tucked behind her ears. Saunders Lee looked older than Billy had expected. Most of his hair was gone, his high forehead and rimless glasses giving him a professorial appearance. His hands lying clasped in his lap touched his daughter's hands, creating a connection between them. All the emotion in the portrait came from Caroline, but there was no mistaking how Saunders Lee felt about his daughter. Caroline was his heart.

Billy wondered how an overnight guest sleeping in Caroline's bed would feel about a portrait of her father staring at him. Perhaps intimidated. Caroline may have hung it there as a test.

"I thought rich Southern women were all about ritual, tradition, and really good monogramming," Frankie said. "Our victim appears to be more complex than that."

"Use her name, please," he said. "It's Caroline."

"We agreed first names make the case too personal."

"This *is* personal."

"Got it," she said. "I have something to show you."

She led him to the spa-like bathroom—the walls covered in marble tiles, a claw-foot soaking tub, heated towel bars, and a seamless glass shower big enough for a couple to use together.

"I was going through her closets," she said, opening a door. "Here we have Oscar de la Renta, St. John, and Armani. Lovely business attire for a woman in her forties but not a young woman like our victim . . . I mean Caroline. Everything still has Neiman Marcus tags attached. Not one suit has been worn."

She opened the door next to it, a much larger walk-in closet. "These are the clothes she wore, all classics from the sixties and seventies—Pierre Cardin sheath dresses, Gucci Italian leather jackets and slacks, Yves Saint Laurent suits, dresses and blouses by Pucci, Chanel jackets. Mixed in are these great current pieces—ripped jeans, custom leather jackets by LA designers, that sort of thing. And this." She pulled out a drawer. "French lingerie, very expensive."

"How do you know these designers?" he asked.

She gave him a look. "I just do. The first closet reads like a Memphis matron. The second says rebel with style."

They left the closet. She directed him to the bathroom counter. "Here we have the pharmacy." She opened a cabinet hidden behind mirrors, four shelves lined with prescription bottles.

"Some are duplicate scripts from three different doctors going back five years. I've recorded everything by drug type. The earliest scripts were Lithium, an antipsychotic, and Klonopin for panic attacks. The most recent are Prozac, Paxil, and Zoloft. Those are SSRIs for anti-anxiety. A doctor, a psychiatrist, wrote the last group. Seems he was searching for the right cocktail."

"What's your take after your walk-through?" he asked.

"There's a thousand in cash in a lettuce safe and more stuck in drawers about the house. It's around two thousand total. There's no real food in the house, and she has a neatness obsession. Between her job and her nutbar family, I'd say she was a highly stressed basket case with epic behavioral disorders. The pills and her doctor-shopping certainly indicate script abuse at some point."

He thought about Caroline's position as a trust and estate attorney responsible for the transfer of millions of dollars from one generation to another. The implications were troubling. Still, this was his Caroline they were talking about.

He thought back over the years, remembering when he was seventeen and Caroline had called to say her parents were out of the house for a day trip. She'd wanted him to come over. He made up an excuse to his uncle and borrowed the car.

That day they had Airlee to themselves. They ate beef and cheddar cheese sandwiches in the front parlor, drank her daddy's good bourbon, and slow danced. Odette surprised them by coming in early to start supper. They snuck out to the barn where they made love in the loft surrounded by sweet-smelling hay and the sound of horses shifting and blowing in their stalls. They fell asleep. He had awakened to Caroline dozing in the crook of his arm.

He looked up to see Frankie staring at him in the bathroom mirror.

"I see what's happening," she said. "You're reliving your own experiences, getting hung up on the human side of this case. We should hand this off to Kloss or Johnston."

"We'll do a better job," he said.

"Not if you can't let go of the Caroline you knew."

"I'll take care of it," he said and walked into the bedroom. *She had no idea.*

"Detective Malone," a voice called from down the hall.

"That's Snackbar," Frankie said, coming out of the bathroom.

"Who?"

"The big cop on the porch. I call him Snackbar." She went to the entry and came back.

"He says there's a woman outside. She wants to speak with you."

Snackbar was in the driveway, a young woman standing next to him with her hands jammed in the pockets of a lime green trench that she'd pulled on over a pink ankle-length night-gown. Her cloud of frizzy dark hair moved around her face in the breeze. As soon as she saw him, she started across the yard. Snackbar reached for her arm. She shrugged him off and kept coming, flip-flops slapping against her bare feet. Billy gave the cop a nod. He couldn't place the woman but had a feeling he should know her.

She bounded up the steps. "Where's Caroline?" she asked, eyes dark and startling.

She was taller than he expected. "Your name?"

"Zelda Taylor. I got this weird text telling me to come to work immediately. I stopped here first. I had this feeling." Her hand darted out to take his. "Was it a home invasion? Did those shits hurt Caroline?"

This was the cousin Rosalyn had mentioned. He wondered

what kind of person drives to work after an emergency call dressed in flip-flops and a nightgown. And why come here first? Her explanation didn't cut it. "Let's step inside," he said.

"Tell me now."

This was the hard part, telling someone that a person close to them has been murdered. Rosalyn Lee had been strangely stoic. A lot could happen with this one. She could start swinging, run away, or pass out.

"I'm sorry to tell you that your cousin was murdered last night," he said.

Her lids fluttered, but she stayed on her feet.

"Where? Here?"

"At Shelby Farms."

"No way."

He kept a steady gaze on her.

A breeze rippled the hem of her gown. "Caroline?" she said. Her color drained.

He figured this time she'd go down, so he took her upper arm and guided her through the door. She made it to the sofa before her legs gave out. He pulled a chair close to the sofa to sit almost knee to knee with her. He wasn't going to push. He'd let her work through the news first.

She brushed hair from her face. "Murdered? How?"

"Shot."

"Shot? Goddamned guns." She wiped tears and sniffed. "I need a tissue."

Frankie, who'd been standing in the doorway, left and came back with tissues and a cup of water. She set them on the table and backed away to perch on the arm of a chair across the room.

Zelda drank the water, her attention staying on Frankie. "Who are you?"

"Detective Malone. We're partners."

"Oh." Zelda set the cup down. She pressed her palm to her forehead. "Wait a minute. What was Caroline doing at Shelby Farms at night?"

"Maybe you can help us figure that out," he said, taking out his memo book. "You up to it?"

She held the cup out to Frankie. "May I have another?"

With Frankie gone, Zelda leaned in. "I don't like your partner hovering over us."

He shifted in his chair, wondering why Frankie made her uncomfortable, but it didn't matter. He needed her confidence. "Detective Malone will be in and out. Let's talk about your cousin. You got the text from your office and came here first. You said you had a feeling."

She dabbed her eyes. "Her life's been pretty rocky since she called off that wedding. Raj flipped out. Big ego you know."

Frankie came back with the water. He inclined his head toward the door. She took the hint and went outside.

"You were saying about the breakup?"

"He sent flowers, begged. Called and called. Then he started showing up at her house in the middle of the night. She wouldn't let him in. He was yelling at her in the parking lot at the office last week. Some attorneys went out there and made him leave."

"Any physical abuse you know of?" he asked, writing.

"No. Raj is temperamental, but then Caroline's no patsy. You know Southern belles—they're dangerous when they're being agreeable. She's been meeting with an attorney named High-smith, who's opening a litigation department at the firm. He advised her to file a protective order against Raj."

"Did she?"

"Last I heard she couldn't decide. She didn't want to damage Raj's reputation."

Caroline had been right about his reputation. A deputy would slap Sharma with a warrant compelling him to appear in court. He would protest his innocence. Caroline's attorney would produce records of phone calls, messages he'd left, snapshots of him parked in front of her house. He would be publicly humiliated, ordered not to call, harass, or visit Caroline's workplace or be within a hundred feet of her. If he did he'd be arrested and held in contempt of court.

Highsmith was the attorney Rosalyn had said was out of town. Billy would request Caroline's file on the doctor's harassment be sent over.

Zelda frowned. "You think Raj did this?"

"We're not drawing conclusions."

"Sure, I understand why you won't say. People can't keep their mouths shut." She ran both her palms down her nightgown. More tears. "My mother died a year ago. An accident. Now Caroline. She called last night to say she was leaving town for a couple of days. I can still hear her voice in my head."

He stopped writing. "Did she say where she was going or if someone was going with her?"

"All she said was she had a lot to do to get ready. I asked what that meant, and she answered in that teasing way she used when we were kids, 'Yooou'll see.' Maybe you remember her doing that."

She twisted a strand of hair, watching him. "Uncle Saunders used to take us to the diner on Saturdays. I remember you from there. You probably don't remember me."

He flashed back to Caroline coming through the door with a dark-haired girl behind her.

"You *do* remember. I see it in your face," she said.

"You would order a Dr Pepper with a squeeze of lime, lots of ice."

She smiled.

"Did Caroline say whether she was meeting someone?" he asked.

"Are you going to do that cop thing where you keep repeating questions?"

She was more perceptive than she appeared. "You've had a shock. Sometimes it takes a couple of passes for details to come back."

She hunched forward, resting her forearms on her thighs. "Okay."

"When did Caroline have her locks changed?"

"About two weeks ago. Raj had a key. He let himself in trying to find out if she'd been seeing another man. Stolen woman syndrome, you know? The woman walks away and the man goes nuts thinking it's because she's sleeping with someone else."

"Was she?"

"I hope so. I hope Caroline was madly in love." She sniffed.

"Were the two of you close? Did you share confidences?"

"Sure, we're cousins. We talked."

"Did she ever talk about reconciling with Dr. Sharma?" he asked.

"No, but that doesn't mean she didn't think about it. Raj is a persuasive bastard. People trust him to cut into their brains." She plucked a tissue. "What makes you think he shot her?"

She'd put it so casually he almost responded. He flipped through pages. "Let's go back. Did she say anything to you that might indicate how long she'd be gone?"

"No."

"Where were you last evening?"

"I went to bed early. Alone."

No alibi. He considered bringing up the argument she'd had with Caroline at the office but decided to wait. Frankie walked in.

Zelda sat back. "Detective Malone. I saw you on YouTube last year taking down that thug at the library. You're the big guns on the team."

Frankie gave her an enigmatic smile that he knew meant she wasn't amused. "Sorry to interrupt. An officer wants to speak with you, Detective Able. Outside."

He wasn't sure whether the interruption was real or if Frankie was making an excuse to get him out of the room so she could grill Zelda.

On the porch, a young patrol officer with puffy eyelids and a sparse mustache came forward. "I thought you should know about the neighbor next door. She was sorry to hear about Miss Lee, but she said she was also tired of being kept awake at night by Miss Lee being in the backyard."

Billy wasn't sure he'd heard that right. "Miss Lee was trespassing?"

"No sir, in her own yard. Miss Lee took to gardening at night, digging, fertilizing, and watering the roses. The neighbor said roses get black spot if you water them at night. She thought it was creepy so she mentioned it."

"Thanks, Officer. Send your notes to me."

Billy was almost to the front door when his mobile broke into the ringtone "Hail to the Chief." It was Deputy Chief Middlebrook calling from the crime scene.

Chapter 10

Billy went to the side porch to answer the call.

"You made the Lee notification?" Chief Middlebrook asked.

"Yes sir. Mrs. Lee was at her office. Mr. Lee is ill." He heard the sound of chopper blades over the phone.

The chief grunted. "Damned helicopters and their telephoto lenses. CSU is standing by while the tent goes up. Hang on."

Billy heard a car door slam and the chief's clipped directions. He came back. "I'm told you interviewed a suspect."

"Roscoe Hanson, gated out of Turney Center four months ago. In for armed home invasion."

"Bastard," the chief said. "I'd like to wring his neck. I didn't know the victim, but I've served on a committee with her father, Saunders Lee. A real gentleman. Their firm represents most of the Old South families in the city. That circle of people won't stand for the endangerment of their women. They'll ring the director's phone off the hook."

"Yes sir. That sentiment runs deep in the South."

"A woman murdered at Shelby Farms is going to spook the public," the chief said.

Now was the time to admit his connection to the Lee family.

"Chief, I knew the Lees when I was a teenager. Saunders Lee drafted my uncle's will. Caroline Lee, the victim, became the attorney of record. She called a couple of days ago to tell me a piece of property had sold, and she was closing out the file. I thought I should tell you."

"Are you a beneficiary under the will?" Middlebrook asked.

"No sir."

"Have you had any other contact with the family . . . damn it. Hold on."

More voices in the background. He hoped the chief wouldn't continue that line of questions. If he had to reveal his teenage relationship with Caroline, he'd be yanked off the case.

"Copy me on that, Lieutenant," Middlebrook said, coming back. "Sorry, Able. Where were we?"

Billy waited, holding his breath.

"Right," the chief said. "Have you had other current dealings with the victim or her family?"

"No sir."

Middlebrook paused, thinking. "If I have to replace you and Malone, I'd bring in Johnston."

"Johnston is a solid detective," he said.

The chief sighed. "Oh, hell. We both know those Old South whites aren't going to accept a black detective investigating this murder. What's your caseload?"

"Four gang shootings, all related. We cleared two cases yesterday."

"I'll have the others reassigned so you can concentrate on this."

They hung up. Billy scrolled through his contacts to a friend, a surgical nurse at the Baptist Hospital. A couple of months ago she'd asked him to lean on an amorous orderly who wouldn't take no for an answer. She told Billy that she'd return the favor when she could. He texted, asking if she was working with Sharma today. If so, would she get in touch?

He went to the living room expecting to see Zelda and Frankie but saw only Zelda's crumpled tissue on the sofa. A sound drew him to the study. Zelda was there with her back turned, crouching beside the gift boxes on the floor. She picked up a small box and tore into the tissue then turned to stare at him like a fox that had been caught raiding a chicken coop. She stood holding the box in both hands as Frankie swung in the doorway.

"I told you to stay put," Frankie barked.

Zelda's hand tightened on the box. "Caroline didn't return my gift. I want it back."

"Give me that," Frankie said, and started toward her.

Zelda dropped the box and pushed past them to go into the living room. They followed her there. Zelda turned and gave him an imploring look. He wasn't buying it.

"You had a disagreement with Caroline yesterday," he said.

"Who told you that? Caroline's assistant?" She dug in her pocket and held up a key for them to see. "We had an argument. So what? She gave me this. I was to come by and feed her cat while she was out of town."

Frankie took the key and stepped into the entry. She came back. "It fits, but it doesn't explain the fight."

"Where were you last night?" he asked.

Zelda's mouth pursed. "I told you I was at home, which is where I'm going now. You can save your questions for later."

"Now is better," Frankie said.

"Not for me," Zelda snapped.

"It's better," Billy said. "Trust me."

"Trust you!" She moved past him and held her hand out to Frankie. "Key, please."

"No one has access to a crime scene," Frankie said.

"Then you feed the cat." Zelda cut her eyes at Billy. "I remembered you as a good guy. Don't disappoint me."

"I'll give that some thought," he said. "I'll call you to come downtown. We'll continue this conversation."

She made sure to slam the door on the way out.

Chapter 11

S o you plan to put a positive spin on her murder," Martin said with a smirk.

"Knock it off," Rosalyn snapped. Her son's sense of humor had soured recently. His old lady clients might overlook it, but she wouldn't. "Caroline didn't die from a ruptured appendix. She cancelled the biggest wedding of the year then got herself murdered wearing the damned dress. Imagine what the media will do with that. We have to control the story."

She'd set this meeting in the privacy of the bank's conference room so they could put together a strategy to protect themselves and reassure their clients. She'd seen this kind of PR disaster before, clients taking flight like startled pigeons. Other firms in their situation had spent hundreds of thousands trying to recover from scandal. Some didn't make it.

"Relax, Mother. Next week's plane crash will wipe Caroline's murder out of the public's mind."

"Not out of our clients' minds. Not the people at the club. I'll be damned if I'll let them pity me as that poor Rosalyn Lee with a sick husband and a dead daughter."

Martin thought for a moment. "You gave Raj's name to the cops. Do you believe he did it?"

"Who else?"

"I don't know. Was she seeing another man?"

"Not a chance. Your sister was too transparent to hide a lover from me."

He tapped his nails on the table, thinking. "Instead of controlling the story we'll change the conversation. If Raj is arrested, it will come out that he was stalking Caroline. We'll write a fat check to some non-profit do-gooders who oppose violence against women. We'll insist they create a fund in Caroline's name. You show up at events and make a few speeches. People will focus on your humanitarian spirit rather than the murder."

She envisioned having to dress down and engage in sympathetic conversation with battered women at abuse shelters. How morbid. "And if Raj is cleared?"

"The media will soon dredge up Finn's disappearance. Our family will look like an episode on *Law and Order*."

The thought made her shudder. "Let's stay with the present. I've hired a publicist to write Caroline's obituary and a glowing bio for the media. Kitty Townsend is brilliant at handling events. She'll take over the funeral arrangements."

She made notes, annoyed by Martin drumming his fingers on the table. A drop in business at the firm would cut the bank's income and his paycheck. He was right to be anxious. Caroline's murder was a threat to his lifestyle—his extravagant wardrobe, his expensive women, his home in Chickasaw Gardens, an apartment in Rome, his Ferrari, a Jaguar XKSS, a Bugatti Veyron, and all those other exotic sports cars. The art in this conference room alone cost more than most people's houses.

Four years ago, Martin had taken over the position as head of Airlee Bank and replaced his aunt Gracie Ella as senior trust officer. He had made it clear since then that he resented the tedium of overseeing day-to-day operations and creating annual reports for trusts. However, Martin understood the power of wealth and the pedigree of the Lee name. Combined they were formidable. He let it be known that he was making a bigger sacrifice for the family than Caroline and thought it was unfair for her to inherit an equal share of the Lee estate. Rosalyn didn't believe Martin would hurt his sister over money, but he hadn't responded when she'd texted last night, behavior that was very unlike him.

She pushed the thought to the back of her mind and noticed he'd been studying himself in the mirror hanging on the wall across from the table. He adjusted his tie, practiced his smile. She had favored Martin over Caroline when they were children, recognizing his narcissism early, which made him the easier child to manipulate.

"We need to discuss how to deal with Detective Able," he said. "Do you remember him?"

"Jackson Able's son. He used to work at that seedy diner we'd pass on the drive to Airlee. He was involved in Buck Overton's case, and he exposed Sid Garrett."

Judge Buck Overton had been a dear friend of the family who visited Airlee many times to work the dogs with Saunders. Three years ago, he was convicted of beating a child into a coma.

Sid Garrett had been her closest ally on the board of the Memphis Bar Association. He'd thrown himself under a train rather than face murder charges. Fortunately, their relationships with Buck and Sid had not come to light during the reporting of either case.

"Detective Able is a Mississippi redneck in a cheap suit," Martin continued. "He's also the best investigator on the homicide squad."

"Then he'll arrest Raj soon, and we'll be done with this night-mare."

"Maybe. But until then the media will be all over this case and not just because of Caroline. Able and Malone are media darlings. After the Garrett case, the department made Malone the new face of Memphis law enforcement. Her photo was on the side of city buses for months. Both of them are media hogs. I warned Able I'd have the mayor step in if he doesn't wrap this up quickly and quietly."

"Threatening the man who can give us what we want was a stupid move," she said.

"He's not on our side. If Raj isn't arrested, they'll expand the investigation to your law firm and my bank."

She sat back. "You're right. He asked for all the client files in Caroline's office."

"You didn't give them to him!"

She gave him a cold look. "Of course not."

"We don't want Economic Crime investigators going through our records."

Outside the windows a fifty-year-old oak stripped of leaves waved its skeletal branches in the wind. She recalled the deter-mination on Able's face when he'd asked about the files. Caro-line's death was personal for him. She knew the reason. Martin didn't.

"This could be real trouble if we don't handle it the right way," she said.

Chapter 12

I t was midafternoon. The day had turned hazy and noncommittal. Billy drove back to Shelby Farms. The medical examiner had signed off on the scene. Caroline was being transported for autopsy at the Regional Forensic Center. It was a blessing he hadn't seen her removed from the car, the train of her dress wrapped around her legs, and her body lifted onto the gurney.

He'd seen countless bodies taken from the place where they had died—swimming pools, burned-out cars, bodies folded and stored in basement freezers. One had been stuffed into the pit under an outhouse and covered with lime, another hauled up in a tree and picked clean by birds. They found a ninety-year-old man who had been dead for weeks. His body liquefied in the blaze of summer heat and had soaked through the floor of his trailer.

As he predicted, the bison had trampled the footprints around the car, making it almost impossible for CSU to cast impressions. Despite the rain the techs had lifted a few prints from the car's exterior, and they'd searched the field with metal detectors for the murder weapon. They found only the blade of a broken hoe used by a prison worker years ago.

Frankie told him she would stay with the house while CSU made their sweep and the neighborhood canvass wrapped up.

The cat had either slipped out a door or knew a great hiding place where no one could find it. Frankie said she would put down plenty of water and dry food before Snackbar drove her to Shelby Farms for her car. There, she would take possession of Caroline's purse and the overnight bag in the trunk.

After the initial shock at the crime scene that morning, he'd done his best to move forward and push away his feelings. Now he felt a gathering in his gut, a dull ache.

Hoping food would make it go away, he went to Patrick's East and picked up a couple of vegetable plates—turnip greens, fried eggplant, potato salad, and black-eyed peas with extra cornbread and rolls. Driving through Midtown, he passed Wiles-Smith Drug Store, one of his favorites. After decades of helping thousands of people and years of hassling with insurance companies, old Charlie Smith had decided to close down for good at the end of the month.

Thinking Frankie would enjoy one of Charlie's chocolate malts made at the last authentic soda fountain in the city, he drove back to the drugstore and came out carrying two cold, waxy cups. Before starting the engine, he sucked up the rich chocolate malt through the straw.

Maybe it was the stillness inside the car or the shock of the freezing malt hitting his brain, but something triggered the jolt he'd managed to hold off all day. The unthinkable had happened, and it had gotdamned happened to him. A woman he'd loved for a very long time had been murdered. The city around him seemed disgustingly normal, traffic lights blinking, people walking along the sidewalk behind his car. He felt ridiculous going about his day and enjoying a malt while Caroline lay dead in the morgue.

Nothing could make him rest his head back and close his eyes while he was on the street, but he had to take a minute to pull himself together.

As a rookie cop, he'd been a "blue flamer" racing around like he had a Roman candle up his ass. At the time he felt he had something to prove. A veteran cop had taken him aside and said, "Son, this is a tough job. If you want to survive it, slow down. Make chaos your friend."

He felt the chaos now, like a rat running an emotional maze. He shook his head, wanting to clear it. Time to man up and grab hold of his fortitude. He had a duty to perform.

Back at his desk at the Criminal Justice Complex, he started the process by writing suspect names on a yellow pad in order of interest: Dr. Raj Sharma, Roscoe Hanson, and Martin Lee. Hanson was on hold until the residue swabs came back. He wanted to check Martin Lee's alibi. On the next line down he added Zelda Taylor. Her fight with Caroline had taken place only hours before the murder. He wrote the words "second interview" beside her name.

Dr. Raj Sharma, the name at the top of the list, was the one he circled. The doctor was about to have his gold-plated cage rattled.

He called the charge nurse at the hospital's surgical desk and learned that his friend was on Sharma's team today. He sent a second text, asking for a half hour's heads-up before Sharma came out.

Next he checked the database for guns registered to the doctor. Bingo. Sharma bought five pistols over a three year period: a .45 Colt, a 9mm Glock, a Beretta 92F and two .32 revolvers. Owning guns didn't make him a criminal, but that kind of firepower would give the case against the doctor instant traction.

He dialed central booking to confirm that Hanson had been transported from the MED to lockup. Next he left a message for Hanson's parole officer letting him know one of his parolees was behind bars.

He ran a background on Zelda Taylor not expecting to find anything. Turned out she had a short sheet. First was a DUI while she was a freshman at Rhodes College. No one made her bond, so she had to spend two days in jail, a tough place for a young lady. A lot of bad crap goes on in lockup. A year and a half later she was arrested for disorderly conduct, obstruction of traffic, and refusal to obey an officer's command, all misdemeanor charges. She could've been bonded out for $250, but this time she'd refused. He checked the date, recalling a protest involving Rhodes College students against the president of the NRA. The dates matched.

The NRA president had flown in as keynote speaker at the Ducks Unlimited annual board of directors meeting. Students got wind of his arrival and decided to stage a "stop gun violence" protest by blocking his limo at the airport. They cuffed themselves together and lay down on Airways Boulevard to stop traffic. Kind of an extreme act, but Rhodes was a liberal arts college attended by freethinkers. TV news showed the NRA president standing outside his limo, looking mad as hell, while the cops peeled students off the asphalt. The president missed the meeting.

When ten protesters had refused bail, local headlines read "Student Protesters Remain Incarcerated." Apparently, kooky Zelda had been one of them. Sure didn't sound like someone who would shoot her cousin in the face. Still, her quarrel with Caroline and her lack of an alibi warranted a second look.

He checked his e-mail. Middlebrook had copied him on the draft for a press release that included the type of crime, its location, and the victim's name. The chief gave his own name as contact person in the release, placing himself between the investigation and the media, a move Billy appreciated.

About the time he thought he couldn't wait any longer to eat, Frankie showed up with the handbag and suitcase from the scene. They sat in the break room with their warmed-over plates, reading their memo books, and bringing each other up to date.

"The ME's preliminary report came in," she said. "Estimated time of death is between 9:00 pm and 11:00 pm. The bullet recovered from the overhead headliner board was slightly disfigured. The second bullet should be recovered intact."

Frankie had phrased her last comment as delicately as she could. The second bullet would be removed from Caroline's brain.

"Her mobile is an iPhone with iOS 8 software," she said. "We can't get her texts or messages even from Apple. Her carrier has the call logs, but a response to a subpoena will take a few days. Apple has everything she's backed up in the Cloud, but they'll drag their feet giving it to us."

Frankie cut a slice of fried eggplant into exact quarters. "There's a sapphire ring with diamonds set on either side zipped into a side pocket of the handbag."

"An engagement ring?"

She took a bite of eggplant and thought about it. "Sharma seems more like the five karat diamond type."

He carried his food container to the trash and came back. "Caroline was about to file a protective order against Sharma."

"Whoa. That's significant."

"I've requested the file. The attorney who was handling it is out of town."

"What's our approach with Sharma?" she asked.

"Best case, we catch him later tonight coming out of surgery. He'll be tired and won't have his story straight. I'm counting on a nurse at the hospital to text me when he's about to wrap it up."

She took a last bite and closed her container. "Where are we on Hanson?"

"The swabs came back clean. No prints on the money clip and no weapon at the scene. He'll be released by noon."

"You've pegged him as a long shot from the beginning." She tossed her food container and continued talking while she rinsed her hands. "What's the status of the laptop?"

"A tech at the computer lab said the law firm uses a VNC server to give their attorneys remote access," he said. "It uses multi-factor authentication to keep out hackers, but he'll be able to crack her personal password and search her banking and credit card records."

"What about a marriage license?" she asked.

"Harrison Pete has taken that one. There's no registered license in the database, so he'll have to contact every county court clerk's office within one hundred miles of Memphis to find out if there's been an application. That includes Arkansas and Mississippi."

Billy's mobile pinged. He looked at the Channel Five Breaking News app and held the mobile for Frankie to see the helicopter video. "Here we go," he said.

The voice-over gave a "sources say" account of a Good Samaritan who'd found a woman's body in the car at the scene. The Samaritan was then attacked by a bison bull.

"Damn it," he said. "Either an EMT blabbed to the media or someone let Hanson leak it at the MED."

"I hope Sharma doesn't see this footage before we get to him," she said. "What time do you want to leave for the hospital?"

"In four hours unless I hear from my contact at the hospital before then. There's a chocolate malt from Wiles-Smith Drug Store in the freezer if you need a boost." He expected to see her face light up.

"Maybe later. I'm stuffed."

Billy went back to clear his desk. He slipped on gloves and set the suitcase on top of it. The negligee still lay on top. When he pushed it aside, the scent of perfume lifted from the lingerie beneath. Inside were slacks, a blouse, a jacket, and a pair of flats. Zelda said she thought Caroline would be gone a few days. This was not a honeymoon in Jamaica bag. It was for overnight.

A cosmetics bag at the bottom held bottles of B-12, folic acid, and travel size tubes of shampoo and makeup. He unzipped a pocket on the left side of the case and dug out a prescription bottle labeled Xanax. A small glass vial with a metal stopper shaped like a dragon rattled inside. He popped off the bottle's lid and slid out the vial. A tiny amount of white powder had clumped along its bottom edge. It looked like cocaine.

Frankie was at her desk across the aisle staring at her monitor. She glanced at him. "The tech at the scene showed that to me. We'll have it tested. Maybe it's foot powder."

"Foot powder?"

"Sorry. Trying to lighten things up. It's coke. To be fair, the date of the prescription is four years old. She could've played around with coke in the past, zipped the bottle in the pocket, and forgot about it."

He thought about the statement given by the neighbor saying Caroline had been gardening in the middle of the night. Was it insomnia from wedding jitters or had she been too ripped on blow to sleep?

Frankie turned her chair to face him. "I've run a background on Sharma. You want to hear?"

"Absolutely."

She took pages from her printer and handed him the *Commercial Appeal*'s engagement announcements from the previous year. He studied the photo. Raj Sharma, considerably taller than Caroline, was standing behind her with his hand on her shoulder. He wore a suit. She wore a sleeveless dress with a string of pearls and her blond hair falling loose on her shoulders. She was smiling. Sharma was not. Compared to Caroline's glowing presence, the doctor appeared foreign and intense. His personality dominated the photo as strongly as it apparently had the relationship.

"Forty-one years old," Frankie said. "Born in New Delhi. Sharma is the surname of most Rajput royalty. The doctor is from the Jodhpur line, descended from Maharajah Jaswant Sharma II, which means he merits the title Maharajah or 'great ruler.' I'm sure that can also be translated as 'arrogant surgeon.' He graduated Cambridge, Oxford medical school, and did his residency at Johns Hopkins. He's the youngest ever chief of staff at the Bathe Neurology Clinic. He travels to India once a year to train surgeons in outlying areas."

"Impressive," he said. "He may be a humanitarian, but he may also be a man who insists on having his way. We've seen the attitude before—if you're not going to live with me, you're not going to live at all."

"You think he has the stones to pull the trigger on the woman he loves?" she asked.

"He cuts people open for a living, doesn't he?"

Frankie went back to typing. "Yep. Slash is our best statistical suspect."

He laughed. "You've nicknamed him Slash?"

"Okay . . . Saint Slash. Let me know when it's time to go."

Chapter 13

I t's the text from the nurse," Billy said, holding up his mobile for Frankie to see. The screen lit up the darkness of her Dodge Charger. "Sharma should be out of surgery in fifteen minutes. He'll be in the doctor's lounge, or we'll catch him in the parking lot at the south employee exit."

Frankie turned out of the CJC parking lot and hit the Charger's LED lights. He noticed her fingers squeezing and releasing the steering wheel.

"Stay loose. It's our game," he said.

"I'm good."

She wasn't good. Her voice sounded tight, which was strange, because she was usually so confident.

At nine o'clock at night the traffic was light, so they made good time to the hospital. The emergency room's red and blue sign appeared on their right. Frankie cruised through the hospital's back lanes and slowed at the physician's parking lot. Sharma's black Escalade sat in the middle of the lot under the blazing lights.

"Got 'em," she said, and grinned.

They took an elevator down two floors beneath street level. The doors slid open to the chilled air and overly bright hallways of the surgical area. They went right and then left into a much longer hallway, passing several unmarked metal doors and a bay of vending machines for drinks and snacks. An orderly came around the corner pushing a rattling transport cart. Behind him were four women carrying handbags and wearing their jackets over their scrubs. The hallway ended in heavy-duty automated doors with a sign across the top that read Personnel Only. Behind the doors were the operating and recovery rooms, and the lounge where doctors made calls and cleaned up after surgery.

Frankie forged ahead of him, her earlier nerves having turned to eagerness. She passed the group of off-duty nurses just as the ringtone on one of their phones began shrieking like a parrot. *Get the phone! Get the phone!* The nurses laughed.

The automatic doors down the hall levered open, and Dr. Sharma walked out. He was easy to recognize from the wedding announcement—tall, with sharp features, deep-set eyes, and skin the color of smoked almonds. He had on dark running pants and a jacket with reflective strips, his arms swinging and his steps surprisingly vital after twelve hours on his feet. Beside him strode a shorter man in a suit, Jerry Vanderman, the highest-priced defense attorney in the city. Vanderman checked his watch and frowned.

Someone must've seen the Camaro on TV and called in Vanderman to run interference with law enforcement. Frankie didn't know Vanderman, but she sure as hell would recognize Sharma.

"Hey Malone," Billy called. She must not have heard him over the rattle of the transport cart and the nurses' laughter. Vanderman saw her coming. He touched Sharma's arm. The taller man stopped and bent to listen.

"Malone!" Billy called again, but he could tell by her walk she was too fired up to listen.

She waved her badge at Sharma, ignoring Vanderman. "Dr. Sharma, I'm Detective Malone. We need a word with you concerning Caroline Lee. Please come with me."

As Billy approached, Vanderman flashed a surprised look at him then switched back to Frankie. "Dr. Sharma has asked me to represent him. Unless you have a warrant you are to have no further contact with him."

"This is a murder investigation. We're not going away," she said.

Sharma started to answer. Vanderman raised his hand. "Young lady, what don't you understand about the word 'no'?" He glared at Billy, who was now standing beside Frankie. "Good evening, Detective. I'm surprised this woman works with you. She needs to be reined in."

Billy felt Frankie go rigid at his side.

A code of civility existed between defense attorneys and homicide cops who oppose one another year after year. In this case, Vanderman was asserting himself at Frankie's expense to impress his client.

"Doctor Sharma and Miss Lee were close," Billy said. "He may have information we need to bring down her killer."

"You know better than to use this approach," Vanderman said. "Direct any questions you have to my office."

Billy gave Sharma a cold stare. "Advise your client my partner and I will be talking with him real soon."

They left the hospital, Frankie marching beside him with her hands stuffed in the pockets of her jacket.

"Guess we'll write that one up as 'failure to properly engage the suspect,'" she said, and gave him a pinched smile.

"Vanderman was posturing. He needs to justify the fifty-thousand-dollar retainer fee he's about to extract from Sharma."

She scowled. "I sure made it easy for him."

"We'll get him next round." He put up his hand for a fist bump.

"You know I don't do that," she said.

"Come on."

"Why should I?"

"It's what successful partners do who support each other. Like Michelle and Obama."

"I'm a Republican," she said.

He processed that and decided to drop it. "It's late. How about some comfort food?"

They were in the Dunkin' Donuts drive-thru waiting on their coffee and grilled cheese sandwiches when a security officer working the CJC entrance called.

Billy put him on speaker. "Go ahead."

"Got a guy here with a shitload of files. He wants to talk about the Lee investigation. Claims to be related to your victim."

"Did he give his name?"

"Judd Phillips."

Frankie shrugged.

"Keep him there. We're twenty minutes out."

Chapter 14

They drove downtown beneath the star-studded sky. Traffic from the Grizzlies game was streaming out of the FedEx Forum and jamming up Poplar in both directions. They ate their grilled cheese sandwiches while they waited.

Billy worked through the family names he knew that were connected to the Lees. Nothing clicked. Phillips could be a Memphis branch or someone related by marriage. The guy showing up like this might be involved in the murder or just plain nuts. There was no shortage of crazy in this town.

Frankie parked in the garage next to the Criminal Justice Complex. The elevator took them to the mezzanine level overlooking the atrium. During the day defendants packed the place for General Sessions Criminal Court, traffic court, and Judge Tim Dwyer's drug court where he authorized alternative treatments for non-violent offenders instead of jail time. At night the atrium echoed with the sound of the custodians running floor buffers.

They peered over the mezzanine's rail at the guy seated on a bench near the door with a stack of files next to him. He had a solid presence, sturdy shoulders and thick forearms. He wore a beat-down canvas hat, a white shirt with the sleeves rolled to the elbows, a leather vest, and tan trousers.

Phillips looked around, studied his knuckles, jigged his knee.

"Nerves," Billy said.

"That's Judd Phillips from *Nighttime Poker*," Frankie said.

"You watch TV poker?"

"I watch him play no limit-hold 'em tournaments. He's good."

"The hell you say."

She smirked.

Phillips slipped a flask from his pocket and took a swig. He might be a poker-playing TV star, and the ladies might see him as the rugged romantic type, but Billy had him pegged as a drunk.

They took the stairs, the whir of the floor buffers covering the sound of their steps. Phillips jumped to his feet when he saw them coming and knocked into the stack of files. Two slid to the floor, spilling their contents.

"Sorry," he slurred. "I'm a little under the weather. Name's Judd Phillips, Caroline Lee's second cousin." He dropped his head and widened his eyes as if exhausted. "Can't believe this is happening. Finn's gone. Now Caroline's dead."

Alarms went off in Billy's head. "I'm Detective Able. This is Detective Malone. Who's this Finn?"

"Our cousin. He disappeared five years ago. All they found were his folded clothes beside a rice field."

"I remember the case," Billy said. The media had played down the disappearance after the Crittenden County Sherriff's Office suspected suicide. The tragedy was never connected to the Lee family.

Judd swayed. "I was in Vegas this afternoon taping a show. A video on a Memphis news app came up showing Caroline's

Camaro. I caught the first flight out and drove directly here."

"You have information about her murder?" Frankie asked.

He looked surprised. "No, I haven't talked to Caroline in months."

"Then why are you here, Mr. Phillips?" she asked.

"Please. Call me Judd." He shook his head. "Guess I didn't think it through."

Bullshit, Billy thought but kept his mouth shut. Frankie was back in the saddle after the incident with Vanderman. Let her run.

She nodded toward the bench. "What's in the files?"

"Finn's case. I hired an investigator after he disappeared . . ." Judd paled. He glanced around.

Billy pointed to the bathroom. "That way."

Judd hustled off and through the door. They heard retching, silence, and then sink water running.

"We can't talk to him in this shape," Billy said. He tapped a number into his mobile and gave the address for the CJC.

Frankie knelt to gather the spilled files. She stopped to read a document and held it up. "He hired Walker Investigations. That's a good firm."

"The best. Walker has moved on. Oregon I think."

Judd came out of the bathroom carrying his hat. He ran his hand through his hair. "Man. I must've gotten hold of some bad fish on the plane."

"Yeah, right." Billy could smell whiskey fumes three feet away.

Frankie held up the files. "You're thinking your cousin's disappearance is connected to Caroline's murder?"

"They both hooked up with a really bad man when they were at Rhodes College. The investigator I hired believed the guy was involved in Finn's disappearance. He's been incarcerated but now he's on the loose. So yeah, I think it's possible." He dropped his gaze and turned the brim of his hat in his hand. "I apologize for coming here in this condition."

"Detective," the officer at the door called. "You ordered a cab?"

Billy fixed Judd with a stare. "You better have fifty bucks on you, because you're not driving home."

Judd nodded, took the files from Frankie, and handed her a card. "Here's my number and address. Whatever you need, I'm available." He picked up the rest of the files and walked away with as much dignity as he could muster.

"I saw a photo in Caroline's study, five kids with Easter baskets," Frankie said. "I'll bet Judd was the tall one." Her eyes widened. "Hold on. Something just hit me. I'll meet you upstairs." She took off after Phillips.

Like hell, I'll meet you upstairs. Billy stood there and waited. A few minutes later she came back cradling all the files in her arms.

"Was he ever embarrassed," she said. "He never loses his cool on TV. Nothing shakes him." She waggled a second card in her fingers. "Here's his producer's mobile number. I'll check out his alibi tomorrow."

"What's your interest in those files?"

She shifted the files to her hip. "The piece of paper I found in Caroline's car? It had the name Finn Adams on it."

Chapter 15

hree in the morning Billy and two night shift detectives sat at their desks in the squad room, the click of their keyboards and the occasional cough the only disturbances. Frankie left after one o'clock with the Adams files under her arm. He worried she might get sidetracked with the cold case but decided not to bring it up after her skirmish with Vanderman. She was going to make mistakes, not because she cut corners—there was nothing imprecise about Frankie—but because she believed she had all the answers. It's important to control the need to be right. Most of the time you aren't.

He'd stayed at his desk to review the neighborhood canvass reports. One woman said she'd seen Sharma's Escalade parked on the street in the middle of the day three houses down from Caroline's. It stayed there for about forty-five minutes. Billy figured that was the day Sharma had entered Caroline's house looking for proof she'd been cheating on him. Motive isn't a legal element of a crime, but it's a big part of the story, something he always looked at. The neighbor said she'd left a note in Caroline's mailbox. If Caroline kept the note, it was a piece of physical evidence that would impress the hell out of a jury.

Physical evidence reports had begun to trickle in. The prints

CSU lifted had matched Caroline, Roscoe Hanson, and the park ranger. Everything else, including latents from the passenger's side door handles, was unusable. The techs took soil samples from the field and made casts of eleven shoe impressions. A footwear examiner would compare those to any evidence they submitted from suspects. The examiner would then report his conclusions as a match, inconclusive, or elimination.

CSU had recovered blue fibers stuck in the fabric of the driver's seat protector. The same fibers were found in the lace on the back of Caroline's dress. Had the fibers been on the seat protector and contaminated her dress? Or had she been wearing something over the dress sometime that evening?

He made sure Frankie had been copied on all physical evidence reports before moving on to Caroline's appointment schedule.

Her assistant had included a profile of clients listed on the calendar. Most were wealthy couples over the age of fifty. He would pass the calendar to another detective to review, and he would interview clients who'd been in contact with Caroline the day she was murdered.

His last act was to text Frankie and say he'd be back at seven in the morning.

On the street he bought a *Commercial Appeal* from the sidewalk box. The headline read: "Bizarre Murder of Socialite Attorney."

The article gave Caroline's full name and cause of death as gunshot wound. The reporter went into her relation to the Lee Law Firm and the prominence of the Lee family in the city. The "bizarre" reference in the headline was about the bison attack on Hanson. The last line mentioned Caroline's engagement to "highly regarded neurosurgeon, Dr. Raj Sharma, who had not returned the reporter's calls." Perfect. The article would turn up the heat on the doctor.

Billy folded the newspaper and drove to the barge, fighting to keep his eyes open. He drank milk from the carton while standing in front of the refrigerator and then slept on top of the covers.

Wake from river traffic rocked the barge until the alarm went off at 6:15 am. In the shower, he started with the water as hot as he could stand it then ran it cold, letting the jets pound his face and chest. That's when a memory came to him so clear it played like a movie.

It was a Saturday afternoon, mid October. He was fourteen at the time and spent every Saturday ringing up tickets at the diner's register, wiping tables, and washing dishes. Mr. Lee and Uncle Kane were having their talk at the table by the diner's front window. Five kids—three boys and two girls—had gone outside to the picnic table to eat their pie and ice cream. He remembered stepping outside with a load of trash and noticing the three boys trooping across the field to the train tracks that ran across the back of the property. The four o'clock Illinois Central was rolling past with boxcars, tankers, flat beds, and cattle cars. One boy stopped to pick up a stick and brandished it like a sword. The others marched across the field toward the train, the smell of burning leaves hanging in the air. He would've given anything to be one of them. Free.

He was rinsing out a mop when he noticed the girl with the dark hair seated at the picnic table with a book propped in front of her. Caroline was picking blackberries from the bramble growing at the edge of the parking lot. The dark-haired girl closed her book and walked to the car, calling something to Caroline. Caroline answered and raised both hands cupped full of berries. Then she turned to him, her face golden in the afternoon light. That was the image he would always hold on to. Caroline lifting the berries for him to see as if she'd known he was watching.

She was standing near the opening of an animal trail used by coyote and fox to get to a creek in the backwoods. A movement caught his eye where the trail broke through the undergrowth. A big raccoon lurched into the open. It stumbled and flipped on its back, paws shuddering with spasms, jaws snapping. The coon rolled up on all fours and staggered toward Caroline in a sideways crabwalk. A city girl, she stared at the coon not recognizing the symptoms of rabies. He jumped off the porch and ran toward the coon, swinging the mop and yelling. Caroline, finally understanding, bolted for the picnic table. His uncle Kane had come running out the front door with his .45 revolver. He shot the raccoon dead.

Billy shaved, dressed, brewed coffee, and went out on the aft deck to watch the dying moon spin its way down to the western horizon. The woman in the Camaro and the golden girl he'd watched picking blackberries were the same, only this time he hadn't been there to protect her.

His mobile lit up. He expected it to be Middlebrook, but it was the top cop calling, Director Jefferson Davis.

"Sergeant Able, my phone rang last night until ten o'clock. The mayor said he's getting the same kind of heat from important people—bankers, lawyers, and country club fat cats. They want the person responsible for the murder hauled in front of a firing squad by tonight. I assured them the investigation was our number one priority. That shut them down temporarily. What's your operating theory?"

"We're looking hard at Miss Lee's former fiancé, Dr. Raj Sharma."

"Christ almighty. The doctor who heads up Bathe Neuro Clinic?"

"Yes, sir. Miss Lee broke their engagement right before the wedding. The doctor was humiliated. He started harassing her. She was about to take out a protective order against him when she was murdered."

"My God. Have you talked to Sharma?"

"He's hiding behind Jerry Vanderman. I'll try to get some answers today."

"Not with Vanderman on board. What about that parolee you caught at the scene?"

"He says he happened on the car by accident, and a bison trapped him there. We've got no physical evidence to prove different. We'll have to cut him loose later today. In my opinion, Sharma is our guy."

Davis let several seconds pass before he spoke. "I'm leaving this in your hands. I expect you to bring charges sooner rather than later."

Chapter 16

Frankie opened her eyes to the dawn light illuminating the room. The clock read 6:32 am. She sat up in the bed feeling stiff and cold. She'd fallen asleep in yesterday's clothes with a pen still in her hand from making notes on the Finn Adams case. Her mobile beside her pillow showed a 3:00 am text from Billy saying he would be back in the office by seven. She came to her feet, stuffing files and her notes into her satchel. Billy's text had sounded like a challenge. If he was in early to the office, she wanted to be earlier. Competition makes for a great detective team or it kills the deal.

Five days' worth of work outfits hung in the closet set to go. She snatched a hanger and hurried to the bathroom. Her short hair and minimal makeup allowed her to shower, dress, and walk out the door in fourteen minutes. She knew because she'd road tested her routine until she had it down. This time she was backing out of the driveway and munching a PowerBar in record time, thirteen minutes and three seconds.

Details of the Adams case ran through her mind as she drove. Finn had disappeared eight days before his twenty-first birthday. A black-and-white headshot included in the file had given her the impression of a young nineteenth-century scholar, his coat collar turned up, long hair, chiseled romantic features, and a grave, earnest expression. He struck her as someone who hadn't engaged in conversation. He debated.

A crime scene photo showed an Arkansas rice field flooded after the harvest to protect the soil. She knew the fields became a habitat that attracted thousands of ducks migrating south. Duck hunters leased the fields during hunting season. Good income for the farmers, deadly for the ducks.

A second photo was of Finn's clothing—pants, a shirt, a jacket, and underwear, folded and neatly stacked beside the water's edge. A pair of blue Nike Free Trainers had been placed on top.

A third photo was of a 1968 Chevy Camaro that had been found abandoned at the scene, the same car Caroline had driven to her death.

The Sherriff's Office investigation appeared to be thorough at the outset, but once it was determined that the disappearance was due to accident or suicide the investigators had moved on. Judd had hired Walker Investigations, a top agency; however, even Walker couldn't prove what had happened to the young man.

In the last file, she'd found a transcript of a telephone interview between Caroline Lee and one of Walker's investigators that had been taped a few months after Finn's disappearance. The investigator had first made Caroline comfortable with a few softball questions. Then things got interesting.

INVESTIGATOR: I understand you and Finn were close while attending Rhodes College.

CL: Oh, sure. We had a great time until I left for Vanderbilt Law. Finn was in his last semester when he disappeared. I was first year law, so we were both busy. God, I wish we'd stayed in touch.

INVESTIGATOR: Do you know anyone who had reason to harm him?

CL: Not Finn. He had strong opinions, but he'd back off before he made someone too mad. He had these high standards, especially for himself. He would've made a great prosecuting attorney. Or a priest. (laughter) But he was determined to join the Lee Law Firm. He was old school when it came to family and tradition.

INVESTIGATOR: What do you know about Clive Atwood?

CL: Clive? He's great. The three of us hung out together. Clive flew in from Miami when Finn disappeared. He helped with the search.

INVESTIGATOR: We've been looking into Atwood's background. I'm sorry to tell you, he's not who he claimed to be.

CL: (long silence) That's crazy. Clive graduated from Princeton and completed the Stanford Journalism Program. He was the one who convinced Finn to apply to Harvard Law. I don't understand. Judd told me you people were good investigators.

INVESTIGATOR: Atwood was kicked out of Princeton, and he never attended Stanford. He's a con artist and a drug dealer.

CL: For God's sake. He smoked pot and sold a little on the side. That doesn't make him a dealer.

INVESTIGATOR: What do you know about his sexual relationship with Adams?

CL: That's disgusting. Finn wasn't gay. Neither is Clive. Where are you getting this crap?

INVESTIGATOR: Judd Phillips, your cousin. He claims Finn and Clive were lovers. Finn's roommate verified it.

CL: You should call Clive. He'll straighten this out.

INVESTIGATOR: We tried. His number's been deactivated.

CL: That can't be. I'll call him.

INVESTIGATOR: You two stay in touch?

CL: We talk sometimes.

INVESTIGATOR: It's my understanding he's left the state.

CL: Judd's behind this. You tell him to call me immediately.

INTERVIEW TERMINATED BY CL.

Frankie walked into the squad room at 7:05 am. Billy was at his desk with a coffee in front of him, his head down, frowning over a file. After several minutes, he looked up from the pages and gestured at Judd's files she was unpacking from the satchel.

"Come up with anything useful?" he asked.

"Interesting reading. I spoke with the producer of *Nighttime Poker* last night. He confirmed Judd was taping a show on Monday."

"Good to know." He leaned back and locked his hands behind his head. "I left a message for Vanderman. He'll call back, but I'm sure he won't budge on Sharma giving a statement. I'd love to see the doc drag Vanderman in here and try to clear himself. Defendants like Sharma won't listen to their attorneys. Their egos usually take them down."

"What's our plan for the doctor?"

"We'll talk to the hospital staff and other doctors Sharma works with. I'm sure he's crossed swords with a number of them. Maybe one will rat him out."

"I'll give Martin Lee's girlfriend a call and check his alibi," she said.

"Good. I'll have another conversation with Zelda Taylor."

She wondered if this was the time to jump into the Adams case. Actually, she felt like an idiot for hesitating. "I have something else."

"Yeah?"

"A transcript of a conversation between Caroline and Walker's investigators." She gave him a pared down version, emphasizing Caroline's emotional responses to the investigator's questions about Clive Atwood. "It's nothing we can take to court, but in my mind it creates reasonable suspicion," she said.

He dropped his hands from behind his head and got this serious look. "Director Davis called this morning. He's catching hell from every quarter. That means you need to focus on what we have in front of us, not a cold case out of our jurisdiction."

"That's not fair."

He gave her a hard look. "Fair? What are you, in third grade?" He picked up the phone as a backhanded way of ending their conversation.

Her cheeks burned at being dismissed. She was the skeptical one. She relied on analysis and logic. Billy was the one who lived off hunches. Now *she* had a hunch that the cases were connected. She just didn't know how.

Day shift detectives drifted in around eight. They picked up the natural deaths cases, suicides, and accidental deaths like the one last week where an old man shot his grandson out of a tree because he mistook the kid's red ball cap for a cardinal. Ten detectives handled the whodunit murders. She and Able were two of them, and they were the best.

Nationwide, cities were competing for the highest murder clearance rates. The top-ranked squads saw promotions for management and detectives. That was Frankie's objective. Advancement. Coming to Memphis, her goal had been a spot on the homicide squad. Now she was quietly enrolled in Boston University's online Masters of Criminal Justice degree program. With the squad's clearance rate keeping them in the top ten in the country, she hoped to move up in rank. If that didn't happen, she would see what TBI or the FBI had to offer.

Was she being disloyal to the department? No. To Billy? She considered that. She was being loyal to herself by focusing on goals instead of dwelling on mistakes, like what had happened with Vanderman. She would never allow another lawyer to use her that way again.

The computer techs had worked through the night to hack Caroline's FileVault encryption. They sent two thumb drives to the squad room. Frankie handed off the drive with Caroline's banking and credit card information to the economic crimes division. She took the personal documents, her e-mails and iCalendar. Scanning subject lines, she found the majority of e-mails, five hundred of them, dealt with the wedding.

The guest list had run over two hundred, many of them living overseas. After the cancellation, Caroline had to unwind contracts with caterers, hotels, dressmakers, florists, and reservations at restaurants for pre-wedding parties. After the breakup, e-mails from the groom's side had admonished her, one calling her a self-involved American bitch. Frankie was beginning to understand how Caroline had ended up on anti-depressants and watering her roses at night.

Not much evidence of a social life—no book club dates or meeting friends for cocktails and dinner. Wedding plans and physician appointments for her father and herself had dominated the last six months of her life.

Frankie had fifty emails to go when she stopped to make the call to Martin Lee's girlfriend. She hung up from the conversation to see Billy on the phone, his back turned to the room. He finished the call and turned around.

"That was Vanderman," he said. "No contact with Sharma unless we bring charges. No statement and no alibi." He scribbled something then slammed his hand on the desk.

"Vanderman knows how to play the game," she said. "We'll crack Sharma some other way. The techs sent up thumb drives from Caroline's laptop. Other than the wedding eruption, she led a boring life. Of course she could have a secret account on her mobile for the racy stuff."

Billy huffed. "That son of a bitch Sharma. The attorney's assistant sent over Caroline's file on the harassment. She recorded some of Sharma's calls, very manipulative stuff trying to break her down. She saved his texts. He sent up to twenty a day. She has photos of his car in front of her house at 2:00 am. The file confirmed Zelda's story that he tossed her place looking for evidence of a rival."

"Any physical abuse or threats?"

"Intimidation and emotional abuse. The attorney believed Sharma was escalating toward violence. Caroline was dragging her feet on the protective order. I'd like to talk to this attorney, Robert Highsmith. His assistant needs to get him in touch with me."

"While you were talking with Vanderman, I spoke with Martin's girlfriend. She's Italian, here on a visitor visa. She insists Martin was home with her on Monday night."

"Did you press her on it?"

"Sure. The lady didn't budge," she said.

"That's too bad. I would love to break that punk's ass, but Sharma is a better bet."

She stood. "The fibers recovered from the car's seat protector were wool off of some type of clothing or a blanket. I'll go by Caroline's house to look for a match. And I'll try to find the cat. After that, I'll do a search of Caroline's law office. While I'm there, I'll ask Highsmith's assistant to have him contact us."

Chapter 17

By 2:00 pm Billy had spoken with the three clients who'd met with Caroline on Monday. He was hoping to hear comments she'd made about taking a trip or if she'd mentioned someone's name. One client said she seemed less engaged than usual. The others said she seemed happier than usual. Both behaviors were reasonable for a woman planning to be married later that evening.

The governor's campaign manager called to verify that Rosalyn Lee had been present at a fundraiser on Monday night. Rosalyn wasn't a suspect, but it was good to know.

Billy's interviews with the hospital staff were more fruitful. One nurse commented that Sharma had been losing his temper over nothing. Another pulled Billy aside and said that three weeks ago a female intern assisting Sharma during surgery had made a minor error. Sharma got in the intern's face and began cursing while waving a scalpel around. The incident had shaken everyone in the OR.

An anesthesiologist who worked with Sharma on a regular basis was evasive at first, but then confided that Sharma, who had conducted himself professionally in the past, had become volatile. He'd bragged about his gun collection and said that everyone in Memphis should be carrying one for protection. He told the anesthesiologist he carried a revolver under his car seat and suggested the anesthesiologist do the same.

Back at his desk, Billy was reaching for the phone to call the ME's office when it rang, the call coming in with a Mississippi area code.

After years of investigative work, he could pinpoint in each case when interviews, evidence, and chance had intersected like lines on a graph, and the case jumped forward. This time the lines crossed at a call made by an old friend.

He picked up the receiver.

"Billy, it's Blue Hopkins. I'm at Airlee Plantation. I heard on the news about Caroline. I can't believe it."

He'd known Blue Hopkins forever. They played on the same high school baseball team, sang in the church choir together. The last time they'd spoken Blue had been working as head of operations at his brother's security firm in Jackson, Mississippi.

"I'm afraid it's true. What are you doing at Airlee?"

"I manage the property for Mr. Lee and work his bird dogs. He lives here now." A sob came over the line. "Sorry, man. Caroline comes down almost every weekend to see her dad. I've gotten to know her. The news hit me hard."

"Take your time."

Blue cleared his throat. "Caroline called on Monday around noon. She knew I'd been reverenized. She asked if I would officiate at her wedding that night."

"Where?"

"The chapel on the property. I was to meet her there at nine. She asked me to open up the guesthouse and get it ready for her honeymoon night."

"Married to whom? Did she say?"

"No, I figured it was Dr. Sharma she was talking about. She called back later and moved the time to ten o'clock. I waited in the chapel till midnight." His voice broke. "Lord. What happened to that girl?"

Blue's pain triggered his own stab of grief. "I'm coming down. I want to talk to you and Mr. Lee."

"He's sick, Billy. Parkinson's disease. The nurse told me Mz. Rosalyn wants to come tell Mr. Lee herself, so we're supposed to say the phones and cable TV are shut down. Mr. Lee doesn't know his Sparrow is gone."

"How did you hear about it?"

"On the radio driving home from Georgia. I left here early yesterday hauling bird dogs and horses to the Westmoreland Plantation field trials. Mr. Lee still wants his name out there on the bird dog circuit. I just got in."

"All right. You take it easy. I'm heading your way."

Billy decided to drive down in his personal car, a matte black 1986 Turismo that he'd resurrected from a barn during summer break from Ole Miss. He had no money back then, so he and Blue rebuilt the engine themselves and added serious power with a nitrous oxide kit that gave it a boost for short durations. He could blow the wheels off any muscle car on the road, but knew when to back off so he wouldn't throw a rod from going too fast. He loved the speed, but his favorite thing about the car was the back seat that folded down, making the trunk big enough for him to camp under the stars while looking through the massive rear window.

Plus, the car reminded him of where he came from.

He took Third Street to Highway 61 South, following the legendary road bluesmen had traveled for decades from New Orleans to Vicksburg to Memphis. On the way he passed the

Crystal Palace Skating Rink, and the old Malco Drive-In The-
atre with double screens that was now a flea market. At the
Mississippi–Tennessee state line, the bluff dropped off seventy
feet. The temperature cooled ten degrees, and the land began to
flatten to miles of pancake fields punctuated only by telephone
poles and tarpaper shacks. This had been the landscape of his
childhood—land flat as the bottom of the ocean, hot green fields
where kudzu grew six inches in a day, and poverty and racism
that exhausted all hope.

Eons ago swamps and lush vegetation had choked the Mississippi and Yazoo River floodplains. Over thousands of years,
the vegetation broke down. Silt spilled over the banks of the two
rivers during winter runoffs and filled in the basin. The soil of the
Mississippi Delta grew broad, rich, and deep. Billy read about a
farmer who'd claimed he was drilling a well when his bit brought
up chunks of tree trunk buried a hundred feet down in silt.

The delta between the rivers had remained untouched until
wealthy planters, including Saunders Lee's ancestors, moved
from their spent plantations in South Carolina and Virginia to
vast tracts of land in the Mississippi Delta. They forced slaves
to drain the fetid swamps and clear the forests despite floods,
raging malaria, and yellow fever. The plantations spawned the
South's feudal system, which in some rural pockets has barely
changed.

Growing up in Mississippi it had all seemed normal to Billy.
Not until he'd moved to Memphis did he realize how much the
people in the Delta feared change. Memphis was only a rung or
two better.

In an hour, he left Highway 61 for a two-lane state road that
served sharecroppers, juke joints, and plantation owners alike.
Twenty more minutes and he pulled into the gravel parking lot of

the diner, his first time back in sixteen years. The FOR SALE sign that had been posted for years was gone. The Kane's Kanteen hand-lettered sign his uncle had been so proud of lay facedown in the weeds beside the steps.

For twenty-seven years the diner had done a solid business serving breakfast and plate lunches. He'd grown up working there, his uncle having given him a home in the shotgun house set far back from the road. He wondered if the new owner would try to bring the neglected diner up to code, or if the place would be bulldozed for a gas station or cable TV satellite office. A part of him regretted not having bought the property and reopened the business, but he would've burned up the Mississippi highways trying to work his job and keep his eye on the place.

Before going to college, his uncle Kane had pushed him to become a lawyer like Saunders Lee, expecting him to raise up the Able name in the eyes of the community. He'd graduated from Ole Miss and entered law school. He was finishing his first year when Blue's two little sisters disappeared. The county Sherriff ignored leads that would have taken deputies into the basement of a Baptist deacon where the girls' bodies lay.

The murders had shocked him into realizing that his uncle's expectations for his future weren't going to be enough for him. He wanted to work in law enforcement instead of writing legal contracts or litigating divorces. He'd driven to the diner and told his uncle that he'd quit law school and signed up for the Memphis Police Academy. They went out back of the diner to argue so the customers wouldn't hear. His uncle had taken a draw on his cigarette, thrown it in the dirt, and crushed it then ordered Billy to leave, saying, "You're just like your father. Don't come back."

He'd driven to Memphis, uprooted by the hot wind of his uncle's anger. Over time the homicide squad had become his proving ground. The diner and tiny house had once been his home, but now all he felt was a hollowness where sadness used to live.

He pulled out of the diner's parking lot and drove through what was once the old forest. Now a pine forest grew in its place as a cash crop. The pines opened up to fields along the highway and rows of abandoned sharecropper shacks, then mammoth grain elevators, then metal sheds that housed the combines used to harvest grain crops. One more turn and he reached Airlee Plantation's long driveway with cedars crowding in on either side.

The Lees' two-story ancestral home had been built in 1857 in the Greek Revival style with heavy cornices, gables with pediments, and columns. It survived being plundered during the Civil War but a lightning strike in 1911 burned out the front parlor. Timber on the property was cut and milled for the repair. They added an upper balcony with balustrades and replaced the four Ionic columns.

Blue was at the front of the house in the circular gravel driveway hosing down the flaps of a Ram HD pickup when Billy pulled in. He shut off the water, wiped his hands on a towel, and came over to Billy to shake hands.

"You still driving that heap?" Blue grinned and pointed at the Turismo.

"It can outrun anything in this county. What about you? You're back home from Jackson."

"My dad has congestive heart failure and dementia is setting in. Mom needs one of us close by."

"I'm so sorry. Your folks have been through a lot."

Blue nodded, furrows cutting across his brow. Premature gray curled in his sideburns. The murder of his sisters had taken its toll.

Billy changed the subject. "How's Mr. Lee doing?"

Blue lifted his chin toward the house. "He's resting, so I haven't spoken with him. It's just as well. I'm afraid I might break down over the sad news. The Parkinson's has taken so much from that man. Now this."

"Can he get around?" Billy asked.

"On his good days. Mz. Rosalyn hired a nurse and a house-keeper. Odette cooks for him seven days a week. We inspect the property and visit the barn and kennels when he feels up to it."

Blue smiled. "My dad used to run Mr. Lee's bird dogs. They campaigned three dogs, traveling the bird dog circuit all over the South and Northeast. They took me with them to some of the field trials. Two of his dogs were national champions. Nowadays, it's a minimum of fifty grand to take a dog to the national level." He laughed. "Wouldn't my great grand pappy spin in his grave knowing his blood was back working on a plantation."

They walked to a curved concrete bench to sit beneath the massive oak at the front of the house. A crow glided out of the sky and landed on a limb above them. "Guess we'd better get to it," Billy said. "What can you tell me about Caroline?"

"She came most weekends. If Mr. Lee had a doctor's ap-pointment during the week, she'd carry him to it. They were real close."

He nodded, thinking of the portrait of Caroline and her father hanging in the bedroom.

"She wanted Mr. Lee to be at the wedding," Blue said, "but he was off his feet on Monday and had to go to bed early. I was leaving the next morning at five, so she decided to go ahead with the ceremony. She asked Odette to make a big wedding breakfast and was planning to tell Mr. Lee the next morning."

"Why the rush?"

"I can't say. She was in one of her high moods when we talked."

"You think the marriage was her idea or was she pushed into it?"

Blue shrugged. "I don't know. She sounded mighty happy."

"And then she didn't show up."

"No. She didn't call and didn't answer her phone. I waited at the chapel till midnight, mad as hell that she'd left me hanging." He stroked his thumb down his jawline. "I should've known something was wrong. I should've done something."

A second crow landed on the limb beside the first and began to caw. Blue picked up a rock and threw it at them. "Damned crows. They're listening. Those birds understand more than is natural." He shook his head and looked down at his hands.

"There's nothing you could've done for Caroline."

"You know the bastard who did this?" Blue asked.

"I've got a pretty good idea."

"The doctor?"

"He's on the list."

"That's where I'd start." Blue ran his hands down his thighs and stood. "Mr. Lee's sister Gracie Ella Adams is here. That's her station wagon parked next to the house." He gestured toward an older green Mercedes. "She and Caroline were real close. They talked on the phone a couple of times a week."

Billy remembered Gracie Ella Adams although it had been fifteen years since he'd seen her. She was a tall woman with capable hands and a perpetually tanned face from showing her horses in the summer and fox hunting in the winter. During fox hunting season, she stopped at the diner on Saturday mornings and ordered egg and cheese sandwiches to go. He'd always admired Mrs. Adams. Felt he could trust her.

"Odette said she found her sitting in the rocker in the guest-house, cold and exhausted, her boots covered in mud," Blue said. "She goes to Arkansas a couple of times a week to walk the rice fields where her son disappeared. She must've driven straight here. Odette built a fire and fed her lunch."

"Does she know Caroline's been murdered?"

"I can't say, but I thought you'd want to talk with her. I spoke with her through the door, told her Billy Able from the diner was on his way down. She didn't answer, but I'm sure she'll remember you."

They started walking toward a tiny cabin secluded behind a pecan grove some distance from the big house. Billy knew about the cabin, but he'd never been inside.

"You need to know she hasn't been the same since she lost her son," Blue said. "She's been hospitalized. They keep her on meds. She gets things real confused."

After housing field workers for more than a century the cabin stood abandoned for years. He heard the Lees had renovated it as a guesthouse and retreat.

He thought about the pain endured in that place. So much history had to be glossed over for everyone to live together.

Before knocking, he stood at the door thinking through what he wanted to say. He wouldn't offer his condolences. She might not know her niece was dead. If she did know, she might not be handling it well. He'd keep in mind Blue's warning that she gets things confused, but if she had talked to Caroline in the last few days, he wanted to know what was said.

He took a breath and knocked. "Mrs. Adams, it's Billy Able. May I come in?"

He heard the lock turn and waited for her to open the door.

Several seconds passed. "Mrs. Adams?" He opened the door and stuck his head in. She'd gone back to the rocking chair that she had pulled up next to the bed.

He barely recognized her face, now tight and shiny with the bloat of powerful medication. Her shoulders were hunched forward, her erect posture gone. Her jaw jutted like that of a crone twenty years older. She had on a field coat, the toes of her muddy boots sticking out from under a long dress.

He stepped into the cabin and glanced around. Shiplap covered the walls, the wide boards oiled dark with age and wood smoke. The floor of the sleeping loft had been removed to expose rafters and give the room height. Skylights flooded the space with light to make up for the two small windows in the front wall. A rough stone fireplace stood at one end of the room and a queen-sized bed at the other. A lean-to had been added to accommodate a sink, toilet, and tub.

Blue had set out candles, fruit, bottles of wine, and crystal glasses for Caroline's wedding night. Orchids, violets, and bird of paradise from Airlee's hothouses overflowed the mantel. The room was chilly. The fire Odette built earlier had burned down to embers. He imagined Caroline sweeping through the door in her beautiful dress, anticipating her wedding night, but to him, a honeymoon night in this place was a terrible contradiction.

He took a seat at the foot of the bed next to the rocker, the mattress sagging under his weight. Gracie Ella began to rock, not looking at him. She kneaded a lump of blue wool in her lap.

He was figuring where to start when she spoke up.

"Yes, I remember you. You're Jackson Able's son. Your mother passed away, and you went to live with your uncle." She shook her head. "You were such a quiet boy."

His mother had died in a car accident, leaving town. Leaving him. He'd moved in with his uncle at age twelve and started helping out at the diner. Mrs. Adams had gone out of her way to ask him how he was doing in school or if he planned to play baseball in the summer. He'd felt terribly alone in those days. The attention she paid him had meant a lot.

"I saw your mother socially before she moved to Pontotoc." She frowned. "I didn't like her. No, that's not right. I liked your mother well enough, but I don't trust women who drink in secret. She should've taken better care of herself and you."

He remembered wishing at the time that his mother had been stronger, more like Mrs. Adams. He didn't want to think about that now, so he changed the subject.

"It's good to see you," he said. "It's been a long time since you came to the diner. Your nieces used to come too, Caroline and Zelda."

She gave him a small smile. "Caroline has a good mind. I knew she'd do well. Zelda went into the arts. No one told her she doesn't have the talent for it. Saunders will look after her."

From the way she spoke about Caroline, he had to think she didn't know about the murder. He'd have to be careful.

"Have you talked to Caroline recently?" he asked.

She stopped rocking. A shudder went through her. She tugged at the collar on her coat. "Are you cold, son?"

"No, ma'am, I'm fine."

Her head dropped forward and she began to rock. "Caroline told me she was cold."

She spoke so quietly, he wasn't sure he'd heard her right. "Caroline said she was cold? When?"

Her head came up. She frowned again.

"What else did she say?" he asked.

Her gaze wandered the walls. "You may remember my son

Finn. He used to come to the diner with his cousins. A smart boy. Always so curious. You remind me of him."

Her fingers began to loop in the air above the wool in her lap as if she was holding needles and knitting. The bones of her hands were visible, the flesh sagging away from her wrists.

Her eyes softened. "Caroline wanted her wedding to be a surprise. The baby, too."

Baby? "Was Caroline expecting?"

Gracie Ella stopped rocking, her head cocked as if listening for someone. "Where *is* that girl? She should be here by now."

"It's okay, Mrs. Adams. Can you tell me anything she said?"

She dropped her hands to her lap, perturbed. "Run on now, Finn. I can't pay attention to my knitting while you're talking to me."

Chapter 18

The only vacancy in the Lee Law Firm's parking lot was a low spot in the back corner swamped by a pool of rain. Frankie parked and grabbed her satchel, opened her car door, and looked down at green and brown walnuts bobbing in the standing water. Good thing she bought shoes off the half-price rack at discount stores. The department's clothing allowance covered only a third of what she ruined while on the job.

She'd noticed the black wreath hanging on the firm's front door, the reason every parking space in both lots had been taken—people stopping in to offer their condolences. She was certain the Lees would have a register at the front door for visitors to sign and a silver tray for those who wished to drop off calling cards.

Across the parking lot, she saw the office's back entrance door that opened into a glassed-in sun porch, an obvious addition to the original house. A slender young woman, Highsmith's assistant, stood as Frankie walked in. Her desk sat next to a doorway that opened into the main building. Piled at the far end of the porch were boxes, a sofa wrapped in protective plastic, and file cabinets.

"I'm Rachel Noel. You must be Detective Malone." She was

dressed professionally, in a navy sheath dress and a cashmere cardigan with her strawberry blond hair swept up in a French twist.

The young woman waved a dismissive hand at the makeshift office. "We're camped here while the offices for Mr. Highsmith's new litigation department are being remodeled."

Frankie set down her satchel, feeling awkward dressed in soggy shoes and a polyester blend jacket. "I see. The firm is broadening their services."

Rachel smoothed her hair. "Our clients call the Lees when their kids get in a scrape with the law or they're being sued. You know, criminal matters. Mr. Highsmith has joined us to take care of those problems." Her hand moved down to her cheek. "But you're here about Caroline. How may I help you?"

"By having Mr. Highsmith call us right away. He can reach us at any of these numbers." She handed over a card. The assistant's lips compressed.

"Is there a problem?" Frankie asked.

"I've been trying to reach Mr. Highsmith. This was a scheduled leave, so it's not a surprise he's out of touch, just bad timing."

"When was his last contact?"

"Monday evening. He left some instructions on voicemail."

"Do you know where he's gone?"

"Not really. He's taken personal time. I'm sure he has loose ends to tie up from his move from Chicago."

"Or he's someplace with poor cell service," Frankie said. Or . . . now there's a twist. Sharma would detest the person who'd encouraged Caroline to file a protective order. What if the doctor had killed both Caroline and Highsmith?

"Have you called his home?" she asked.

Rachel looked affronted. "Of course. I reached the dog sitter.

She said everything's fine." She pasted on a professional smile. "I'm sure it's nothing. Mr. Highsmith mentioned recently that he was having problems with his mobile." She moved behind her desk. "I'll send the text with your request right away."

Frankie wasn't ready to let it go at that. "Did Mr. Highsmith ever speak with or meet Dr. Sharma?"

"Not that I know of."

She thought a moment. Sharma had broken into Caroline's house searching for a rival. It wouldn't surprise her to learn that Sharma had been following Caroline. "Did Caroline and your boss ever go out, like for drinks or dinner?"

"I don't believe so. They met several times to discuss Dr. Sharma's harassment. After one meeting, Robert—I mean Mr. Highsmith—told me she was under a lot of pressure. He was doing everything he could to calm her down."

"If you don't reach him today, please let me know. Is the information complete in the file you sent over?"

"That's everything." She frowned. "You don't think something's happened to Mr. Highsmith, do you?"

"No. I'm sure your boss is just taking a much needed break."

Voices of visitors in the main reception area carried down the hall. Frankie could see Rosalyn at the front door speaking with a woman using a walker.

"That's quite a crowd," she said.

"The Lees know everyone in town. Caroline was a favorite."

The woman with the walker patted Rosalyn's hand. "I don't need to speak with Mrs. Lee, but you should let her know I'm here."

To avoid drawing attention, Frankie took the back stairs to Caroline's office. She didn't want to add to the staff's tension. There was enough emotional turmoil in the building.

She stopped at the assistant's desk outside of Caroline's office and identified herself. They spoke for a while, the woman answering several questions. She let Frankie into the office, a sunny space with modern furnishings and a wall of windows looking out on a garden. A bright abstract in mixed media and signed by Caroline hung over the credenza. On a table beside the sofa stood a framed photo of Caroline in cap and gown, her father beside her smiling. They had posed in front of a stone archway Frankie recognized as the entrance to the chapel at Rhodes College. Her desktop was completely clear except for a stack of hardcover titles on politics and the Supreme Court. The tidy desktop was no surprise considering the compulsive neatness Caroline had exhibited at home.

Frankie laid out her Nikon and evidence bags, snapped on gloves, and began examining the contents of the credenza and desk drawers. Nothing of interest there except a stack of thick stock envelopes addressed to clients. The assistant had mentioned Caroline's preference for the personal touch of handwritten notes. Frankie opened them all and found nothing of interest.

Next she dug through the wastebasket and discovered an interoffice memo scrunched into a ball so tight it took effort to smooth it out.

FROM: R. Lee
TO: C. Lee
SUBJECT: Yancy III probate

Chester Yancy III has called to my attention your mishandling of the probate of his father's will: late filing of a motion, unprepared for a hearing, having to request another continuance. In thirty-five years, the Yancy family

has never questioned our advice or our fees. Now we're at
risk of being sued or reported to the Bar. Get your head in
the game, little girl, or there will be consequences.

Harsh words from mother to daughter. Rosalyn was tough.
Frankie photographed the note and bagged it, probably not
something that would figure into the investigation, but Billy
should see it.

She made her way around the perimeter of the room inspect-
ing books and poking under cushions on the sofa and chairs.
Her experience in Key West had taught her that important clues
could hide in the strangest places.

Finally, she went to the built-in filing cabinets with six hori-
zontal drawers and pulled on the top one, expecting to feel the
weight of files as it glided forward. Instead the drawer rattled
open. All the drawers were empty. She knew about Billy's show-
down with Rosalyn over the client files. Obviously, Rosalyn had
removed them. They could get a warrant if the investigation went
in that direction, but they would never know what else she had
removed or destroyed.

She took a seat at the desk and pulled the stack of books toward
her. The top three had sticky notes with Caroline's comments
scattered throughout. In the fourth book, Bob Woodward's *The
Brethren: Inside the Supreme Court,* she found a folded page
torn from a legal pad with notes in Caroline's handwriting. What
appeared to be a draft of a letter began:

Dearest Raj,

*I wish to extend a heartfelt apology for my role in our
breakup. We've both made mistakes. I remember the*

*days when love and admiration were the gifts we of-
fered each other. Where do we go from here?*

The next three paragraphs had corrections and entire pas-
sages marked out with notes made in the margins. Frankie
photographed the page and stepped out to ask the assistant if
Caroline had mailed a letter to Dr. Sharma recently. The assistant said nothing had gone out since the breakup, but that Caroline sometimes dropped personal mail by the post office for the
five o'clock pickup.

Frankie went back to sit at the desk and think. Caroline had
been struggling for the right words. Was this a draft for an apology letter or a confession of some kind? Most important, had she
written the letter and mailed it to Sharma?

Frankie was considering the ramifications when Martin
walked in the office, his slim cut Italian suit and gray silk tie an
appropriate choice for the wake downstairs. He took the chair by
the window and crossed one leg over the other, his hand resting
on his knee. She noticed his fingers were curling into the fabric
of his slacks and releasing like cat claws.

"Detective Malone, unless you have a warrant you shouldn't
be here," he said.

His dark eyes and the way he'd combed his hair back from
his sleek brow reminded her of an otter, but there was nothing
playful about this man.

"You're the one who shouldn't be here. I'm conducting a
murder investigation," she said.

He ignored that. "You're sitting in my sister's chair. It's disre-
spectful."

He was taunting her.

"I'm busy, Mr. Lee. Time for you to go."

"But I have a question first."

"Keep it short."

He dropped his leg and leaned forward. "Have you ever shot anyone? I mean killed them."

Now he was trying to provoke her. "Why do you ask?"

"I'm curious. What's it like?"

Bringing up the subject while his sister lay in the morgue meant he believed his alibi was beyond question. Or he was nuts. Or a sociopath.

Four percent of the population functions without a conscience. Some are money managers, surgeons, soldiers, and preachers. They could be your kid's kindergarten teacher, your attorney, or the assistant manager at the AutoZone store. The smart ones will use you up, ruin your career, blow up your marriage, and steal your money. Then there're the underachievers who have no power or money, but they enjoy generally screwing with you.

She was looking at some version of that now, sitting across the room.

Elbows on the desk, she inclined toward him. "Shooting someone. It's like this. You draw your weapon same as you've done a hundred times on the range only this time it's not a target. Your finger wraps around the trigger. You take a breath and hold it, sight your shot. Boom."

He wet his lips. "Fascinating."

The eagerness she saw behind his eyes forced her out of the chair. She moved in on him quickly. He rose to his feet, his hand brushing the length of his tie. She was in his face in seconds, aware of his lack of eyelashes behind those glasses.

"I'm not here to amuse you, Mr. Lee. I want to find who did this terrible thing to your sister. Someone has removed files from this office. Tampered with evidence. We're talking jail time."

He altered his expression, adjusted. "I see. Well, I'm sure the files have been distributed to other attorneys." He moved to pick up a photo of Caroline from the credenza and turned it for Frankie to see. "You may have misunderstood my question. I take this investigation very seriously. My sister was everything to me." He set the frame on the credenza. It fell facedown. He didn't bother to stand it up.

Liar, liar pants on fire.

"I must leave you now," he said. "We have guests."

He glided out the door. Caroline's assistant came in, a tissue wadded up in her palm. "Are you all right?" the woman asked.

She appeared to be unstrung. Martin would have that effect on normal people.

"I'm fine," Frankie said. "I have a question. Who has a key to this office?"

"I do. And Mrs. Lee, of course."

Chapter 19

Billy stood in the doorway of the guesthouse to keep an eye on Gracie Ella while he texted the ME's office:

Victim Lee, Caroline. Case 442976: Pregnant
at time of death? Respond ASAP.

Had Mrs. Adams seen or talked to Caroline on Monday? Was the baby real or fantasy?

He palmed the key so she couldn't lock herself in and started for the house. Blue met him halfway there in the gloom of the shadowy pecan grove.

"I believe Mrs. Adams needs some attention," he said.

"I'll ask the nurse to take her upstairs and give her supper. Was she any help?"

As much as he trusted Blue, he couldn't go into detail. "You were right about her mental state. Do you know where she lives in Memphis?"

"Near the Lees' house about a mile from the hospital."

That fit. Sharma lived near the hospital, too. Caroline could've stopped by her aunt's house on her way to pick up Sharma for the drive down, or she could've called.

"Mr. Lee is awake," Blue said. "I think he's up to a few questions as long as you're careful about it."

"That's great. By the way, did Caroline ever talk about reconciling with the doctor?"

"Never."

"Do you know if she was seeing another man?"

Blue frowned in the twilight. "No I don't. Are you planning to ask Mr. Lee that question? The man's daughter is dead."

Billy didn't answer. He couldn't. He kept walking.

They continued through the pecan grove, the smell of decomposing shells rising from the damp earth. A mockingbird cried in the treetops. He could see Odette moving past the lighted kitchen windows at the back of the house. The Lees weren't his people. This wasn't his home, but a part of him would always be connected to this dark, sweet soil.

They came around the side of the house to find Saunders Lee standing on the front porch in his royal blue bathrobe with gray sweats on underneath. He'd aged even more than in the portrait in Caroline's bedroom, his expression vague and searching. He turned at the clicking sound made by dried magnolia leaves as they waded through them.

"Blue? Is Sparrow driving down?" The old man's voice had a hoarse quality, his movements stiff.

"I'll see what I can find out, sir," Blue said. "Someone you know has stopped by. Billy Able. You'll remember him from Mr. Kane's diner. Billy was his nephew."

"Why, yes." The old man straightened, calling up some of the old glamour from those summer days when he would arrive at the diner, tanned and clean-shaven, in a crisp white shirt and khaki slacks pressed to a knife-edge. Back then his very presence could calm a room.

He clasped Billy's hand in both of his to disguise the palsy. "Your uncle and I had several conversations about your future in the practice of law. I was saddened by . . ." He frowned, searching for the right words.

"Thank you, sir. His death was a shock. Those Saturday afternoon political discussions the two of you had meant the world to him. I took a different route than what my uncle had in mind, but I stayed within the law."

Saunders chuckled then studied him under the porch light, uncertain of his meaning. He turned to Blue. "How did we do at the field trial?"

"Hawk won," Blue said.

The old man clapped his hands. "Wonderful. Let's have a drink to celebrate." Blue placed his hand on Saunders's back as he shuffled inside the foyer.

The layout of the house hadn't changed since the last time Billy had been there. The stairway mounted the wall on the left and opened to the second and third floors. Directly in front of them a long, broad hall ran the depth of the house and ended in wide French doors that let onto a screened porch and the stone terrace beyond. He could smell Odette's good cooking coming from the kitchen and the wood smoke from the fireplace in the parlor on the other side of the entry.

Saunders led the way into the parlor, the main gathering place in the house, furnished with antiquities collected by the Lees on their travels. He remembered the parlor from the day he and Caroline had slow-danced in front of the fireplace when they were teenagers. Chinese vases on alabaster pedestals stood on either side of the doorway. Oriental carpets covered the hardwood floors. There were rosewood screens and ebony chests, beeswax candles and bowls of potpourri, a bookcase full of leather-bound books, scrimshaw carvings, and delicate porcelain figurines.

A Chesterfield sofa stood in front of the fireplace with straight-back chairs pulled up on either side. An ornate sterling tea service and a pair of massive candelabras crowded the top of a sideboard against the wall. The afternoon he'd spent with Caroline she'd told him about the six paintings hanging in the room. They'd been handed down through generations of Lees, painted by famous impressionists and American landscape artists. He'd guessed the paintings were fine enough to hang in a museum but thought it rude to ask.

Blue went to the sideboard, poured three bourbons from the decanter, and handed them around. Saunders raised his glass. "A salute to a dog named Hawk. And to Blue, his excellent trainer."

Blue gave a slight bow before taking a seat on the sofa. Billy and Saunders took the chairs. "How many head of cattle are you running this year?" Billy asked.

"We're out of the cattle business," Saunders said. "Our Charolais bull broke his leg while mating. But he died a happy bull." He stopped, seeming to gather his words. "We're down to the four saddle horses we use for dove shoots and Blue's personal mount for the field trials."

"Horses are more trouble than a pack of kids," Blue said. "The vet bills never stop coming."

"This place burns through money like a sailor in a cat house." Saunders sipped his bourbon and seemed to relax. "Taxes and farm bills take every bit of my income and then some. A real estate developer out of Jackson wants to subdivide the place. When I'm gone, Roz might have to move in that direction."

"Your family won't let that happen," Blue said, then frowned and glanced at Billy. By family, Blue had meant Caroline not Martin.

It was an opening so Billy took it. "Speaking of family, you mentioned your daughter earlier."

"Communications are down. I'm surprised Sparrow isn't here to check up on her old man. She works at the firm, you know. I've asked her to handle your uncle's will."

"I remember Caroline. She was to be married recently."

He nodded. "My daughter had a change of heart."

Blue cleared his throat. "I met Dr. Sharma when he came down several months ago. Seemed like a good man. Mr. Lee, you think she'd reconsider her decision and go ahead with the wedding?"

The older man shifted in his chair. "The doctor asked for Sparrow's hand in the proper manner, so I gave my blessing, but she told me last week it would've been the mistake of her life. Probably for the best. My daughter's had her problems. She needs a steady husband, and more than a busy doctor like Raj Sharma can give her."

The fire popped. Blue got to his feet and swept an ember off the hearth. He stole a look at Billy that said, *That's it, bud. No more help from me.*

Saunders sipped his drink. "You know everyone at the club thinks the Lee clan is perfect, but we're like every other good Southern family—'crazy' runs in our blood. We're just better at pretending." He laughed softly.

Billy thought of his mother's delicate, high-strung nature. He knew what Saunders meant. "Maybe your daughter called off the wedding because she found someone else. Someone steadier like you say." He let the statement dangle. Felt like crap doing it.

Saunders took out a handkerchief and wiped the drool leaking from the corner of his mouth. "Are you suggesting that my daughter was seeing another man while she was engaged?" The old man looked down at the glass in his hand and rotated it. "You said you're working within the law. What exactly does that mean?"

"I'm with the Memphis Police Department."

"I see. What division?"

"Investigative." Billy's mobile pinged. "Sorry, sir. I have to check this. If you'll excuse me." He nodded at Blue.

Blue followed him into the entry. "Time you headed back to Memphis. Mr. Lee is worn out."

"Is there a bathroom?" he asked, and kept walking.

"Down the hall, second door," Blue said, exasperated.

Billy passed sepia-toned photos of Lee family members— men with stern expressions and handlebar mustaches, their wives draped in ropes of pearls and posing beside vases of overblown roses. The women looked passively sweet, unlike Rosalyn Lee. Saunders had gone against type when he married.

In the washroom he checked the text:

Regional Forensic Center. Lee, Caroline, 442976.
Findings: positive ten weeks pregnant.

He pocketed his phone. Five weeks pregnant when Caroline had called off the wedding. Had she known about the baby early and decided against being trapped in a bad marriage? Did Sharma learn about the pregnancy and persuade her into a last minute wedding? Or had she told him it was another man's child, and he killed her because of it?

Gracie Ella had known about the baby. What more did she

know? Right now she was upstairs with the nurse. After she had supper, he would try for another conversation.

Those plans changed when he came out of the washroom and heard Rosalyn Lee's voice shattering the peace of the house. He started for the parlor, not surprised she was in full cry with a stranger's car parked in the driveway. At the door he saw Blue and Saunders on their feet with glasses in hand and their backs to the fireplace. Rosalyn was standing beside the sofa, pointing at a cushion.

"I come here and find you sitting on my furniture in your dirty work clothes," she snapped at Blue. She went to the sideboard and picked up a crystal decanter, holding it for Saunders to see. "Half gone. He's drunk up our best bourbon."

Then she turned her eyes on Billy, steel points behind tortoiseshell-rimmed glasses. "What in the hell are you doing here?"

"Do you really want me to answer that, Mrs. Lee?" he asked.

Her body stiffened but she didn't give an inch, only glanced at her husband.

"Now, Roz, I invited these men in for a celebration. Hawk won the field trial—"

"You *know* the doctor said alcohol fights with your medication."

Saunders drew himself up, the wobble of his head growing more pronounced.

"Where's the nurse," Rosalyn said. "Lucille! Lucille!"

Billy knew no plantation owner's wife would ever speak to her husband in that manner, especially not in front of the help. Every man wants to hold on to the way he's always seen himself. The damage Rosalyn was inflicting was painful to watch.

"Coming, Mz. Rosalyn," a stout woman in a gray uniform

called as she came down the stairs. Behind the woman, Gracie Ella leaned over the handrail, a fierce expression directed at Rosalyn.

"You killed my Caroline," she screamed.

Rosalyn cut her eyes to Saunders. "Don't listen to anything your sister says, dear. She's confused. Now let's say goodbye to these gentlemen, and we'll go into supper."

Gracie Ella pushed past the nurse on the stairs to run across the entry, her robe flapping behind her like wings. "It's your fault," she screeched at Rosalyn. The nurse ran after her and grabbed her by the shoulders from behind. Gracie Ella struggled to throw her off.

"Control yourself, Gracie," Rosalyn spat. "Or I'll call the clinic and they'll come get you." They stood toe-to-toe, both radiating hatred.

Saunders's voice cut through the drama. "What's Gracie talking about?"

Gracie Ella eased in his direction, her hands turned up in supplication. "Caroline was coming here to be with you, sweetheart. She didn't make it."

Saunders looked around the room, disoriented and shaken. "Roz?"

"Take that bitch upstairs," Rosalyn said to the nurse. She turned on Billy. "You and Blue wait on the porch."

Blue raised his eyebrows and waited for Billy to take the lead. Out of respect they did as Rosalyn asked and went outside.

On the porch Blue paced in and out of the light from the two hanging lanterns, the glare shining off his maroon jacket. Billy pressed his back against a column. He could only imagine the words being spoken in the house, reliving his own shock when he knew Caroline was gone. Then came the heart-wrenching cry. Blue closed his eyes and dropped his head. The old man's pain cracked and bloomed and spread itself throughout the night.

Minutes later Rosalyn came out and closed the door behind her. Her face was as pale and hard as marble. Billy wanted to feel compassion for this woman who'd lost a daughter and was slowly losing her husband, but he'd seen the damage she could do. Sympathy for her plight wasn't in him.

"My husband needs you," she said to Blue.

He nodded and went inside.

She turned on Billy. "He's a very sick man. You came here without permission and questioned him with no regard for his welfare. He told me you suggested our daughter had been chasing around with a man other than her fiancé. It's unconscionable. Tomorrow I'll phone Director Davis. By the time I'm through, you'll be demoted to hosing down the cellblock."

This woman was a dirty fighter. He thought about the pills in Caroline's bathroom and had a better understanding of where her problems had begun.

"Caroline was on her way here to be married the night she was murdered," he said. "Did you know that?"

Rosalyn glared at him. "Of course. I'm her mother."

"Yesterday you were surprised when we told you about the wedding gown. In fact you disputed it. She was ten weeks pregnant. Did you even know that?" A cruel question, but he didn't care.

Rosalyn's eyes narrowed. "I know your people. Your father was useless. He wanted a rich wife, so he tricked your mother into marrying him. Then he tomcatted around with anything wearing a skirt. He left your mother with a bankrupt business and a child. No wonder she drank."

That stung. Too much truth in her words. "Don't talk about my family, Mrs. Lee. It's unhealthy."

Her chin went up. "I see your father in you, Detective. You're trash just like him. Get off my property."

Rosalyn watched as the detective stalked to his car. She knew that walk, body angled forward, graceful and aggressive. He could thank his mother for his good bone structure. His hot temper came from his daddy. The car door slammed, the engine cranked, gravel spun away from the tires. The taillights winked between the cedar trees like burning match heads. His father, Jackson, had been the most reckless man she'd ever taken into her bed. She'd never gotten over the thrill of him.

They'd started as teenagers meeting on the sly at the drive-in on summer nights. In the daytime the place was a dirt lot with speaker stands lined up in rows like parking meters, half of them decapitated by patrons driving off with the speaker still hooked to their door frames. Even though the big screen was falling down and pocked with shotgun shells, at night the place was magic. Movie stars were twenty-feet tall. Richard Gere in *American Gigolo*. Kathleen Turner and William Hurt in *Body Heat*. Sex on the screen was new, hot. The sex in the cars was even hotter. She craved Jackson Able, carnal, mysterious, erotic. She'd loved the risk of being with him.

She'd been Rosalyn Taylor then, the Taylor lineage just as august as the Lees' but not nearly as wealthy. The Taylors had been plantation owners until they moved to Memphis two generations earlier and began parceling off their land. The hunting lodge and fifty acres east of the levee was all that was left. When she and Saunders were teenagers, the Lees and the Taylors would spend summers at their Mississippi homes and share Thanksgiving turkeys shot on the property. They attended the same church and voted Republican. The families had taken it for granted that she and Saunders would eventually unite the clans.

She'd never loved Saunders. She wasn't capable of it. Love never found a way of entering her. Saunders knew this and accepted her as she was. Producing children was expected although she knew she'd have no talent for raising them. Martin and Caroline recognized her shortcomings early. She'd quit pretending with them a long time ago.

But in between training bras and her boring marriage, she'd had Jackson Able.

She would go with a carload of girlfriends to the drive-in on Friday nights. Partway through the movie she would slip out of the car, slip off her panties, and find Jackson's blue Impala waiting at the end of a back row. He would be ready for her. His hands cupped her bottom as they pounded themselves into noisy climax, relying on the movie soundtrack to cover their passion. She would return to her girlfriends, redolent with sex, the idiots buying the story that she had gone for popcorn and run into friends. She thought if she were careful, she wouldn't have to give up sex with Jackson for a year or two.

In July, *Dressed to Kill* was the second feature of the evening. By the time she'd found Jackson's car, the opening credits had rolled and naked Angie Dickinson was pleasuring herself in a steamy shower scene. Jackson went crazy. He pulled her onto his lap and took her roughly. When he was done, he'd pressed his hand against the small of her back and breathed into her hair. He'd said, *Let's get married. We'll figure out the rest later.*

She'd known how his mind worked. If she said no, he would shove every dirty thing they'd done in Saunders's face. Saunders would have no choice but to walk away. Jackson thought he'd trapped himself a rich girl who would be a ticket into the society that had been closed to him.

She'd buttoned her blouse and told him if he shot his mouth off within a mile of Saunders she would turn him in for stealing electronics out of the back of a delivery truck. He'd given her a Walkman and Betacam, both still in their boxes with barcodes, so she had proof of the theft. He kicked her out of the car without her panties and skirt. She had to walk back to her girlfriend's car half naked. They laughed in her face, saying they had known all along she'd been sneaking off to hump the white trash stud.

Those bitches were all wearing size eighteen now. They had to pretend their husbands weren't cheating alcoholics and that they liked being saddled with a pack of grandkids every week-end. The wheels of justice grind slowly, but they do grind.

On the porch, the night wind blew off the lawn bringing with it the scent of cedar trees. She should go back inside to Saunders. Without Caroline to take care of him, she would have to move him back to Memphis. A developer had made an offer for the property. She'd let the house go and keep the leased acreage for income. Losing the place would take the heart right out of Saunders, if it hadn't already been broken by Caroline's murder.

She started inside, thinking about Jackson Able's son. He'd said it was unhealthy to run down his family. He didn't know the meaning of unhealthy. But he was about to find out.

Chapter 20

He'd sped away from Airlee, six miles gone before he let off the gas and cruised to a stop on a logging road deep in the forest. Shutting off the engine, he rolled down the window and inhaled the night air. Around him pulsed the memories of primordial swamps filled in and covered over by silt from the Yazoo and Mississippi Rivers. Panthers, bears, and wildcats once moved among the ancient trees. The Chickasaw and Choctaw tribes had ruled the forests. Break the levees, let the winter floods run wild, and the taming of the Mississippi Delta would be undone. "Wild" wins in the end.

In the silence he heard Saunders's cry of grief. The sound would visit his dreams, the place where he had no defense. Everyone touched by murder becomes its casualty. The longer a case drags on, the deeper the wound. He could feel the killer ahead of him, around the corner, out of sight, doing away with evidence. He clicked on the dome light and took out his memo book to complete the notes he'd started earlier.

Gracie Ella Adams—Saunders Lee's sister
and Caroline Lee's aunt. Mental breakdown
after disappearance of son. Delusional during

interview. Knew about Caroline's pregnancy.
Did Caroline visit or call her aunt the night of
the murder? Accusation made against Rosalyn
Lee—You killed my Caroline. Meaning what??
Unreliable witness.

He thought about Rosalyn Lee's behavior. She'd been like a rattlesnake striking anything that moves. She could stir up a stink with Director Davis over his conversation with Saunders if she wanted to. He rolled up the window and started the engine. He'd have to deal with that later.

Ten miles down the road his mobile rang. It was Blue.

"We just loaded Mr. Lee in an ambulance."

"What happened?"

"Slurred speech. His left arm went weak. It's happened before. The docs will run a CT to find out if it's a TIA or a stroke. They'll keep him overnight."

"Anything I can do?" *A stupid question.* Stay away from a sick old man whose daughter has been murdered.

"Find the son of a bitch who killed Caroline, okay? I'll let you know if the test shows anything significant."

They hung up. A text popped up from Frankie:

5:03 pm. Call me.

That had been two hours ago. Cell service was spotty. He started to call then decided he needed time to think. Thirty minutes later on Highway 61 and his mobile rang again. He grabbed it expecting an update from Blue. It was Frankie.

"Did you get my text?"

"A little while ago. I'm driving."

"Can you pull off? It's important."

She sounded excited. A sign on a pole flashed Pal's Gas in the sky farther down the highway. He put the phone on speaker and took the winding access road to the aging truck stop and parked by the front door. A heavyset man came out carrying a case of Tecate hooked under one arm with a Chihuahua riding on top of the box.

Billy leaned forward and rested his forearms on the top of the steering wheel. "What's up?"

"I searched Caroline's office and found what looks like a draft of a letter. It starts out 'My Dearest Raj.'"

He sat up. "Whoa."

"It's handwritten on a page torn off a legal pad. She crossed out lines, added words. Here's the gist. There'd been a lot of good things between them in the past. She wants the fighting to stop. She was contacting him against the advice of her attorney who recommended she file a protective order. She would prefer they work things out."

"That opens a lot of doors."

"She wrote several versions of the next lines: 'I wasn't truthful about the reason I called off the wedding. I apologize for not telling you in person. I was embarrassed to tell you. I have something important to tell you.' In the margin she wrote 'couldn't admit and ashamed to admit.' She crossed out both of those phrases."

"Sounds like another man in the picture," he said.

"Not definitively, but I agree."

"Have you seen the ME report?"

"Yes," she said. "The baby. That's a real twist. I wondered if she knew she was pregnant when she called off the ceremony. If Sharma was the father she might have been trying to draw him in with this letter."

"Or these notes could've turned into a phone call," he said.

"I don't think so. She's a letter writer. Her assistant said she broke up with Sharma by letter. From the sound of it, she never told him why she walked."

Caroline breaking up by letter was no surprise. She'd left a note for him on the counter at the diner. *Sorry. I can't do this anymore.* She'd returned to Memphis for her fall school term and never came to see him at the diner again.

"Do you know if a letter went out to Sharma?" he asked.

"Her assistant said nothing has been mailed to him since the breakup, but Caroline dropped off her personal mail on her way home, so it's possible. Wish we could get a sample of Sharma's DNA. We'd know if it was his child," she said.

"That won't happen."

A semi parked behind him released its airbrakes with a pop and a whoosh.

"Where are you?" she asked.

"A truck stop off Highway 61. A friend who manages the Lee's plantation had information for me, so I drove down."

He briefed her on Caroline's wedding plans, his talk with Gracie Ella Adams, and Rosalyn's blowup. He didn't mention her threat to call Davis. He was tired and had a taste for a burger and a cold Tecate.

"We'll go over all of it tomorrow." He put the car into reverse. Two kids appeared out of nowhere, running from behind the semi. He slammed on his brakes.

"Let's talk now," she said. "I want to think about this overnight."

"Not now, Frankie."

"This is business. I'm not a girlfriend you can put off."

He started to fire back then remembered Frankie's persistence was one of the reasons he'd wanted her for his partner.

"It's been a long day," he said, hearing the drag in his voice.

She paused. Her tone softened. "Okay, drive safe. I'll be in early."

He hung up. *Drive safe.* He felt like he'd been driving on the wrong side of the road all day. One more call to make. He dialed Jerry Vanderman and left a message about the existence of a letter. Ten miles from Memphis his mobile rang.

"What's this about a letter?" Vanderman asked.

"It's in Ms. Lee's handwriting. Starts out 'My Dearest Raj.'"

"I'm in criminal court in the morning. I'll come by after. My client has a right—"

"He has no rights unless he's been charged. If he cooperates, he can see the letter." He heard muffled profanity from Vanderman. The phone went dead.

He slapped his palm on the steering wheel. Damn that felt good. He clicked on a Trace Adkins CD, the best company a man can have on the road.

Chapter 21

Forty-five minutes after leaving the truck stop, Billy was driving up Riverside Drive. He had a quarter tank of gas left, which was more than he had going for himself. A Green Beetle burger and a cold Tecate were on his mind. One thing he liked about downtown, plenty of late-night joints where his nerves could uncoil and he could half listen to the jukebox. The Beetle had exactly what he needed tonight.

The Glenn Miller and Benny Goodman Orchestras used to play at Hotel Chisca down the street from the Green Beetle. The hotel was now a renovated apartment building after standing for years as a decaying hulk. After their shows the Miller and Goodman band members would head for the Green Beetle, which was then an illegal speakeasy during Prohibition. Later it became a hangout for B.B. King, Hank Williams, Sam the Sham, and Elvis.

He walked through the tavern's double doors smelling the resin of the aged pine paneling and the grease coming from the fryers in the kitchen. He signaled the bartender nicknamed "Fish" for his usual. Fish nodded, a man in his forties with the hangdog looks of the old detective on the *Barney Miller* TV show.

A handsome, young guy would've been out of place in the Beetle.

He ordered a burger and took a seat at a table even with the bar with his back against the wall. It never hurt to have your guard up. Memphian Machine Gun Kelly got mad one time and shot up the place leaving bullet holes in the paneling.

Fish came from behind the bar with his beer and slapped him on the shoulder. "Hey, Detective. Catch any killers lately?"

Billy closed his eyes. The crowd was slim and focused on their own conversations, but he felt his anonymity was shot.

"Thanks for the beer. We're working on it," he said.

"Listen," Fish said. "I read in the *CA* about Roscoe Hanson getting trapped on the roof of a car by a damned bison with a dead woman in the driver's seat. So I says to Mamie"—he jerked a thumb at the server—"that's the Roscoe who used to wash dishes in the back. Not long after that he walks in bragging how he'd fought off this giant bull. Son of a bitch had his arm wrapped in a bandage. I'm looking at his arm and thinking the bull probably came out all right.

"Anyway, Roscoe keeps slinging the shit and buying drinks for anyone who'll listen. The guy was dead broke most of the time he worked here. Tonight he flashes a roll of fifties when he pays the tab, shit-eating grin on his face. Go figure."

A flood of adrenaline hit Billy so hard he had to set his beer down. A fry cook four months out of Turney and living in a trailer on his sister's property, why the hell was that dirtbag flush with cash?

Billy dropped a five on the table for the beer. "You know where the bastard went?" he asked Fish.

A guy who looked like he'd been sitting at the bar so long he was built into it leaned over to Billy. "I heard him say he was heading for Earnestine and Hazel's. He's probably shooting off his mouth like he was doing here."

Billy parked in the lot next to Central Station across the street from Earnestine and Hazel's. Hard to believe the history of the place was even more infamous than the Green Beetle. It began as a pharmacy then became a bar with an upstairs brothel that serviced WWII soldiers traveling through Memphis by train. Musicians—some of the founding fathers of the blues, R & B, and rock and roll—used to come to E & H daily for plate lunches of pig's knuckles, collard greens, and cornbread. They treated the place like home. Ghosts of prostitutes and overdosed heroin addicts are said to haunt the rooms upstairs. They play the piano and scare the fool out of the staff, everyone except Karen the manager. Karen knows the ghosts are on her side.

Walking across the street to the bar, Billy was picturing the crime scene all over again—Hanson's truck, the gate, the Camaro's tracks in the mud. No weapon, no residue on Hanson's hands. What had he missed? Had there been someone else at the scene, a shooter who carried off the gun and left Hanson stranded?

A crowd was standing on the sidewalk at the door, which meant the front of the E & H house was packed. The 5 Spot Cafe backed up to the bar, so he entered by their side door and walked down the hall to the bar's rear entrance. It took two seconds to spot Hanson. He was shooting pool under the incandescent light hanging over the bar's lone pool table, bent over the side rail with his cue jacked up to shoot over another ball. He had on a red shirt with pearl snaps down the front and jeans cut so tight they gripped his crotch. He took his shot. The balls clicked and rolled down the cushions. He whooped and shuffled his cowboy boots in a sideways scoot that took him to the other end of the table.

Billy knew the player Hanson was shooting against, a guy named Spuds, a frequent flier for narcotic busts who was currently out on bond. Cops called him Spuds because his shaved skull looked like a Mr. Potato Head with the white plastic teeth glued in the middle of his face and a gold earring hanging off the side. Spuds put the heat on and cleaned up the table. The eight ball dropped in the pocket. He shoved out his dentures with his tongue and waggled them at Hanson.

"Rack 'em up," Hanson bellowed. "You're deader than fried chicken."

"Even up first," Spuds growled.

Hanson stowed the cue under his bandaged arm and threw a handful of bills on the table.

The sight of the money set Billy off. He pushed through the bystanders and grabbed Hanson's bandaged arm.

Hanson pulled away. "Hey, asshole!" His face beamed with a chemical shine, his pupils dilated to the size of black pennies. He focused on Billy and licked his lips, amped on crank or bennies.

A salty taste hit the back of Billy's throat. "You're coming with me, shithead."

Hanson swiveled toward two fat guys slouched on the vinyl sofa against the wall. "Here's the cop I told you about tried to bust me for killing that woman. Had to kick me loose." He turned back, grinning. "I made you look like a dick. Suck on this, Detective."

He stuck out his middle finger and jerked it up and down. Then he puffed out his cheeks like a blowfish. One of the guys on the sofa laughed, tipped up his beer, missed his mouth and poured it down his chest.

Billy grabbed Hanson's finger and bent it back. Hanson yelled and yanked it away.

"You're shooting pool with a convicted felon," Billy said. "Get moving or you're back at Turney Center faster than you can fart."

Hanson was ripped, but he wasn't stupid. He dropped his cue on the table. Billy shoved him toward the door, staying behind him, jabbing stiff fingers in his back all the way down the hall. They crossed the street with the Arcade Restaurant's neon sign burning in the night. A chilled dampness hung in the air.

Ten feet from the car the drugs floating in Hanson's brain took over. He dropped to a crouch and swung around, his fist catching Billy in the ribs.

That was all the excuse Billy needed.

He spun Hanson back around and hiked up the bandaged arm behind him. Then he drove him face forward into the car's rear fender and smashed his head onto the trunk. Hanson's legs collapsed from under him.

"Let up, let up," he begged, voice muffled against the flat of the trunk.

A man and woman passing by on the sidewalk hurried on.

Billy grabbed him by the back of the belt, turned him around, and threw him against the side of the car. "Where'd you get the cash?"

Hanson coughed. His breath smelled like gasoline. "The fuck you care?"

Billy backhanded him. Hanson's head snapped to the right, spittle flying from his mouth. "What do you think, asshole? You're connected to a murder."

Hanson's hand went to the side of his face. "Shit, man, all right. Those people at Shelby Farms paid for their bull banging me up. They cleaned out petty cash and gave me a paper to sign."

"How much?"

"Four hundred."

He grabbed a fistful of shirt and bounced Hanson off the car again. "You threw eight bills on the table. Who paid you to kill the Lee woman?"

Hanson's hands came up in front of him. "Back off. I hit the long shot Superfecta at the dog track today. The payoff was fourteen grand." He wiped blood from his mouth with his sleeve.

"You had a partner Monday night. You stopped Caroline. He shot her. He took off with the gun leaving you stranded. I want his name and the name of the man who hired you."

Hanson was sweating and looking incredulous. "What're you smoking, man? Swear to God you got it wrong."

Billy flipped him around and hooked him up. He opened the back door, shoved Hanson in, and locked it. He got behind the wheel.

Hanson's voice came from behind him sounding tight like piano wire. "You gonna shoot me or what?"

"Not another gotdamn word." He started the engine and drove west by way of the new bridge over the Mississippi River toward the lights illuminating the clouds above Southland Greyhound Park. He parked out front and dragged Hanson through a crowd at the entrance and into the lobby in cuffs. A guard checked Billy's shield and radioed the manager his question about Hanson's Superfecta win. They walked through the lobby to the sound of slot machines and a race being called. Down a hallway, a manager came out from behind a steel door that looked like it could withstand a nuclear blast. He was as big as a pro linebacker and wore a pinky ring with a large ruby in the center. His hands were manicured, his suit pressed, and his shoes were polished. Billy was expecting a Bronx accent. Instead he got proper British.

"Good evening, Officer," the manager said.

"It's Detective. I'm with the Memphis Police Department."

"I see." The big man looked Hanson up and down. "Most of our winners aren't returned to us in handcuffs. You gave my guard the name Roscoe Hanson."

"Right. I want to verify his win," Billy said.

"I understand. I've checked the cashier's video. Mr. Hanson had a spot of luck today. He collected fourteen thousand. Taxes deducted, of course."

Hanson took it quietly with his head down, knowing better than to gloat.

"Anything else, Detective?" the manager asked.

"No, sir. That'll do it. Thanks."

"Then may I ask that you exit through a side entrance? A man leaving in handcuffs will give our clientele the wrong impression."

"Not a problem," Billy said.

They followed the guard down the hall. Billy had a decision to make. The fact that Hanson had big bucks didn't tie him to the murder, so now he had nothing. He could have the idiot's probation revoked based on gambling and consorting with a felon at E & H, but the paperwork would take time away from the investigation.

Before they entered the lobby, he removed the cuffs. Hanson rubbed his wrists, his eyes bouncing around as if looking for an avenue of escape.

"We're done," Billy said. "Call a cab."

Hanson wiggled his brows. A smile twisted his mouth. "Don't believe I will. I've had a hell of a lucky day. Looks like it's my lucky night."

Billy walked out, leaving Hanson gazing at the tote board.

The rest of the money would be gone by morning. In the parking lot, he realized he'd never gotten that cheeseburger. Now it was too late to eat. He decided to call Frankie. She answered, still at her desk at the CJC. He told her about the last two hours, even the rough stuff in the parking lot.

"E and H and the dog track?" she said. "Wish I'd been there. Where did you come out?"

"Bad news. Our suspects list just got shorter. Good news. Give Hanson a week, and he'll be back at Turney in the program."

Chapter 22

The next morning Billy and Frankie sat at their desks reading each other's notes from the previous day's interviews. Hers were short and precise. His read like pulp fiction.

"Rosalyn has a watertight alibi, so why is Mrs. Adams accusing her?" she asked.

"The woman had a breakdown. Never recovered. She's delusional. She was right about the pregnancy, but we can't rely on her as a source."

"Got it." Frankie went back to reading.

"Rosalyn removed files from Caroline's office," he read aloud. "I specifically told her not to do that."

"Do you want to push back?"

"If we need to. Let's stay with Sharma for now." He read on. "How seriously do you take Martin Lee's question about killing someone?"

"Not at all. He was trying to get under my skin."

"And what's this about Highsmith being out of touch with his assistant all week?"

Frankie put down the notes. "It's a scheduled leave, but here's what I'm wondering. He advised Caroline to take out a protective order against Sharma. If Sharma found out about it, or if he had some reason to be jealous, Highsmith could be a second victim."

Billy picked up the baseball he kept on his desk. "Just what we need. What do we know about him?"

"I did a quick search. He was an assistant State's Attorney in Chicago for five years. Not sure why he moved to Memphis except that the Lee Law Firm probably offered him top dollar for his litigation credentials. Defendants love a lawyer with prosecutorial experience who's jumped the fence."

"Let's not make this complicated," he said. "He's probably on vacation and roughing it where there's no cell service. Or he's into dope, booze, or gambling, and he doesn't want to think about real life. When's he due back?"

"Monday."

"If he's not back by then we'll look into it."

"I'll run a deeper background on him just in case." She stood. "By the way, Caroline's security control panel showed no one entered her house on Monday night. And I found a sweater that's a possible match for the fibers in her car." She held up a paper bag. "I'll run it to the lab now."

His phone rang. It was the department's receptionist. "Detective Able, Dr. Sharma is here. Something about seeing a letter."

Oh, hell. He called out to Frankie, who was almost to the door then spoke into the phone to the receptionist. "Is his attorney with him?"

"He's alone and very anxious," she whispered.

Frankie was back and standing in front of him. He covered the phone. "I called Jerry Vanderman last night about that draft letter you found. He must've told Sharma. He's out front without Vanderman asking to see it."

"Vanderman's going to flip out," she said. "You know he's already reeled off that speech attorneys give their clients to keep them in line— 'Don't talk to the media, or the police, or even your family. Not one word unless I pull your string.'"

"It's not smart to come here without Vanderman, but Sharma hasn't been charged. He can do what he wants."

"If he's here asking about the letter he must not have seen it," she said.

"And he's not going to. Not until it's made available in discovery. But I won't tell him that until I get some answers out of him."

He put the phone to his ear. "Send him in." He looked at Frankie. "I'll take him one-on-one. Set your mobile to record and look busy."

She put her mobile on his desk and walked over to the filing cabinets where she could see and hear.

Sharma stormed through the door, his blue scrubs stained with sweat at the armpits and chest, blood spatters on his pants, his hair flattened from wearing a surgical cap. His eyes flicked left and right over the desks looking for Billy. Detectives around the room hung up their phones and went quiet. They wanted to hear this one.

Billy stood. "Over here, Doc." He pointed to the blood on the scrubs. "Did the patient survive?"

"You have a letter addressed to me. I want to read it," Sharma said, ignoring the taunt. Might as well have snapped his fingers.

You want to play this game? We're good at this game, Billy thought. He placed his fingers on a file on his desk. Sharma's gaze dropped to it. The draft wasn't in it, but Sharma didn't know that.

"I'd like to offer my condolences on the passing of your ex-fiancée," Billy said. "I know the Lees are devastated. They're a fine family."

"Damn the Lees," Sharma snapped. "My family is held in

higher regard in a city twenty times the size of Memphis. When Caroline cancelled the wedding they lost face. Important people were ready to fly in from all over the world for the ceremony. I had to tell them not to come. One of them mocked me. Now this shameful murder."

Caroline was dead and this creep was upset about being embarrassed. He saw Frankie glance over her shoulder at Sharma. Her mouth tightened.

"My attorney explained what you're up to," Sharma said. "In America broken romances end up in murder. Caroline left me, so I'm your target."

"Actually, the statistics on men murdering women are the same in most countries," Billy said, standing up. "I'm glad you're here. We could use your help clearing up a couple of things. It won't take long."

Sharma stepped back. "I want to see that letter now."

Billy picked up the file and a legal pad and moved from around his desk. "I understand, sir. We'll get to that." He gestured toward an interview room.

Sharma wagged his head, recognizing the trap. "I have no time for questions." He shifted on his feet as if working through what he wanted to do next then extracted a cream-colored envelope from his pocket. "Caroline had this note delivered to me by courier. She broke our engagement without giving me a reason."

Billy eyed the note. The assistant had told Frankie that Caroline had sent Sharma a Dear John note. It might be useful in building the case. "We need to discuss all this in private. Step this way."

Sharma didn't budge. "I've read this note many times. It doesn't say she no longer loves me, only that she wanted to cancel the wedding. I believe this was meant to shock me, because I wasn't paying her enough attention. She wanted to be pursued. She wanted me to prove how much I cared." He stopped for a moment, seeming lost. "I'll never understand it. I would've given her everything. All I asked was that she give me children and behave like a proper wife."

Billy became aware of the doctor's sunken cheeks and the pallor beneath his dusky complexion. The hand holding the note looked unsteady. Could be exhaustion from a long surgery. Could be guilt. Why had he risked coming here unless he thought there was something damaging in the letter?

He fanned the note at Billy. "I'll give this to you in exchange for a copy of the letter."

This was going nowhere. "I can't do that, sir."

"What will it take to persuade you to let me read the letter?"

"It's not up to me. It's the law." Sharma slipped the envelope in his pocket and surprised Billy by stepping in.

The doctor spoke softly. "For God's sake, tell me man-to-man. Does she say in that letter there was someone else?" His voice quavered.

Now Billy had it. Sharma came in because of his monstrous ego. The son of a bitch was still jealous even though Caroline was dead.

"Doctor, there's a situation I'd like to tell you about. A woman broke up with a man, much like Caroline did with you. Later the man found out it was because she'd been sleeping with someone else. How do you think that man responded?"

"He killed them both," Sharma said without hesitation. He gave the room full of detectives a deadpan shrug. "But of course, I'm not that man."

"You went into Caroline's house looking for evidence she was cheating on you. You're still not sure and it's driving you crazy. That's why you're here."

Sharma's eyes flared, but he tamped it down quickly. He made a show of looking at his watch. "I have rounds in an hour. I'm leaving."

Billy flicked the back of his hand toward the door. "Take off, Doc. Just remember everyone in this room knows you're good for this murder."

Chapter 23

Sharma walked out of the squad room a dissatisfied and jealous man. Human emotions make people dangerous. After their conversation, Billy was even more certain the doctor had killed Caroline.

She may have told him about the baby—forget the big wedding, she wanted to be married right away, and she wanted to wear her dress. Sharma agreed then shot her believing she'd gotten pregnant by another man. A man's wounded pride is a powerful motivator.

Detective Kloss had closed a similar case a year ago, a woman who ran off with the captain of her husband's bowling team. Three weeks later she called her husband, said she was pregnant with his child, and wanted to come back. He'd said, "Sure baby, come on home."

He met her in the garage and cracked her skull open with his bowling ball. When officers pulled up, the man was waiting for them on the front steps. He said that not knowing if the baby was his had sent him over the edge. He'd apologized to them for the mess he was leaving in the garage.

The heart can be an assassin. Billy knew that from experience.

Frankie returned from taking Caroline's sweater to the lab. While she was gone, he'd transcribed the recording from his conversation with Sharma. A copy would go into the case file as insurance against Vanderman's possible attempt to use Sharma's visit as an excuse to have the case thrown out.

Billy picked up the phone. Zelda Taylor was his next target. She knew things about Caroline he couldn't find out anywhere else, plus he wanted to know what had provoked the argument between Caroline and her at the office. She answered.

"Ms. Taylor, it's Detective Able."

"I'm glad you called. I'm worried about Caroline's cat."

"He's fine. We put out plenty of food and water. I want you to come to the CJC this morning. I need your help clearing up some details."

He heard flamenco guitars playing in the background. "Ms. Taylor?"

"Leo is a rescue cat. He hides from strangers."

He thought a moment. "That's no problem. Meet me at Caroline's house in an hour."

"Great. And call me Zelda."

When Billy pulled up, the cruiser he'd requested as a safeguard against a "he said, she said" incident was waiting in front of the house. He wasn't about to risk a compromised investigation. The officer followed him up the driveway to wait on the porch.

Inside, the entry hall felt lifeless. The essence of Caroline in the house was beginning to seep away. He was uncomfortably aware that the CSU team had jostled her personal things, drawers left open in the living room, magazines scattered on the table. He took a moment to look at the photos in the library of kids grouped in front of the big house at Airlee. Finn Adams came back to him now, a skinny, earnest kid. A young Judd Phillips stood next to him. Another shot was of Caroline and Zelda, teenagers in cowboy hats and bikinis goofing around on horses bareback.

In the corner the gift boxes on the table had been re-stacked after the techs had gone through them. He picked up the top box. Buried inside the tissue he found an antique spoon, the bowl shaped like a clamshell with an "S" for Sharma monogrammed on the handle. The spoon was a sugar shell used for formal teas. Probably not what Zelda had been searching for.

His mother had taught him about sugar shells, pickle forks, and asparagus servers. He knew the proper placement of the fish knife, a pastry fork, and dessert spoon. The afternoons she'd been sober, she would lay out the family's sterling flatware and instruct him on its proper placement for formal meals. He was confident Caroline had been given the same lessons. They weren't the last generation who could tell the difference between sterling and silver plate, but the pool of people who cared about such things was drying up. Lose your family's culture and you lose yourself— like knowing the origin of every Christmas ornament on the tree and knowing what kind of pie people expect to see at Thanksgiving. He hadn't grown up with that kind of tradition, but because of his mother, he could set a hell of a nice table.

He considered the critical comments made by Rosalyn and Gracie Ella Adams about his mother. Yes, she drank. Some days he'd come home from school and find her in the kitchen polishing the Wm. A Rogers flatware and weeping. She would pull him to her side and recite her family's lineage. His great, great grandfather had been a governor of Arkansas. He'd moved to Georgia and bought a thousand acres near Atlanta, worth millions now. Dementia had taken hold and the land was stolen from him. She would tell the story of her great, great uncle, Dr. Tom Rivers, who had assisted Dr. Jonas Salk in developing the polio vaccine.

His mother had begun drinking well before her visit to friends in Tunica one summer after graduating from college. She'd met Jackson Able. They ran off and got married. Her parents had been appalled but made a wedding present of thirty thousand dollars for a down payment on a house. Jackson used the money to buy an appliance store in Pontotoc, Mississippi.

He ran the store into the ground, left town owing money, and abandoned his wife with a young son to raise. Billy had wondered why she stayed in Pontotoc instead of going home to her folks in Georgia. Later on he understood it had been about alcohol and shame.

Hard to know the direction your life will take when you fall in love. What Rosalyn said about his father had been true. His mother had come to that realization too late.

He was in the kitchen checking on the cat's food and water when he heard Zelda speaking with the officer on the porch. He wasn't prepared for the change in her appearance as she came through the door. Instead of flip-flops and a nightgown she had on a russet suede jacket, skinny jeans, and high-heeled boots. He hadn't noticed on Tuesday how slender she was. She came toward him swinging a cat carrier, her vulpine features reminding him of a friend's pet fox that used to nip his ankles. Sometimes it drew blood.

"Thank you for meeting me here," he said.

"Glad to. Is the guy on the porch your backup in case I try to take advantage of you?"

"Good guess." He took the carrier from her.

She peered around him into the kitchen. "Any sign of Leo?"

"Just an empty food bowl and a full litter box from the smell, so he's around."

She wrinkled her nose. "You check the guest rooms for him. I'll take the master."

She strode down the hall and into Caroline's bedroom like a perp who knew exactly where to find the loot. Whatever she'd been looking for in the library she now thought was in Caroline's bedroom. He waited one minute then went down the hall and found her in the large walk-in closet poking through a drawer full of costume jewelry.

"Shopping?" he asked.

She straightened. "You scared me. I can't stand sneaky people."

"Me either."

She slammed the drawer. "I'm looking for a ring. A big sapphire."

"Diamonds set on either side of the stone?"

She came over to stand in front of him. "Where is it?"

He'd noticed Zelda hadn't mentioned Caroline, not a single sign of grief, not a question about the investigation.

"In Caroline's handbag," he said.

She frowned. "The one she had with her the night she died?"

He nodded.

"That's my mother's ring. When will I get it back?"

"I can't say. But if it's so important, why did you give it to Caroline?"

"I didn't give it to her. She borrowed it for the wedding as her 'something borrowed, something blue' item. Then she refused to return it, so I assumed she'd lost it. We argued about it."

"Is that what the fight was about on Monday?"

She scratched her nose. "Yes."

"Why didn't you say that earlier?"

"I was upset. You were acting like I'd killed her."

"Did you kill her?"

She narrowed her eyes outlined with black kohl. Stage makeup. He reminded himself that this woman was a performer.

"You think I shot Caroline over a ring?" she asked.

"Just answer the question."

"I *didn't* kill her. I told you how I feel about guns." She blinked rapidly and bit her lower lip. "I don't want to discuss this."

The nose scratching, the blinking, the lip biting—they were all signs of lying. He decided to let her stew for awhile. "There's a closet full of expensive suits with tags still attached. What can you tell me about that?"

She rolled her eyes. "That was Raj. He disapproved of Caroline's wardrobe. She has these great retro finds and custom leather jackets from LA. She'd tone it down when she went to court, but otherwise she loved dressing in edgy clothes. I'd kill for a wardrobe like that." She winced. "I didn't mean it that way."

"Go on."

"Raj had those stuffy suits delivered without even asking her. He wanted her to dress conservatively like the wife of an important doctor. She refused. He wouldn't take them back so she left them in the closet. The bastard tried to bully her into giving in."

Billy glanced around. "I don't see her wedding dress. You think she sold it?"

"No way. It was custom-made with heirloom lace. She probably stored it in one of the guest rooms. I'll check."

She started past him. He put his hand on her arm. "Caroline was wearing the dress the night she died. She was on her way to be married."

Zelda shrugged off his hand. "To whom?"

"We don't know."

She sucked in a breath and pushed past him. He found her

seated at the foot of the bed, staring at the portrait of Caroline and Saunders. Tears streamed down her face. He found a box of tissues in the bathroom and brought it back.

"You think it was Raj?" she asked.

"Do you?"

"It doesn't make sense. She'd cut ties with him." She stopped, reasoning it through. "A wedding. That's why she wanted to keep the ring." She covered her face with her hands then dropped them. "This hasn't seemed real until now, but thinking of her dying in that dress . . . I have to confess—I lied about Caroline and me being close. We weren't even friends. It's been that way since we were kids. I admired her and I was envious. Sometimes I hated her. Now I feel really rotten about it."

She swallowed. "Uncle Saunders indulged her. He called her Sparrow like she was a helpless little bird, but she wasn't. The girls at school got her into coke. She craved the stuff. It kicked off the first of her manic episodes. She started shoplifting, sneaking out of the house to party. Then a cop stopped her for a broken taillight and busted her for a gram of coke. Aunt Rosalyn inter-vened with the DA. They wanted to 'protect her future.'" Zelda made quote marks with her fingers. "The charges were dropped."

She looked out the window and wiped her cheeks. "My fresh-man year at Rhodes I drank too much PGA punch at a frat party and got so drunk I plowed my car into the back of a dump truck. Aunt Rosalyn told my mother that a few days in jail would be a maturing experience. They left me there for two days. They weren't so worried about *my* future."

"What about the time you and your buddies waylaid the pres-ident of the NRA?" he asked.

She sighed. "I'd forgotten about that. We wanted to make a point about guns. You can't open a closet in my family's houses without seeing a shotgun. My dad owned shotguns. He—you don't understand how much I hate guns." She turned watery eyes on him. "I shouldn't have told you about Caroline doing drugs."

"Why?"

"It makes her look bad. And I can tell you still have feelings for her. First love and all."

"No harm done. But I'm curious. Did Caroline talk about me?"

"Yeah. She said you're a really good kisser."

He studied her. "You're lying again."

She gave him a half smile. "I was guessing. I always thought you guys had something going with the way you looked at her."

That pissed him off. "This isn't a game. She called you on Monday evening. You're one of the last people she spoke with. Tell me again where you were that night."

She stopped smiling. "I didn't kill Caroline so quit asking me."

A muffled meow came from under the bed. A large black cat—scrappy-looking with a bony skull and an ear half chewed off—jumped on the bed. He padded across Zelda's lap to sit on a folded blanket beside her.

"Hi, Leo," she said.

The cat blinked at her then blinked at Billy.

"He likes you. Caroline said he prefers men."

A gray scar zigzagged across the top of his head and swooped down to his left eye. "What happened to his head?" he asked.

"A Rottweiler got him down behind the air conditioning unit in the firm's parking lot. But Leo got his licks in."

The cat switched his tail.

"Tough guy, huh," Billy said.

"Caroline had a vet patch him up and she took him home. Raj said she had to get rid of him before the wedding. I think that was the final straw."

Zelda sneezed and scooted away from the cat. "What's going to happen to him?"

"You brought the cat carrier. You're taking him home."

"No way. I signed up to feed him and empty the litter box." She sneezed again. "I'm allergic."

Leo yowled from the back seat all the way to the barge. Billy wondered how he'd ended up with the cat even temporarily although he admired the way the cat had landed a cushy home with Caroline. He didn't mind helping out as long as Zelda did as she'd promised and found a home for him in a few days.

At the barge he set up the litter box in the bathroom and gave Leo a can of salmon fillet. The cat knocked back the whole can and looked for more, which Billy gave him.

"You ready to chill?" he asked.

The cat groomed his whiskers and ignored the question. Billy had never owned a cat, but knew they were good at working their own agenda. Not too often a human gets something over on a cat. As a cop, he couldn't fault that behavior.

Leo slept on a towel in the bathroom while he made coffee with chicory, heated a can of Stagg Chili, cut a big wedge of cheddar, and grabbed a handful of saltines. A breeze was blowing off the water, so he pulled on a jacket and took his food out on the deck. Sunlight sparkled on the eddies behind the bridge pylons. A flock of Canada geese flew downriver in squadron formation while he ate. He saved his coffee for last and made notes on his conversation with Zelda.

No alibi, he wrote. Angry about the ring, clueless about the dress. Hard to know if she's telling the truth or doing a good job of acting. Honest about her DUI, dishonest about her relationship with Caroline. Dishonest/honest. Interesting woman.

Beautiful woman. He couldn't help but wonder what was going on under that hood. He scratched out the part about her being beautiful. Not the place for that observation.

Had she exaggerated Caroline's drug use and behavioral issues? Difficult to verify. She'd admitted being envious and even hating her cousin. Zelda didn't fit the profile of a murderer, except that she was part of Caroline's long-term inner circle, which meant she didn't need to develop a reason to kill her.

He took his dishes inside and heard the cat meowing in the bathroom, so he opened the door. Leo jumped on the bed, stretched out, and began to purr.

"Good idea, bud," he said. "Wish I could join you."

Chapter 24

Sitting at her desk, sipping her third coffee, Frankie flipped through a summary of Caroline's banking and credit card statements. Multiple cash withdrawls popped up reminding her of the hundred dollar bills in the money clip and the cash Caroline had squirreled away around the house. Caroline appeared to be as obsessive about having cash available as she had been about her housekeeping.

Billy was on his way to meet Zelda Taylor at Caroline's, a smart move. The woman would be difficult to handle in the interview room. Frankie found her quirkiness—not to mention the obvious childhood crush she had on Billy—irritating. He would work that relationship to his advantage with his sincere tone and slow smile. She'd seen tough offenders give up the damnedest information to him, because he'd slipped under their guard.

She put away Caroline's records and moved to her search on Highsmith. Nothing remarkable there, not even a speeding ticket. Robert Highsmith had grown up in Lincoln Park and attended University of Chicago Law School, graduating third in his class. He then joined the Cook County State's Attorney's Office. With those credentials and visibility as an assistant state's attorney, he must have been planning a political career. If that was the case, the move to Memphis was a veer off course.

She signed onto Friend Feed and Search Systems but found little information. No Facebook or Twitter account, but then on an initial pass Highsmith hadn't seemed like the social media type. An article in the *Chicago Tribune*'s archives pictured him and two colleagues participating in a Toys for Tots drive. All three wore Santa hats and business suits. Highsmith—barrel-chested with a high forehead—gripped a three-foot-tall Big Bird in front of him like he'd taken the bird hostage. Not a handsome man, more the dependable type.

The most telling piece was an article published in the *Tribune* seven weeks before Highsmith had left Chicago. A city council-man was in court being arraigned on bribery charges. Highsmith was the prosecutor. Immediately after the councilman and his attorney were given a trial date, the councilman stood up and began to curse at the Cook County State's Attorney, who hap-pened to be in the rear of the courtroom. The reporter implied that the councilman had seemed astonished when prosecution of the case moved forward. The article also noted that the council-man had twice before been arrested on felony charges. In both cases, the State's Attorney had, without explanation, dismissed the charges. Soon after that Highsmith was out of a job.

It smelled rotten. Frankie imagined the Cook County State's Attorney had instructed Highsmith to tell the judge they had decided to drop the charges. Highsmith may have objected. As a result the state's attorney fired him. On the other hand, High-smith could have quit in protest or disgust.

That had been seven months ago. Highsmith moved to Mem-phis and had been with the Lee Law Firm for around five months. She copied the article, submitted requests for more documents from the Cook County Clerk's office, and moved to Caroline's phone logs from her office and mobile.

Starting with the day Caroline died, Frankie cross-referenced her office calls with her list of clients. All incoming and outgoing calls had been work-related. During the afternoon and evening hours, she'd made five notable calls on her mobile. The first was to Blue Hopkins, presumably about the wedding arrangements. The second was to Robert Highsmith. According to his file, he had repeatedly urged her to allow him to file the protective order. Since she was planning to leave town, it was possible she'd called to put that on hold. The third was to Zelda Taylor, the fourth to Gracie Ella Adams, her aunt. The fifth was to Judd Phillips. That one put up a red flag. Judd said he and Caroline had been out of touch.

Frankie tapped in Judd's number. "Mr. Phillips, this is Detective Malone. I need to speak with you . . . Oh, really." She listened. "That *is* a coincidence. I can come there. Sure. I have the address."

S omeone had done a masterful job updating Judd's 1930s cozy craftsman bungalow by enlarging the paned windows and adding peaked roofs and stone pillars to the porch. The yard had been extensively landscaped. And there was the red BMW Z4, Frankie's all-time favorite car, sitting in the driveway.

Judd was waiting for her on the porch, seated in a wicker chair with a coffee cup and reading a newspaper. He folded his paper and stood as she came up the walk, carrying her satchel. She could tell he was attempting to read her face the same way she'd seen him do with other players around a poker table.

"Cool day to be reading outside," she called.

"I needed some air."

She took the steps up to the porch.

"Let me take that," he said, relieving her of the heavy satchel on her shoulder. She picked up on his bloodshot eyes and the smell of the rum he'd poured in his coffee.

She'd grown up with her father's alcoholism and the smell of Flor de Caña rum as he drank himself into a stupor every night. Alcohol had been his way to blunt his anger toward a wife who'd left him with a daughter he had not wanted in the first place.

She wondered what pain Judd was trying to bury. She understood. She'd done the same for a brief time with pills. The struggle to get past it had given her a new kind of courage, something she hadn't expected.

Judd held the front door for her. The oak floors and the sun flooding through the windows and skylights made the space warm and inviting. They passed through a rustic, tasteful living room with a fireplace and a sofa deep enough to curl up in. This was a real home, not what she'd expected from the drunken man she'd met two nights ago at the CJC.

A Georges Braque painting, *Vase, Palette and Mandolin* done in charcoal and oil, hung over the mantel. The logic of the geometric shapes in his work had always fascinated her.

"You're a student of art?" She stepped closer to study the painting.

"More a student of poker."

"I've seen a photo of Braque. You look a lot like him."

Judd laughed, pleased.

She followed him through an arched doorway into the dining room where the rustic elegance stopped. This was a war room—chairs pushed against the walls, their seats loaded with boxes and binders, a computer and desk chair positioned at the end of a ten-foot farmer's table, lists written on whiteboards, and news articles tacked up.

Aerial photos of rice fields took up most of one wall. On an adjacent wall hung a geological survey that mapped the flood inundation of a river basin. Yellow and blue sticky notes with directional arrows festooned the edges.

"I've read the case files," she said, indicating the satchel he'd laid on the table.

Judd dipped his head. "I was sure you'd find them interesting. Finn was a great guy. He deserved more than to vanish without a clue."

A two-foot by four-foot photo of shoes and folded clothes lying near the water's edge dominated the room. She'd seen the shot in the file. Enlarged it was even more unsettling. She walked over to look at several snapshots Judd had pinned around it. In one of them, Finn was sitting in the Camaro, leaning out the driver's side window and waving. Caroline and Judd were standing next to the front fender, both of them grinning.

"Finn bought that car with his own money," Judd said. "He was a wizard in the stock market."

"Looks like the three of you were close."

"Best friends."

"How did Caroline end up with the Camaro?"

"Seeing it in the driveway every day made Finn's mother heartsick. She let Caroline take it as long as she promised to give it up when Finn came home."

He pointed out a photo of Finn and Caroline, the Gothic architecture of the Rhodes College campus in the background. A man stood between them, one arm around Finn's shoulders and the other around Caroline's waist. In his thirties, he was fit and tan with angular features and thick dark hair cut short on the sides. Frankie thought of the Argentine polo players who used to fly into Key West to compete in the local field polo tournaments. At night they would take over the bars on Duval Street with women practically throwing panties at their feet. This guy had the same cocky smile.

"That's Clive Atwood," Judd said. "Finn came down with mono the fall of his junior year and had to sit out seven weeks. Aunt Gracie Ella hired Atwood as a tutor to get him through the semester. He claimed to have graduated from Princeton and earned a Masters in journalism at Stanford. Finn came out of the semester with a 4.0 average. We were impressed. After that Atwood hung around as a mentor."

"Why do you say 'claimed'?"

"After Finn disappeared I got suspicious and looked into Atwood's background. He'd been expelled from Princeton and never attended Stanford. He had a minor possession charge in Florida and an arrest in Georgia for selling counterfeit DVDs out of his trunk. Got probation for that.

"Our family has lived in a bubble of power and privilege for many years. It didn't occur to us that someone with Atwood's background could work his way inside."

"It happens. Con artists seek out smart, wealthy people like your family and worm their way in. They rely on your good manners."

"Finn trusted him. We've calculated that Atwood talked him out of at least thirty grand."

She studied the photo, the way Finn's gaze cut possessively at Atwood. "The PI report indicated Finn and Atwood were lovers."

Judd's eyes softened. "That explains a lot, doesn't it?"

"What makes you think Atwood had a role in the disappearance?"

Judd's gaze jumped around the room over the charts and stacks of files. "Atwood started dealing drugs. We believe he talked Finn into making a pickup. It got him killed."

"You're certain he's dead?"

"Without a body . . ." He shrugged. "Walker's investigators believe he's gone. The day Finn disappeared the landlord overheard him yelling on the phone. Records show Atwood called Finn from Miami three times that day. Walker believes Atwood convinced Finn to drive to a place in Arkansas where meth labs had been operating. Meth cookers have shit for brains. You know what I'm talking about."

She nodded, not wanting to interrupt.

"I'm sure Finn didn't know what he was walking into. It would be like him to balk when he realized he'd been sent to mule meth. He'd be furious."

Frankie looked around the room, aware of the resources Judd had thrown at the case. She caught him rubbing his eyes. "Headache?"

"No sleep. It's under my skin. Finn and Caroline gone. You're wondering why I think the cases are connected. Take another look at the photograph of the two of them standing with Atwood."

She leaned in. Atwood had pulled Caroline close, his hand around her waist, two fingers slipped deep into her waistband.

"She had it bad for him," he said. "She'd done a lot of drugs as a teenager, but it was behind her. Atwood found out. He roped her in with coke."

"You're sure?"

"I'm sure," he said.

"She had to know Finn and Atwood were lovers."

"No one in the family knew Finn was gay. Maybe Zelda did, but she'd never bring it up. Finn wouldn't want Caroline to know about him and Atwood, although she was so infatuated I don't think it would have mattered. Atwood must have realized Finn's money was limited and that Caroline's folks were the ones with the deep pockets."

Frankie thought about that. "You believe Atwood wanted Finn out of the picture?"

"Hard to say. Running drugs out of Arkansas was dangerous business. Walker believed the meth cooks killed Finn by accident or for the hell of it. Knowing they'd screwed up, they called Atwood. He was smart enough to make the murder look like an accident or suicide.

"I ran into Atwood at a bar downtown after the case went cold. I hauled him out into an alley and knocked him around, gave him Walker's theory about the meth labs and Finn's murder. I accused him of being responsible. He took off running. I couldn't catch him. He disappeared after that. Caroline found out what I'd done. That's why she quit talking to me."

"I picked that up from the transcript," she said.

"Walker tracked him to a California prison where he served 120 days for a simple possession charge. He gated out. Walker lost him." Judd fell silent. He ran his palm across his forehead, sweating. The rum and conversation had taken its toll.

"On the phone you said you had information about Caroline," she said.

"Right. It's in the kitchen if you'll follow me."

He showed her to a kitchen with a beamed ceiling and brick fireplace. Sitting on a stack of old phone books at the end of the counter was a dusty answering machine.

"I just found this message Caroline left on my landline. It's time stamped Monday afternoon. I was concerned I might lose the recording if I unplugged the machine to bring it to your office."

"Good thinking," she said. She took out her mobile and set it to RECORD.

He hit PLAY.

Chapter 25

aroline's voice came over the speaker sounding elated. She spoke in a hurry.

"Judd, it's Sparrow. It's been too long. That's my fault. I'm leaving town for a couple of days. If you're in Memphis when I come back, let's get together. I'll have some happy news. At least I'm happy about it. I've missed you, Cuz."

Judd hit the STOP button.

Caroline's good news probably referred to the baby, but Judd wouldn't know about that. "What are you thinking?" she asked.

"Atwood's back."

"Why jump to that conclusion?"

"The excitement in her voice. If you'd seen how wrapped up she was in Atwood, you'd understand. Before Finn disappeared, she confided that Atwood had come to Vandy and proposed. She wanted to graduate from law school before they married, so they kept it secret. Then Finn disappeared and Atwood took off."

"There's nothing in that message that points to Atwood."

"There is." He played it again. "Only three people ever called her Sparrow—her dad, Finn, and Clive Atwood. She never used the name between us. I think she'd been talking to Atwood."

"That's pretty thin."

He regarded her. "I'm at a dead end with Finn's case. Atwood knows what happened to him. I think he came here to seduce Caroline and wound up killing her. If we find him, we may wrap up both cases." He was more clear-eyed now. He held her gaze, didn't flinch.

What the hell, she thought. He could be right. "Tell me what you think happened."

"Atwood found out about her engagement to Dr. Sharma and got in touch. A call from him would have turned her world upside down."

"You think she would've gone back to Atwood that easily?"

"In a heartbeat. Especially if he played on her sympathy and fed her a plausible story about where he'd been."

"You have evidence he's been in Memphis?" she asked.

"After I heard the message this morning, I hired an investigator to look for him."

Frankie considered a possible scenario. Atwood showed up with a good story and a supply of coke. That could explain the vial in her overnight bag. She partied with him a couple of times and decided to cancel the wedding with Sharma. When she found out she was pregnant, she chose to marry Atwood. On the way to Airlee, she changed her mind and rejected him. Would he kill her? Murder isn't the typical profile for con artists.

"Do you think he'd kill her?" she asked.

"I have a report on Atwood written by a prison psychiatrist. Read it and you'll understand.

"What kicked off my investigation was a visit with Aunt Gracie Ella four years ago after she'd been released from the hospital. She was like a bonfire burned down to ashes. She was suffering. For both our sakes, I had to find out what happened to Finn. That hasn't changed."

He cleared his throat. "Would you consider riding over to the scene with me tomorrow to take a look?"

At the CJC Frankie stowed her satchel under her desk and went to check on Harrison's progress with the marriage license application search. When she came back Billy was on the phone with his shoulders up around his ears. He hung up and began scribbling on a pad.

"How'd it go with Zelda?" she asked.

"Good. She explained the closet of suits with the tags on them. Sharma wanted his wife-to-be to dress more conservatively. That fell flat with Caroline. I think Zelda is going to try and talk Rosalyn into giving her Caroline's wardrobe. She's an enterprising woman."

Frankie leaned her backside against the edge of her desk. *Sheesh.* Men could be so bloody stupid. "What else?"

"The sapphire ring belonged to Zelda. She loaned it to Caroline for the wedding to Sharma. Caroline wouldn't give it back. Zelda says that's what the fight in the office was about."

"You believe her?"

"About the ring? Yes. But there's more to the fight than she's telling. And she sure changed her story about being best buddies with Caroline. Caroline went to the top of the family firm. Zelda got stuck in the file room."

"I'll bet she said the family spoiled Caroline and treated her like a dog."

A funny look crossed his face. "Yeah, sorta. She said Caroline picked up a coke habit at her private school. Bored little rich girls looking for trouble. The coke triggered manic episodes that never went away. And she had some legal problems."

"Manic episodes," Frankie said. "That explains her dependence on scripts. The coke screwed up her neurochemistry. Judd told me she'd been clean then started back with coke in college."

"You've talked to Judd Phillips?"

"I did. But let's stay with this."

He frowned, not used to her controlling the conversation.

"Is Zelda on our suspects list?" she asked.

"The fight over the ring still bothers me. I think she showed up at the house on Tuesday to push her way into the investigation."

"We'll see how it rolls. Hold on. I have something else." She went to her desk to pick up her mobile and two files.

"Here's Caroline's phone log." She gave him a marked up copy. "Caroline made five calls on Monday evening. Three we've confirmed—Blue Hopkins, Zelda Taylor, and Gracie Ella Adams. The fourth was Highsmith. We'll assume she was on her way to marry Sharma and wanted to cancel the protective order."

She tapped her finger on the log. "And this one. She left a message on Judd Phillips's landline. I went to his house to record it."

She played it on her mobile. Billy listened with his chin tucked and his brow furrowed. He asked to hear it again. He wanted to listen to the message, but she knew he also wanted to hear Caroline's voice a second time, an observation she would keep to herself.

"Her good news was about the pregnancy," he said.

"Judd doesn't know about the baby. He has a different interpretation."

She summarized the connection between Finn, Atwood, and Caroline including the secret engagement. "Judd thinks Atwood came to Memphis to snake Caroline away from Sharma."

Billy picked up the baseball on his desk, tossed it in the air, and caught it. "You've confirmed Atwood is in town?"

"Judd put an investigator on it this morning."

He tossed the ball up again. "Why would Atwood kill his potential meal ticket?"

"Try this. She dumped Sharma and got back together with Atwood. She agreed to marry him then tried to back out at the last minute. He's broke, he's desperate. He snapped and killed her."

Billy leaned back, thumbing the ball. "You're intrigued with this Phillips character."

She knew this would be coming. "I wouldn't say that."

"Would you say he's an alcoholic?"

"He has a drinking problem."

"He's a rum-dum. He's steering you off course."

She held up her mobile. "We need to rule Atwood in or out. And your comment about my being intrigued with Phillips is out of line."

"Point taken." He set the ball on its stand. "Now I have news. Rosalyn called the director this morning and told him my interview with her husband put him in the hospital. She called me opportunistic white trash. Said I want to see my name in the papers."

"Wow. And Davis repeated that crap to you? He should've thrown it back in her face."

"Here's the thing. Our new director, Mr. *Jefferson* Davis, is as Old South as the Lees. His family ran out of money faster, so he had to get a working man's job. He's going to align with people like the Lees all day long."

"That's unethical."

"You're not from here, so I'll explain how it works," he said. "We have two types of born and raised Southerners—sons of planters who've owned delta soil for over a hundred years, and the sons of the poor whites who moved from the Kentucky and North Carolina hills. The poor whites bought acreage from struggling plantations. They started their farms but couldn't compete with the big planters who still had cheap labor from sharecroppers. Most of the poor whites lost their farms. They had to go into government work or sell burial insurance to the blacks. They ended up living in tenant houses or trailers. That's where the term 'trailer trash' comes from.

"It doesn't matter that the descendants of those families have gone to university and now own businesses and practice law, the Old South folks still resent the fact that their great grandfathers stole land from plantation owners.

"The poor whites blamed the blacks for everything bad that had happened to them. It's human nature to find someone to look down on. The more they burned crosses and lynched people, the more blacks caught the train north to Memphis and Chicago. Here's the twist. The Old South folks depended on frightened and oppressed blacks to maintain their lifestyles. They resented the poor whites even more because they had scared off the cheap labor."

"Where does Rosalyn say you fit in?"

"I'm poor white on my father's side and Old South on my mother's. Her family never forgave her for marrying beneath herself."

Frankie hardly knew how to respond. This was his heritage he was talking about. She could see the discussion was upsetting him. Even if Billy wasn't insulted, she was.

"I don't care if Director Davis believes he's the president of the Confederate States, he's supposed to be in the trenches with us," she said.

"He'll be there with us until someone like Rosalyn yanks his chain."

He picked up the *Commercial Appeal* and turned it so she could read the headline:

Local Attorney Murdered in Bison Field

"Tomorrow the story will be Middlebrook's plea to the public for information. Every kook in the city will call the tip line. We'll have officers chasing bullshit leads instead of digging up real witnesses." He creased the paper and dropped it in the trash. "A waste of time."

She knew that sullen look. "The chief didn't consult you on this."

"That's not the point."

"It's precisely the point. You're angry because Middlebrook and Davis are going around you."

"Which is the reason I don't want you to be sidetracked by your gambling buddy. You and I have to solve this case and get out from under it."

"Damn it, Billy, don't put this off on me."

Detective Kloss walked by, grinning. "You guys fight like a married couple."

"Hey, that hurts," Frankie called after him.

Billy started slamming desk drawers. "Where are we on the marriage license application?"

"The entire staff at one of the clerk's offices got food poisoning from bad potato salad served at a birthday party. They've been closed for three days. The Benton County's office had pipes break in the ceiling. Everything's soaked. But Harrison is staying with it."

Billy took a fresh memo book from a drawer and flung it onto the desk. "Any surveillance shots of the Camaro from Monday night?"

"Not yet."

"Those frigging guys aren't doing their job."

"I'll be sure to pass that along." She handed him pages from a file. "Here's the latest on Highsmith."

"We can't find him either?"

She took a breath, held her tongue. She'd been in his place—angry, frustrated. "His grandfather is some kind of kingmaker in Illinois politics. Highsmith was the golden boy of the Cook County State's Attorney's Office until his departure last May."

Billy flipped through the pages and stopped at the Toys for Tots photo. "He looks like a bore."

"Read the next article. The courtroom fight may have been the reason he moved to Memphis. Looks like the fix was in. I'm still digging. I'll send along anything of interest."

Chapter 26

On the murder squad, you go flat out until there's nothing left to do, or there's nothing left of you.

There were no more field reports to read or calls to make, plus Billy's head felt like a boiled cabbage. A New York strip was waiting in the fridge, but he was too hungry to fire up the grill, so he called the Flying Fish for an order of crawfish chowder, blackened catfish fillets, and a large order of fried jalapeño chips.

When he got to the restaurant, the kitchen was running behind. He took a corner table and put a call into the one friend he'd made the year he attended Ole Miss School of Law. Carson Bicks had wanted to get the hell out of Mississippi, so he'd joined a Chicago firm as a criminal defense attorney. Billy hadn't seen his buddy since they'd run into each other three Christmases ago at the Hollywood Cafe near Tunica, but he knew Carson wouldn't mind a voicemail requesting confidential information. He wanted to find out if ASA Highsmith had a reputation in Chicago's legal community as a fixer.

State's Attorneys can make things happen, more so than most officials. Sometimes they get overzealous with a prosecution. Occasionally, it goes the other way. When a solid case is kicked out of court for no obvious reason, everyone in law enforcement smells rotten fish.

He picked up his order of chowder and took Riverside Drive home, easing down the steep pitch of the cobblestone landing to his home at the edge of the slack water. He'd left the porch light burning. As he walked up the ramp, he could hear the radio he'd left on to keep the cat company. When he opened the door, Leo jumped down from the sofa and trotted over, making guttural sounds in his throat.

"I'm going to teach you how to use the can opener," he said as the cat led him to the food bowl. He opened a can of white fish in sauce. Leo glanced up and licked his chops.

He sat in his recliner with a Corona and switched on a James Bond movie he'd seen before. He watched car chases and bombs explode while he ate his blackened catfish and crawfish chowder out of a foam cup. He drank a second beer and finished off the jalapeño chips before the movie ended, thinking the beer would help him unwind. He considered the pack of Camels he kept in a drawer, but thought better of it and poured three fingers of Jack Daniel's before walking out on the aft deck.

He looked out over the broad Mississippi, the most untamed, indifferent entity in the region. The moon cast white light on the water, and in the distance a bonfire flared on a sandbar on the Arkansas side of the river. He scanned the Memphis skyline with its unique sense of place. He wasn't born in Memphis but felt downtown, the bridges, the river—all of it belonged to him. He'd given up a lot to be a cop in this city.

Two years ago he'd fallen in love with an extraordinary woman named Mercy Snow. He'd met her during an investigation involving her older sister who'd gone missing. Mercy had a growing business in Atlanta that she loved, so when the case was

solved, he went there on an extended leave from the force to give
their relationship a try. After nine months, things between them
had cooled off. Mercy didn't want to leave Atlanta. He wanted
to be a homicide cop in Memphis. They called it quits, and he'd
come back to live on the barge alone.

Leaving Mercy had just about flattened him. Now Caroline
was gone. A wave of loneliness hit. He took a deep breath, cen-
tering himself. He took a swallow of the Jack and sucked cold air
over the warming liquid, tasting the soot and burnt toffee. The
night folded around him like an old friend. He needed sleep. He
needed a lot of things—sex, a weekend in a bass boat, and that
New York strip in the fridge grilled to medium rare.

He was ready to go inside when his mobile rang.

"Where are you?" Frankie asked.

He could tell she was out for a run, her rhythmic breathing
layered with traffic noise. "I'm on the aft deck taking it all in," he
said. Now he could hear her running in place, probably waiting
on a light.

"Glorious moon out," she said. "Two things. The report came
back on Caroline's sweater. It's a match to the fibers caught in
the car seat protector. They must've rubbed off on the lace of
the dress."

"So that's a dead end."

"Appears to be. Second, I've emailed some documents on
Highsmith. The light's changed. Catch you later."

Frankie hung up and slipped her phone into the zippered
pocket on her hip. After so many days of rain, the clouds
had given way to the moon and stars. Driving home, her choice
had been to collapse in bed or go for a run. The bed nearly won,
but she'd thrown cold water on her face and put on running

gear. She was glad now to feel her lethargy disappearing with every step.

She turned south and jogged under the trestle into the Cooper-Young district passing by Soul Fish Restaurant, her favorite place for fried catfish, hush puppies, and Southern style vegetables. Down the block she passed the hundred-and-forty-year-old Burke's Books, one of five independent stores that had supported John Grisham with signings before he became famous. Grisham returned to Burke's Books with every new release to sign books for the line of people who circled the block.

She was about to loop around and head home when she noticed a man across the street lumbering toward her. He was wearing Dockers and a light jacket, his arms swinging slightly out of rhythm with his steps. Judd Phillips. He lived several blocks away and apparently had decided to give jogging a try. He stopped in front of a bar a half block from her and bent with his hands on his knees to catch his breath. He straightened, his gaze rolling upward to the underside of the awning. Then he looked at the door. The flask at the CJC came back to her along with the sound of his retching in the bathroom.

Don't, she thought. Don't go in.

The door swung open. An older man, pear-shaped and walking with a cane limped through the door and turned to hold it open. Judd nodded and went inside. She wanted to kick Mr. Pear-Bottom in the shins. Nothing she could do. Judd's drinking problem wasn't her business. She was about to start jogging again when the door swung open. Judd came out followed by a man with a potbelly and a bulbous nose. Judd picked up something from the frame of the window, handed it to the man, and pointed to where the awning was attached to the wall. She got it. Judd must have spotted a problem with the awning and gone inside to tell the owner. Good for him. The men talked for a moment then Judd slapped the man on the back and took off down the sidewalk at a speedy walk.

She caught herself smiling as she crossed over Cooper Street and headed for home.

Billy went back inside the barge and sat in his recliner with his laptop. The documents on Robert Highsmith contained nothing of interest, so he switched to the last half of the game between the Grizzlies and Mavericks.

The room was warm. He kept drowsing off. Next thing he knew he was startled awake by a knock at the door. The game was over. The clock read 11:39. The knock came again. The cat jumped off the sofa and stalked to the door with his tail puffed up.

Billy dropped the chair's footrest. "Who is it?"

"Robert Highsmith. Attorney with the Lee Law Firm."

Highsmith? What the hell. He came to his feet, retrieved his SIG from the drawer, and slipped it in the waistband at his back. Leo was standing in front of the door. He nudged him away with his foot to open it. Highsmith stood beneath the overhead light, hands visible at his sides. A former prosecutor would know that a cop answering the door this time of night would be armed.

Highsmith was taller than he appeared to be in the Toys for Tots photo, well over six feet. He had a paunch, probably from too many hours sitting behind a desk, but he looked solid through the chest and shoulders, the kind of guy who could surprise you with his strength.

Highsmith squinted under the glare of the bulb as if it was giving him a headache. "This a bad time?" he asked.

"Yep," Billy said.

"My assistant texted that you wanted to talk to me about Caroline Lee."

"How did you find my place?"

"I have my resources," Highsmith said.

"This could've waited till tomorrow."

Highsmith jammed his hands in his pockets. "I was driving back in town. I went out of my way to get here."

Billy scanned him. No bulges that might be a weapon, no smell of booze. Dirty, rumpled slacks and a two-day beard. A swipe of white paint marred the arm of his Cubs jacket. He looked like he'd been through the wringer. Showing up this late, he had some kind of an agenda. Might as well find out what it was.

"Watch the cat," he said, and stepped back.

Highsmith came through the door, his nose twitching with distaste as if the barge was a doublewide with the smell of stale beer coming from the sink. Billy smelled it too, the chowder container he'd failed to rinse out before throwing it away.

He didn't offer the man a seat. "You've been out of touch since Tuesday. Your assistant was concerned when you didn't respond to her texts. Where've you been?"

"I took a few days off. There's no cell service where I was staying. I just learned of Caroline's death on the drive in."

"Must've been a shock."

"Yes. It was." Highsmith's eyes went vacant as if he'd disappeared inside himself.

Detectives and prosecutors think they're prepared for when death comes close to them. Billy knew that wasn't true. Especially when it's murder.

Highsmith wiped the back of his hand across his mouth.

"You look like you could use a drink," he said. "I've got some Jack."

Highsmith got a stern look and shook his head. "You have my file on Sharma so you're aware of the escalating harassment. Why isn't he in custody?"

Billy let a couple of beats pass. "You know I can't answer that."

"Caroline came to me for protection. I feel I deserve answers." His fingers curled at his side.

Prosecutors learn to mask their emotions. Highsmith wasn't even trying. "I get that you're invested, but I'm not discussing the case."

"Has Sharma hired an attorney?"

"Jerry Vanderman."

"I hear he's tough. That should tell you something," Highsmith said.

"It does. It says Sharma knows he's a suspect." Discussing Vanderman was going nowhere. Maybe he could get something useful out of this guy. "Is there anything you haven't entered in the file?"

"Last week Sharma accosted Caroline in the firm's parking lot because she refused to wear the clothes he'd given her. I saw it happening and ran out. He had this wild look and took a swing at me. I grabbed hold of Caroline, and a couple of the other attorneys showed up. They kicked him off the property. If I was the prosecutor, I'd lock him up for life."

"You don't run the show anymore, remember? You jumped the fence."

"I know homicidal rage when I see it. The doc realized Caroline wasn't coming back. In that scenario, a lot of women end up dead."

That's how Billy saw it. A man with Sharma's ego wouldn't let Caroline walk away without doing something about it. However, this guy showing up at midnight and throwing accusations around made him wonder. He'd been the new hire working down the hall when Caroline was considering bailing on the marriage. Something personal could've developed between them.

"You've been at the firm for what . . . five months?" he asked.

"About that."

He studied the man's lank hair combed to the right side, the glasses sitting askew in front of round, rabbit gray eyes. Cleaned up, dressed in a suit, he had looked more like a Presbyterian minister than Caroline's type. But with women you never knew.

"You think Caroline was seeing someone behind Sharma's back? I mean intimately."

Highsmith's chest swelled. "That's insulting."

"The other guy could've been just as jealous as Sharma if she told him she'd decided to go back to the doctor." He pointed his index finger at his temple and pulled the imaginary trigger.

Highsmith flinched.

"You were advising her," Billy said. "Did she tell you about the letter she wrote to Sharma?"

"What are you talking about?"

"It began 'Dearest Raj.' She told him she called off the wedding because she'd fallen for another guy."

Highsmith's head jerked back like he'd been punched. He went to the sofa and dropped as if his equilibrium had been shot out from under him. He looked like an electrical storm was passing through his brain.

Billy had exaggerated the details in the draft letter to get a reaction. By damn, it worked. "You didn't say where you've been for four days."

Highsmith ignored the comment. He nodded to himself as if he'd made a decision and stood. He pulled a business card from his wallet and dropped it on the table. "Give me a call when you arrest Sharma. In the meantime, I have another angle to pursue."

"Meaning?"

Highsmith moved toward the door patting his pockets for his keys. "Sorry I disturbed your evening."

Billy hadn't anticipated this switch, and he didn't like it. "I want you at the CJC tomorrow at nine to discuss your whereabouts."

Highsmith's hand went to the doorknob. He gave Billy a small, stony smile. "That's the shitty part of this business, isn't it? I don't have to tell you a damned thing."

Chapter 27

Early Friday morning Rosalyn's mobile rang during her drive downtown for a probate hearing. Martin wanted her to come to his house immediately. She didn't have time for this, but in thirty-six years he'd never made such a request. She contacted the judge's clerk, was granted an emergency postponement, and drove straight to Chickasaw Gardens, which happened to be only a few blocks away.

The entire historic neighborhood had begun as an estate belonging to Clarence Saunders, founder of Piggly Wiggly, the first self-serve grocery store in the country. After losing a battle with Wall Street speculators in 1923, Clarence Saunders had been forced into bankruptcy. His 36,000-square-foot mansion—built of pink Georgia marble and including a pipe organ, ballroom, a shooting gallery, eight bedrooms and baths—had gone up for sale. Known as the Pink Palace, it became the city's natural history museum. Rosalyn's grandfather had been one of the developers who'd snapped up the twenty-two-acre property and the man-made lake to create what is now known as Chickasaw Gardens, one of the most exclusive neighborhoods in the city.

Two years ago, Martin had purchased a 1940's Tudor style home. He'd torn out the leaded casement windows, stripped the walls down to the studs, and refurbished the house with a mini-malist hand and outrageously expensive finishes. He couldn't boil an egg, but he'd spent two hundred thousand on the kitchen remodel.

Rosalyn picked up the newspaper at the front door and let herself in. Martin was working on a laptop at his desk in the living area, unshaven and still in his bathrobe. His scruffy appearance alarmed her even more than his call. As a teenager, he'd taken interminable showers and thrown clothes on the floor until he'd found what he wanted to wear. Their cleaning bills had been staggering, but they could never break him of the habit. She'd begun teasing him, calling him Martina and Meticulous Martin. He'd hated it.

While he worked on the laptop, she roamed the expansive living area with its modern furnishings and startling art. A nightmarish abstract by Marcel Eichner hung over the buffet. A digitally hybridized image by Jon Rafman took up half of one wall. A life-sized sculpture of a truncated female torso smeared in black, green, and blue gesso stood in the corner. The twist of the torso's spine evoked agony. Martin thought the house was tasteful. She thought it was hideous.

The buzzing sound of a blender coming from the kitchen caught her attention. A gorgeous young woman Rosalyn had never seen before came into the room carrying a frothy drink that she placed on the desk next to Martin. He spoke to her quietly in what Rosalyn recognized as Italian, instructing her to bring an espresso for his guest. The young woman left without acknowledging Rosalyn's presence.

Rosalyn walked over to the brushed steel fireplace with its gas flames, the only thing in the room with warmth. "You didn't introduce us," she said to Martin.

"Elena Lucchesi. She does a little cooking and housekeeping. She's a convenience."

Elena returned with an espresso for Rosalyn and chocolate biscotti on a china plate. The young woman picked up the newspaper on her return to the kitchen and slipped Martin a smile that was too intimate for the position he'd described. Rosalyn knew he preferred his women to be accessories, not attachments. None of them stayed very long. This one would be out the door soon.

Rosalyn sipped her espresso. "You had me rush over. What's this about?"

"In a minute, Mother." One corner of his mouth lifted.

Her son enjoyed occasionally calling the shots.

When he was young, she would come home exhausted from a long day at the law firm. He'd follow her around the house whining and demanding attention until she was emotionally drained. She rationalized yelling at him as a way to toughen him up. Saunders didn't know what to do with him either, so he never interfered.

Sometimes Martin would flare up by slamming doors and smashing plates. She punished him by locking him out of the house until supper. Once he'd stabbed a butcher knife through a valuable painting left to her by her grandfather, a Childe Hassam portrayal of a shoreline full of blue water and light. She'd taken Martin's Scottish terrier to the pound as punishment. Later she felt bad about the dog and had given him two hundred dollars. Money was the best apology. What could he have done with words?

He closed his laptop, straightened his robe, and motioned her to a seat on the sofa across from his flat screen TV. He joined her there.

She leaned in. "If this is about business, be careful what you say. That girl may be listening."

"Elena doesn't speak much English. Besides, I trust her."

"My Mexican gardener acts like he can't speak a word of English, but I've heard him on the phone chatting away."

"I'm not interested in your gardener, Mother."

"You can never be too sure about someone who works for you."

"You should take your own advice." He pointed a remote at the screen. "Balkin Security recorded this at two this morning."

The video footage showed Robert Highsmith entering the firm's foyer and taking the stairs to the second floor.

"You've given keys and individual alarm codes to your attorneys," he said.

"Our attorneys work late and come in very early," she said. "Their codes tell us who's been in the building and when. We've installed hidden cameras in every office. If there's a problem, we're protected."

"I asked Balkin Security to review your after-hours footage. They called me at five this morning. Watch this."

He clicked the remote. Robert Highsmith entered Caroline's office and walked directly to her built-in file cabinets. He opened and closed each empty drawer then took a seat at her desk and dropped his head in his hands.

"What's that jacket he's wearing?" she asked.

"A Cubs windbreaker. He's probably been to Chicago."

She'd never seen Robert Highsmith in anything less than a three-piece suit. Here he looked disheveled and unsteady.

Martin fast-forwarded the recording. "He goes through everything in Caroline's office then searches her assistant's desk. He seemed particularly interested in her files."

"They don't have any clients in common."

"I've checked the firm's database," he said. "Caroline signed out twenty-three sequestered trust files on Monday. Highsmith used his remote access last night to track those files to her office. I think he went there to steal them. Thank God you moved them out."

"Detective Able wanted access to everything, so I took all of her files to my office instead of to the file room. They're untraceable. Why would Robert want them?"

He shook his head. "Was there something going on between Highsmith and Caroline?"

"I don't believe so. You think he was involved in her murder?"

"It's one possibility." He ran his hand through his hair, frowning and blinking.

She knew that look. His guilty look. "What aren't you telling me?"

His features stiffened. "Yes, well. You assigned Highsmith to defend Tarek Merkle in that criminal case. We've hit a rough patch."

Teenager Tarek Merkle had been paralyzed from the waist down after a fall from a hotel balcony due to a loose railing. Rosalyn had administered his trust funded by a settlement of four million dollars. Recently, while driving his handicap-equipped van, Tarek had rear-ended a car and killed the driver.

"Has Highsmith mishandled the case?" she asked.

"It's taken an unexpected turn. The victim's husband has four kids to raise. The prosecutor and victim's attorney have agreed to a favorable plea bargain on the criminal charges as long as a big chunk of cash is included as restitution. Everyone was willing to go along, but they wanted proof the money is available before the prosecutor will recommend the plea bargain to the judge."

"How much?"

"One million."

She thought about that. "Last year's accounting showed over two and a half million in assets. What's the current balance?"

Martin flushed. "Not enough."

"Be specific."

"Seven hundred thousand and change."

She got a sick feeling in her stomach. "Explain."

He met her gaze, broke it off. "The apartment next to my place in Rome was about to go on the market. I had to move quickly, but I was short on cash. I transferred the money out of the Merkle trust because I knew other funds would be coming available in a month, six weeks at most." He tugged at his robe exposing pale skin on the side of his neck. "I learned through an interoffice memo that Highsmith had checked the trust's balance last Friday. It's incredibly bad timing."

She struggled to hold back her anger. "How much money did you take?"

"I borrowed a million eight."

"You didn't *borrow* the money. A first-year accounting student could trace it. Even your sister never made such an obvious blunder."

"Caroline made mistakes. She got herself murdered."

"Don't think you can hide behind her death. We've operated with impunity for years because we're careful, and our clients trust us." She rose and paced the sterile room surrounded by disturbing art. The implications of what Martin had done struck her hard.

"You're not fit to run the bank," she said. "You're fired."

He laughed. "Good one, Mom. Aunt Gracie Ella is nuts. Caroline is dead. Dad might as well be. I'm the only one left to cover your tracks."

She took a breath and let it out slowly. "Has Highsmith contacted you about the money?"

"Not yet. I've set up a secondary account for the Merkle trust and backdated it. After I deposit replacement funds, I'll contact him and say I'm aware of the plea bargain and ask for the amount. When he says one million, I'll give him the balance of both accounts. The total will match the number he was expecting. I'll explain that a computer error had overridden the second account. He'll be so relieved the money is available he won't question it."

"What I don't understand is the connection between the missing money and Highsmith's search of Caroline's office," she said.

"He apparently became suspicious after he saw the balance on Friday. Over the weekend he wrote queries that narrowed his search to those trusts we've placed in our sequestered files. He didn't have a password, so he couldn't access all the information. On Monday he tried to get his hands on the physical files. Caroline must've gotten wind of it, because she pulled all the sequestered files we have on site into her office."

"This is bad, Martin."

"I've blocked Highsmith's remote access to the database until we sort this out." He rubbed his temples. "Balkin Security is arm's-length. I want boots on the ground to make sure no one enters your office without authorization. I've hired the security firm that provides protection for the warehouse where I store my cars."

"You have to replace the Merkle funds immediately."

"I don't have the money. Federal Reserve Regulation O prevents me from borrowing from our bank. I can use the deed on this house as collateral with another bank, but a title search will take at least two days and we're going into the weekend. I need to talk with Highsmith before then."

She knew he was waiting for her to bail him out as she'd done since he was a child. She wasn't feeling that charitable today.

"I had lunch with Pidge Wallace," she said. "She's out of the market and sitting on a mountain of cash. Go see her. Take the deed to this house with you. Make up a story about getting a Russian diplomat's daughter in Rome knocked up. Tell her you need two million immediately to avoid an international incident. She's bored. She'll eat up the drama. Tell her you'll pay her back in two months with interest. If she gets the money into your account an hour after the bank opens, you'll include one of your fancy cars, maybe that red Corvette convertible."

Martin stared at her like she'd lost her mind. "Pidge Wallace is an extortionist. She'll demand twenty percent interest. That's over a thousand dollars a day. And I'm not about to loan her one of my cars."

"You'll give her the car. That's the penalty for being an ass. Fund the Merkle account so Robert has nothing to squawk about. I'll call him in and say we've changed our minds about the litigation division. We don't have the heart for expansion now. I'll write a fat severance check and boot him out the door."

"No," Martin said, shaking his head. "I refuse to give that woman one of my cars."

She walked over to the sofa and slapped him so hard his glasses flew under the cocktail table. When he bent to pick them up, she saw he was naked beneath his robe. That unnerved her even more.

"You listen to me," she said. "You've put the firm at risk. You've put me at risk. I expect results not a tantrum."

He straightened and settled his glasses in place. "This is your fault. All of it." His gaze never left her face.

What she saw there made her take a step back. She remembered his expression the day he'd stabbed her painting with a butcher knife. He'd meant the knife for her.

She no longer felt safe in this house.

"Marteen, Marteen." The young woman's voice carried from the kitchen. She burst into the living room, waving a section of the morning's newspaper.

Chapter 28

The next morning, the ringing phone caught Billy coming out of the shower. Water rolled down his calves as he whipped a towel around his waist. It was Blue on the phone.

"Mr. Lee is having one of his good days," Blue said. "He wants to tell you about a conversation he had with Caroline a few weeks back."

"Good. Put him on the phone."

"He wants you to come down."

For God's sakes. He didn't want to spend half a day driving to Airlee and back, plus if Rosalyn found out about it she would raise hell. But the old man might have something important for him.

"Is Mrs. Lee going to be around?"

Blue chuckled. "I'll make sure we're in the clear."

"See you around one."

"We'll hold lunch."

He dried off and lathered for a shave. Too little sleep last night. His mind wouldn't give him a break. He was up and down making notes about how easy it would've been for a relationship to start between Caroline and Highsmith. She was unhappy. Highsmith was new in town. They clicked and got carried away.

Billy nicked his chin with the razor, flashing back to his lovemaking with Caroline. He couldn't see how that guy was any kind of a match for her in bed or out. If there'd been something between them, they did a good job keeping it secret, which wasn't easy to do at a small firm.

Things would've changed when she realized she was pregnant. She could've told Highsmith he was the father and then decided to marry Sharma after all. In a jealous rage Highsmith abducted her and shot her.

Or Caroline told him the baby was his. Highsmith agreed to marry her but got cold feet. He killed her to save his freedom.

All speculation. Whatever was true, they needed more information on this guy to rule him in or out.

He drank steaming coffee while he scanned the front page of the paper. Middlebrook's public plea appeared below the fold. *Damn it.* He banged his cup down on the table. The day had just gotten harder.

On the way to the CJC, a call came through directing him to an early meeting with Chief Middlebrook, probably concerning a call from Rosalyn Lee. Middlebrook had taken on the job of running interference with the media, but he was too busy to react to every squawk from the victim's family. Billy parked in the lot across the street and was starting up the steps when his phone pinged a text from Frankie:

> Director's conference room. Director and Chief
> on scene. Officer requesting backup.

Uh oh. Both the top brass. He took the express elevator, tucking in his shirttail, and hurried toward the closed door at the end of the hall. He hoped Middlebrook's presence would mitigate the director's anger. He had a lot of work to do before getting on the road to Airlee.

He rapped the door with his knuckles and pushed it open. Frankie was seated at the table facing the door, her body stiff with anxiety. Director Davis sat at the end of the table, a compact, powerful man who liked his suits cut a fraction too small to emphasize the breadth of his shoulders and the bulge of his biceps. It was rumored that on a bet he'd lifted the back end of a Volkswagen Beetle and held it for a count of five. The bet had been for a count of three.

Middlebrook stood at the window with his back to the room. The *Commercial Appeal* lay on the table opened to an inside page Billy hadn't seen. Two photographs appeared at the top—a headshot of him and the photo of Caroline in the wedding gown they'd used for the neighborhood canvass. He didn't need to see the byline to know his old nemesis Terri Cozi had written the article.

"You've seen today's paper, Detective?" Davis asked in a neutral voice. He wasn't the type to show his cards.

"Not that page, sir."

"Read it now."

The article opened with a fairly accurate rundown of the investigation along with an impressive bio for Caroline. The next few paragraphs made the family connection between Finn Adams, the disappeared cousin, and victim Caroline Lee.

The rest of the article read like a tabloid with Billy's name running throughout. That didn't surprise him since Terri, a wickedly attractive investigative journalist he'd lived with three years ago, had written the article. She'd quoted several observations he had made about the Lee family during a conversation they had one evening when the power at their apartment had gone out.

They sat with candles, beer, and cold pizza and talked for hours. She'd told him about her parents' divorce when she was six. He talked about his life in Mississippi at the diner and the glamorous Lee family at Airlee Plantation. Thank God he'd stayed away from the Jack Daniel's that night or he might've divulged his teenage romance with Caroline.

In the last paragraph, Terri revealed that Caroline had been murdered while wearing the gown, the one she would've worn for the wedding she'd called off five weeks earlier.

Billy slipped a glance at Frankie. Her brows lifted. He got the picture. Terri had called Frankie.

Davis steepled his fingers in front of him. "Seems you can't stay out of the papers," he said to Billy.

"The reporter is a former friend. The information was taken from a conversation we had three years ago."

"Pillow talk?" Davis asked.

He paused. "We were sharing an apartment at the time."

"Is the information in the article accurate?"

"For the most part."

"She must've been taking notes," Middlebrook said.

"Knowing Terri, she secretly recorded it. That sort of behavior is the reason I ended our relationship."

Middlebrook walked over to stand beside Davis's chair, his face empty of expression. That worried Billy more than anything.

"Where did the dress intel come from?" Middlebrook asked.

Frankie started to speak. Billy cut her off.

"Hard to say, Chief. The park ranger and EMTs saw the dress. So did Hanson. Cameras were everywhere."

"It was me," Frankie said.

"What happened?" Davis asked.

"Ms. Cozi called yesterday. I made the mistake of speaking with her. I'd prefer to leave it at that."

"Not an option," Davis said.

Her eyes shifted to Billy. The heat in her gaze could've stripped paint. It was killing her to admit she'd screwed up.

"The reporter asked me questions, none of which I answered. I was about to hang up when she said, 'By the way, tell me about the dress.' I said, 'I'm not talking about the dress.'"

"She tricked you into a partial confirmation," Davis said.

"Yes, sir."

Middlebrook cleared his throat. "Malone, you have to know that media will seek you out. Never assume you can manipulate the story a reporter will write. And never become the topic the way Able has done."

Frankie started to respond. Billy interrupted again.

"My partner was aware that Ms. Cozi provided helpful information during the Judge Overton investigation. She may have thought Cozi was a team player."

"You're taking responsibility for your partner's error?" Davis asked.

"This was my fault," Frankie bristled.

Billy glanced over. She'd committed a serious breach. Davis, new on the job, would be looking for an excuse to show the troops he meant business. If he decided to punish her with suspension, Middlebrook's hands would be tied.

Davis tapped his pen on a pad, his eyes narrowed in thought. "Young lady, please step outside."

Frankie rose, her expression neutral but her fists were clenched. The door closed a little too loudly behind her. This was bad. When he'd come back to the force, he'd negotiated with the chief to have Frankie as his partner. He might have to fight to keep her.

Middlebrook took the chair beside Davis and signaled for Billy to sit across from them.

"I have a budget fight with city council in twenty-five minutes, so I'll be direct," Davis said. "I learned this morning, along with the rest of the city, that you have a history with the Lees. The chief tells me you've recently had legal dealings with their firm. Is that correct?"

"Caroline Lee managed probate of my uncle's will. I was never directly involved."

Davis glanced at Middlebrook, who was busy studying his knuckles. "I've read your file, Able. This Cozi woman compromised another case of yours three years ago."

It was true. One night while he'd slept, Terri copied notes in his briefcase and used the information to publish an article about a case under investigation. Fortunately, the defendant had agreed to a plea deal the day before the article appeared. He'd barely missed disciplinary action and could've been fired.

He looked from Davis to Middlebrook. Both men were grim-faced.

Davis pointed to the newspaper. "Rosalyn Lee accused you of being a media hound. A day later your photograph appears beside the victim's. My life will be made easier if I discipline you before the mayor and Mrs. Lee call."

Davis turned to Middlebrook. "And, Bud. You used poor judgment keeping Able's involvement with the Lee family from me."

"You wanted this case closed," the chief shot back. "Able is our best man."

"He has four notations in his file. One official reprimand." He pointed a finger at Billy. "You take too many risks. I won't tolerate any more surprises."

"Yes sir," he said. If Davis and Middlebrook knew he was planning a trip to Airlee without Rosalyn Lee's knowledge, he'd spend the rest of his career monitoring pawn shops and chasing down stolen scrap metal.

Davis came to his feet. "Bud, I'd like a word with you before I leave. Able, you're dismissed but no more screwups. Do what it takes to build a case the DA can prosecute. And in the future when you're with a female reporter keep your fly zipped."

Down the hall Billy found Frankie leaning against the wall next to the water fountain, her jaw working with tension.

She came off the wall, straightening her jacket. "Thanks for stepping in, but I'm not the little lady who needs to be rescued. In the future, you'll have to suppress your Southern gentleman instincts."

"Partners cover each other."

"Maybe I'm not the partner type."

You are, he thought. You don't know it because no one's ever had your back.

"We sink or swim together," he said. "Besides, I should've told you Terri almost got me fired."

Frankie looked off. "She said the two of you had stayed friends after you broke up."

"That's Terri. She lies so much she thinks she's telling the truth."

"Wow. Twisted." She frowned.

He guessed she was remembering how she'd almost tanked their partnership with a whopper of a lie when they'd first begun working together.

"By the way, I had a late night visitor," he said, changing the subject.

He gave her the details of Highsmith's apparent emotional

attachment to Caroline. "He wouldn't tell me where he's been since Monday, and he won't come in for questioning. I've put a call in to a friend in Chicago who is a criminal defense lawyer. He'll know the gossip about the State's Attorney's Office."

"You consider Highsmith a suspect?"

"Sharma's still number one, but this guy will do as a backup."

She nodded. "I'll check for carry permits in Illinois and Tennessee to see if he owns a registered weapon."

"Good. Blue Hopkins called this morning. Saunders Lee says he has information that may help us. I'm leaving for Airlee at noon. Blue assured me Rosalyn isn't scheduled to be there, but if she shows up, Davis will have me barbequed."

"You can't close cases if you don't take risks," she said.

He smiled to himself. *Atta' girl.*

They were heading for the squad room when Middlebrook came around the corner. "I knew I'd find you two in a huddle. Malone, my rookie detectives get a pass on one screwup as long as they haven't killed somebody. Log this and forget it."

The chief knew his people. He'd pegged Frankie as a perfectionist who would chew on this incident unless ordered to let it go. She was hard on herself, but her obsessive side also made for good detective work.

"And you." He pointed a finger at Billy. "Every dog gets one free bite. After that the owner is on notice. Do what it takes within reason to get this case closed. I've assigned two detectives to take the calls coming in from today's paper." He sighed. "Don't screw up. Either of you."

Chapter 29

In the ladies room, Frankie checked her face in the mirror and ran her hand through her hair. Her first face-to-face with Director Davis and she'd come off like a nincompoop. One thing she knew. First impressions last. And this hadn't been just Davis. The Chief and Billy were there, trying to let her off the hook, but she'd been the one who made the rookie mistake of allowing that bitch reporter to trick her into breaching the case.

Shake it off, she told herself. This wasn't her first time to hit rough waters. Take a hard look at every suspect, even the ones Billy hadn't wanted to acknowledge like Clive Atwood. Do the job. Close the case. Success trumps mistakes.

She went to her desk and opened Judd's file on Atwood that included a psychological workup by a prison psychiatrist. In the doctor's opinion—while Atwood tested out with a genius IQ and appeared to understand normal moral standards—he was incapable of adhering to them: *"Extreme abuse during Atwood's childhood has created a sense of rage that can be triggered by feelings of exclusion or rejection."* What bothered her most was the psychiatrist's underscoring of the word "rejection." Had Caroline rejected Atwood and he killed her for it?

On the last page he'd added a notation: *"Incapable of separating reality from his own mental projection of a situation. Lack of emotional control suggests primary weakness in personality structure. Pathological behavioral disorders indicated. Recommend against release into general population."*

God knows how Walker had gotten his hands on the report, but she was grateful he did. So far only Judd's suspicions had connected Atwood to the Lee case. This report supported his contention that Atwood was capable of homicidal rage. She hadn't decided whether to accompany Judd to the rice fields. This report tipped the scales in his direction.

At noon she pulled up to Judd's house and saw he was raking leaves out of the front flower beds. He gave her a quick wave, stowed the rake on the porch, and came down the walk with his chest puffed out and stomach sucked in. She smiled at his touch of male vanity. She'd seen Billy do the same thing.

They took I-40 across the new bridge into Arkansas bypassing the town of West Memphis. Never-ending construction on the interstate meant battling the semis and the concrete barriers that had narrowed the highway to two tight lanes. They turned onto State Highway 147 and headed south through fields of soil the color of wet coffee grounds. Judd asked a few polite questions, but they mostly watched as the farmland swept past.

Frankie hoped to bring fresh eyes to a case that other professionals had shelved. Judd had spent thousands of dollars on the investigation trying to bring peace to Finn's mother. She'd also picked up that Judd had his own issues to resolve about his cousin's disappearance. Possibly this trip would help.

Forty-five minutes later he directed her to turn onto an elevated levee road that ran between the rice fields. The fields were like giant rectangular swimming pools scooped out of the earth and filled with water to irrigate the rice crops. After driving several minutes, the levee road terminated in a spoon-shaped parcel of land broad enough to allow the rolling stock that harvested the rice to turn around. Five corrugated storage sheds lined one side of the circular driveway. Frankie parked in front of the sheds. A tangle of bushes and scrub trees about thirty feet away blocked their view of the fields.

"This way," Judd said, getting out of the car. A dirt path through the patch of trees opened to a clearing. In the center stood the memorial marker for Finn. A handful of orange lilies hung limp over the lip of the zinc vase attached to the marker's base.

"The hunters found Finn's clothes over there to your left," he said. "Beyond those bushes are the rice fields."

Frankie walked through the bushes to where packed earth sloped down to the water's edge. A flock of green-headed mallards dabbled in the shallows for waste grain. The sparkling wetland stretched in front of her. The ducks suddenly burst from the water and flew overhead. Hard to imagine this peaceful place as a murder scene. She went back to where Judd was waiting.

"Gracie Ella drives over a couple of times a week with fresh flowers," he said. "I came with her one time. She brings a chair and spends a good part of the day chatting with Finn. The strange part is when she stops talking and listens to him respond."

"How about if we start with the day Finn disappeared," Frankie said. She took out her memo book.

He nodded. "It was a Friday in November. There'd been too much rain. The Mississippi threatened to crest ten feet above flood stage with more rain on the way. Crazy weather. Finn had no reason to be out here."

He pointed across the water. "Hunters came in from that direction and spotted Finn's clothes. They didn't think much of it until they found his Camaro parked in front of the sheds with the keys in the ignition. They couldn't find anyone around, so they called the Sherriff's Office.

"First theory was he'd stripped down and was wandering around in the cold. Or he could've accidently drowned. Deputies searched for two hours then the Sherriff brought in tracking dogs. You can see there's a lot of acreage to cover, plus there's the ditches and riverbanks, which aren't too far from here. The water in the fields is about three feet deep. A person could drown if he hit his head or was wacked-out on drugs. Suicide was a consideration, but they didn't find a note.

"The Sherriff contacted Aunt Gracie Ella. I joined the search. They brought in boats and dragged the fields and tried to search the riverbanks, but the current was too fast. It started to rain. Poured for three days. I stopped at a convenience store for sandwiches and coffee. This crazy-looking woman in line got in my face and whispered, 'The devil sent the rain.' Then she crossed herself. It was creepy.

"Atwood flew in from Miami. He started shooting his mouth off about Finn being involved with the Silver Elves."

Frankie glanced up then wrote the word "elves," but decided she'd leave that part out when she talked to Billy.

"I know it sounds weird. It's a cult. These two sisters wrote several books on Elven philosophy. One book described a re-birthing ceremony where you're supposed to strip naked and immerse yourself in a river. Atwood told the investigators Finn had the book in his room. They decided he either walked through the rice fields to the river for the ceremony and accidently drowned, or he'd committed suicide."

She stopped writing. "Where was Caroline during all this?"

"Second year Vanderbilt Law in Nashville. She came home every weekend to be with Aunt Gracie Ella. After a while she stopped coming."

"You said Atwood and Caroline became secretly engaged before Finn disappeared."

"That son of a bitch took control. I believe that in a less stressful time Caroline would've seen through his act." He sighed. "Maybe not. Finn was no fool, and he was taken in.

"Aunt Gracie Ella spent the next year walking the fields and riverbanks looking for him. Then she started calling the Sherriff's Office saying Rosalyn had hired someone to get rid of her son."

"What happened with that?"

"Nothing. The cops saw Aunt Gracie Ella as another parent driven crazy by grief. I was living in Las Vegas by then and making it to the final tables at no-limit hold 'em tournaments. When I heard she'd been hospitalized, I came home. I'd met Johnnie Walker when he ran security for the Memphis tournaments. You know Walker?"

"By reputation," she said. "I heard when Walker gets involved in a case he makes the other side look stupid."

Judd stifled a laugh. "You got that right. It's tough to pick up a year-old case, but Walker agreed to give it a shot. Right away he spotted the inconsistencies. The condition of Finn's clothes was the most obvious. His shoes and socks were clean and dry, but his pants had been dipped halfway up the legs in muddy water. That made no sense. The Sherriff's report didn't mention meth activity in the area, and there was no evidence Finn had ever been suicidal. Walker wanted to interrogate Atwood. He tracked him to Avenal State Prison in California, but Atwood had already been released."

Judd pulled a photo from his jacket pocket. It was of him and Finn on a tennis court holding a trophy between them, squinting in the sun with happy grins. They were young. Could've been brothers.

"This was before Atwood got his hooks in Finn. It's how I remember him, strong and confident, a great life ahead."

She wondered if Judd realized the changes in himself since the photograph had been taken. He'd put on thirty pounds and the sparkle in his eye was gone. Not gone. Finn's disappearance had stolen it. She handed back the photo.

"Anything else I should know?" she asked.

"Yes," he said softly. "I could've stopped it."

A vibration ran through her. This was how confessions start. "What do you mean?"

He pocketed the photo and stared at his shoes, breathing hard through his nostrils. "The day Finn disappeared he called and asked if I would ride with him over to Arkansas. He wouldn't say why, but he was pretty insistent. I'd been invited to sit in on a high-stakes game. A producer from *Nighttime Poker* was supposed to be there. I'd built a reputation at regional tournaments. It would've been a chance for some good exposure. I told Finn I couldn't go with him." Judd swiped at his cheek. "If I'd been with him, maybe I could've done something."

"You've kept this to yourself?"

He nodded. "I was ashamed to tell Aunt Gracie Ella." His jaw worked. His heart had to be twisting like meat rolling out of a grinder.

She'd been in his shoes. A man died in a car accident, someone she believed she'd loved. She'd felt responsible. A doctor prescribed pills for her anxiety. The pills took over her life. She'd recovered from the dependency but her guilt over the accident and the shame about the drugs had stayed with her.

No one knows what it's like until they've been through it.

"I drink a lot. That's how I live with myself," he said. "It's not going to change until I find out what happened to Finn."

"In Key West where I was a patrol cop, people would party all night then drive this remote two-lane highway. I don't know how many accidents I came upon where I had to hold the victim's hand and talk to them while they bled out waiting for the ambulance. I couldn't save them. My job was to investigate the accident then clear the roadway. I learned to move on."

"But you didn't cause the accidents."

"You didn't cause your cousin's death. If you'd gone with him, you'd be dead, too."

They drove to Judd's house. Before he got out of the car, he surprised her with an awkward hug. His cheek against hers was clean-shaven. He smelled of soap, not alcohol. He leaned back and smiled. She'd never seen him smile on TV even when he'd taken down a mountain of chips on a big bet. On his front steps, he turned and waved goodbye.

She hadn't been able to shake the guilt about the accident she felt she'd caused. Nothing she could do would make it right. But if Judd found out what happened to Finn, maybe he could beat his guilt. She'd do what she could to make that happen.

Chapter 30

A breeze moved the treetops at Airlee Plantation as Billy got out of the Turismo. Bursts of blue skies showed between fast-moving clouds, a relief after the pall that had shrouded the region. He stopped to look over the vehicles parked in front of the barn. There was Blue's Ram HD truck, four pickups, two late model Cadillacs, three Lexus sedans, a yellow Hummer, and a dented Chevy Beretta with plastic taped over the passenger's side window. He recognized Zelda's Miata from the day of the murder when she'd shown up at Caroline's house. Gracie Ella's green Mercedes station wagon was parked in the yard beside the big house, same as it had been two days ago.

What were these people doing here? He made a note of the Mercedes' and Miata's plate numbers then went to knock on the front door. No one answered, so he walked around to the side porch. The pasture that flanked the house spread like a blanket over the back acreage. Four saddle horses idled beside the pond, all of them white with black and brown spots.

Behind the house a group of men and women milled about on the stone terrace with plates of food in their hands. Most were craggy-looking middle-aged men or older, dressed in camo vests and scuffed boots. A few were in canvas jackets and boat shoes.

They had to be the Lees' city friends who owned hunting camps in the area and came down on weekends.

Airlee's elderly housekeeper was seated in a rocking chair in the far corner of the patio. She had a red cloth napkin spread across her knees and a plate in her lap so heaped with food she didn't seem to know where to put her fork first.

Saunders's nurse, whom Billy remembered from two nights before, sat beside the housekeeper in a straight-back chair sipping a glass of iced tea. He wondered if her perplexed expression meant she was uncomfortable about being treated as a guest, or she was concerned about Mr. Lee who was standing beside the outdoor bar in the role of host.

Today the old man was dressed the way Billy remembered from years ago—cream slacks, a blue blazer with brass buttons, and buff shoes. However, today the jacket hung loose on his stooped shoulders, and he had to hold a glass pitcher steady with both hands while pouring drinks for his guests.

Blue elbowed his way through the screen door with a casserole dish balanced on hot mitts. He set the dish on the buffet table already loaded with platters of food. Noticing Billy, he shook his head and grinned.

Billy took him aside. "What the hell is this?"

"After I called you, Mr. Lee got this idea about throwing a celebration of his daughter's life."

"That's great, but if he has information for me, I need to speak with him now."

"That's not going to happen. This is his show. He's running on adrenaline. He'll make a short speech then he said he'll talk with you."

Nothing to do but go along. Saunders noticed them and waved Billy over to the bar.

"Thank you for coming, Detective. Mint julep?" His lower eyelids drooped, exposing their red lining, and his voice had the soft burr symptomatic of Parkinson's.

Billy never drank on the job, but thought it would be rude to refuse. He rested both hands on the bar. "I'll bet the Lee family has the best mint julep recipe in the Delta."

"You'd win that bet, sir. It was passed down from a distant kin, Mr. Will Percy." He pointed to two highball glasses already lined with sugar. "Always use your best bourbon. Begin by tamping down half an inch of sugar in the bottom of the glass and dampen it. Here's the crucial step. Powder your ice with a mallet quickly so it remains dry. Add two sprigs of mint to the glass then fill it to the rim with ice until there's no room left. Add the bourbon."

Blue pounded the ice in a tea towel until it sparkled like snow. He added the mint and ice to both glasses, poured in the bourbon, and whisked a grate of nutmeg on top.

Saunders raised his glass, the sun filling it with a tobacco-colored light. "To Mr. William Percy and other fine gentlemen of the South. May the graciousness of their culture be regained. And to my daughter, Airlee's fairest flower."

Saunders clinked Billy's glass, his hand trembling so badly he had to set it down. He gestured toward the table. "Make yourself a plate, son. If you'll excuse me, I must see to my other guests."

Saunders shuffled toward two ladies and called their names. Both women held out their hands to him. Caroline's death and the Parkinson's would eventually sap Saunders's strength but not today.

Billy went to the buffet table where Odette was fussing over platters of smoked turkey, barbequed chicken wings, squares of baked cheese grits, pickled carrots, and yeast rolls. Two gentlemen were grazing the platters and stuffing food in their mouths as they went. Odette wagged her finger at them. They all laughed.

Billy spoke to Odette then made up three rolls stuffed with ham and homemade herb mayonnaise. He was spooning up creamed corn soufflé when Zelda came down the steps carrying a salad bowl. She wore a blue sweater buttoned up to the neck against the cool day and a skirt that moved around her legs like silk scarves.

She surveyed his plate. "You need a little acid to balance the fat. Add some marinated black-eyed peas."

"Don't you work on Fridays?" he asked, not liking to be bossed about his food.

"Glenda gave me the day off. They're reviewing filing procedures." She picked up a deviled egg. "These are delicious. Airlee could be a destination restaurant if it ever needed to earn its keep. Isn't that right, Uncle Saunders?"

Saunders joined them, placing his hand on Billy's shoulder for balance. "I see you've found the artist in the family. Zelda is a dancer of some kind. Isn't that right, honey?"

She reddened. "I have a BFA in choreography, and I teach."

"Of course," Saunders said. "I'd like to come to a performance sometime, but right now I'd appreciate it if you'd see that everyone has champagne. I want to make a toast."

Even with Caroline gone, Zelda would always get second billing in the family. But if her feelings were ruffled, she recovered quickly. "Happy to. And I'll take a piece of caramel cake up to Aunt Gracie Ella. It's her favorite."

As she walked away, Billy said to Saunders, "I noticed your sister's car is still parked out front. Is she all right?"

"She's been shut up in her room ever since the other night.

She won't speak. She hardly eats. I'm afraid losing Sparrow has further damaged her mind."

"She blames your wife for your daughter's death."

Saunders studied him. "I had hoped you disregarded that outburst. That's her illness talking. It started after Finn disappeared. For some reason, she's decided Rosalyn was responsible."

"What's behind that?"

He shook his head. "A long-standing dispute that's been going on between them since grade school. Gracie Ella wouldn't speak to me for a year after I married Rosalyn. Then she married late and was divorced, so she went to work at the bank as senior trust officer. She and Rosalyn had to come to an understanding for the family's sake.

"Unfortunately, after Finn disappeared Gracie became so delusional the doctors had to hospitalize her. The psychiatrist said shock treatments were her only hope. I'd just been diagnosed with this damned illness and wasn't up to making that kind of decision. Rosalyn took on the responsibility."

Saunders pulled out a handkerchief and patted his mouth. "My sister is an amazing woman. She raised Finn by herself. She showed her horses and learned to fly airplanes. The shame of it is after those treatments she's never really come back to us."

His hand slid off Billy's shoulder. "It's time I say a few words in my daughter's honor. We'll have our talk after that."

The old man collected himself and shuffled to the terrace wall, Blue joining him with a chair in case it was needed. The group quieted.

"Thank you for coming on such short notice to share this beautiful day with me," Saunders began.

He paused and cleared his throat. "My daughter Caroline was a child of summer. She loved the sun. The day I learned she was gone, the skies grew dark and the rain came down. I thought I would never feel the sun's warmth again.

"When I woke this morning, it came to me that she would be let down by my sadness. She would want the days of her life celebrated, not mourned."

He stopped, eyes glistening. "I'll share a story with you, something many of you may have wondered about. The spring Caroline turned six, our cat brought a baby sparrow into the house. It was unharmed, so my daughter took it upon herself to hand-raise it. She walked around the house with it riding on her shoulder, tucked under her hair.

"The bird grew up. Caroline took me aside one day and said, in that serious way little girls have, 'Daddy, it's almost time for my sparrow to fly away.' I told her she was right, but that she would always be my Sparrow.

"I said those words knowing my daughter would one day grow up and leave me." His voice blurred. "This was not the leave-taking I had imagined."

He raised his glass. "So let's turn mourning into celebration. Please lift your glass to the lovely Caroline Lee, belle of Airlee Plantation, my Sparrow, my heart. She flew away too soon." He turned to the second-story window where Zelda and Gracie Ella were watching and acknowledged them. Zelda waved. Gracie Ella turned from the window.

Saunders took a seat in the chair. His guests gathered around him.

Blue came over to Billy. "I'm to give you a tour of the kennels and barn. Mr. Lee will come down to speak with you in private."

Chapter 31

Billy and Blue walked the gravel path to the eight-stall timber-framed barn, built in the forties with hand-hewn beams. The double doors at either end of the dirt hall had been opened to the sunlight and fresh air after so many wet and gloomy days.

"Beautiful speech," Billy commented. "Caroline would've loved it."

"Mr. Lee did all right," Blue said. "He wrote those words this morning."

Billy had worried the old man would break down during his speech. He should've been concerned about his own emotions. He couldn't help but think that if he had been at the diner the day Caroline came to leave her note, he could have convinced her of how much he loved her. And maybe their fates would've been different.

They walked into the barn hall, fragrant with the sharp smell of fresh wood shavings used as bedding in the stalls. Blue explained his daily routine—feed, muck out stalls, rake the barn hall, wipe down the benches that line the hallway, and knock down cobwebs with a broom. In the mornings he turned out the farm's five saddle horses and brought them in at night. The handmade Tucker plantations saddles and the bridles—each on a stand with the horse's name carved on the front—were cleaned and oiled once a month.

They stopped at the stall of a tall gray horse that was bobbing his head over the door, wanting to be noticed.

"This is Bucky. He's a Tennessee Walker," Blue said. "Mr. Lee bought him for me to ride on the bird dog circuit." He scratched the horse's forehead and gave his neck a pat.

They walked around the barn's shed row to the kennels. Three dogs, quivering with energy, leapt onto the chain link fence.

"You know about field bird dogs?" Blue asked.

"Not my area."

"The two white and liver-colored dogs are English pointers. Hawk there is a tri-colored English setter. We expect Hawk to be national champion this year. These dogs are Mr. Lee's passion. It's my hope they'll keep him going."

One of the pointers stood on his hind legs and rested his paws against the chain link. Blue put his hand to the gate so the dog could lick his fingers. "My dad used to work Mr. Lee's bird dogs. Best trainer in Mississippi back in the day. He had a way with dogs and horses."

"Some folks have the magic," Billy said.

"My dad worked for Mr. Lee five days a week doing whatever needed to be done. Weekends he fixed up old cars and sold them for cash. My mom worked as a nurse's aid at the clinic mopping floors and emptying bedpans eight hours a day. Then she came home to cook and clean for my brother and me and my dad." He shook his head. "It was a terrible time for my folks, losing my sisters to murder that way, but the Lord sustained them. They worked hard to put together a down payment on three hundred acres Mr. Lee had agreed to sell to them. It's good land near the river, not prone to flooding.

"Came time to close the deal, the bank wouldn't give my dad a loan. Mr. Lee took his note. He caught hell for it from the other plantation owners . . . selling prime land to a black man. But Mr. Lee respected my dad. He understood a black man in the Delta had his manhood challenged every day. My dad earned enough money from farming to send my brother and me to college. Dad being in charge of his own future changed things for our family. Mr. Lee made that possible. Even after my dad left Airlee, he came back every week to help Mr. Lee work his dogs."

A breeze blew leaves against the side of the barn. The two pointers circled the kennel, heads up, catching a scent.

Blue checked his watch. "I have to go. My folks are due back from the doctor, and Mom's going to need help with my dad. Mr. Lee said he would be down soon."

Blue left. Billy went to the barn hall to sit on a bench with his head resting against the wall. The pervasive, warm scent of horse-flesh comforted him. He listened to Bucky inside his stall licking his feed box and the clink of the dogs jumping on the chain link. He was trying to picture himself returning to this slowed-down Mississippi life when Saunders stepped into the barn hall, the afternoon light behind him emphasizing the stiffness of his gait. He sat heavily on the bench beside Billy and picked up a length of bailing wire. He bent it in a coil as he spoke.

"I appreciate the time you took to come here and talk with an old man. My wife wants to protect me from the details of our daughter's murder. She means well, but I have to know how my Sparrow died."

Billy understood a father's need for information. Grief demands answers. "Two shots fired, small caliber. One bullet penetrated the car's headliner board. The second was fatal. We believe your daughter fought her assailant."

"Where did the bullet enter?"

"Her right cheek. It was contained, very little damage. Death came quickly."

"Was she armed?"

"She had a loaded derringer in her handbag."

The old man pondered that. "I gave every woman in the family a .32 for self-protection. Appears it did my daughter no good."

"Every woman?"

"Rosalyn has a sweet little derringer, diamonds imbedded in the grip, a wedding present. She keeps it in her lingerie drawer, refuses to carry it. My sister already owned a shotgun and several handguns, but I gave her a pearl-handled derringer with some riverboat-gambler history behind it."

"What about Zelda?"

"I gave her a .32 derringer for her sixteenth birthday. Sparrow and Zelda both know how to use a gun." He set down the coil of wire. "I'm told my daughter was on her way here Monday night to be married. Was the groom Dr. Sharma?"

"I don't know for certain."

"That's why you insinuated there might be another man in Caroline's life."

"I have to consider all possibilities, sir. I meant no disrespect to your daughter."

Saunders gave him an appraising look. "Two weeks ago Sparrow and I had lunch in Memphis at Houston's. Robert Highsmith was seated at a nearby table. He joined us. I once saw a man walk into a tree because he couldn't take his eyes off my daughter. I found it odd that Highsmith ignored her all during lunch. He spoke primarily to me."

"You think he wasn't interested in your daughter?"

Saunders scoffed. "The man was so smitten he was afraid to look at her. If you're searching for another man in her life, put Highsmith at the top of the list."

The sound of hooves on packed dirt stopped their conversation. Zelda entered the barn leading a black and white horse by a belt she'd looped around its neck.

"Houdini opened the gate and joined the luncheon," she said.

Saunders nodded. "Damned smart horse. Will you bring in the others? Blue had to leave to take care of his dad."

She beamed. "My favorite chore." She turned the horse into his stall and took three halters from their hooks, giving Billy a quick smile.

Saunders watched her leave. "You know about Zelda?"

"I don't."

Saunders stretched his legs out in front of him and leaned his head against the wall. "Her father was Rosalyn's brother. He traded commodities, a real gambler by nature. Did okay until he bet big that a drought would raise soybean prices. He took a colossal loss. He bet again, lost the rest of his money, and ruined several clients. Zelda was seven at the time. His wife Julie was four months pregnant. A boy.

"He went hunting on a Sunday morning alone. He wasn't back by four so we went looking for him. We found him at dusk tangled in a barbed wire fence. He'd tried to climb through and shot himself in the chest. The coroner ruled it an accident, but he'd recently bought a big life insurance policy, so we knew the truth. Julie miscarried because of the stress. I stepped in where I could for Zelda. She's an odd one. She needs guidance." He looked over at Billy. "Did she tell you her mother died a year ago?"

"She mentioned it."

"Julie took a midnight swim at a Miami hotel pool after too much champagne. She drowned. That's a lot for a young woman to handle, but out of all the kids I believe Zelda is the strongest."

As an attorney, Saunders Lee was a practiced judge of human nature. He'd picked up on the emotional connection between Highsmith and Caroline. That confirmation was important, but Saunders had given him even more significant information.

Zelda owned a .32.

Billy walked with Saunders to the terrace where guests were beginning to leave. He excused himself on the pretense of using the bathroom in the house. He searched around until he found what he was looking for in the kitchen—Zelda's purse and her car keys beside it. He took what he needed and went outside to the porch to check his mobile. Kloss had texted that several potential leads had come in on the tip line. The second text was from his friend in Chicago:

In court all day. Answer to your question: I defended three clients against Highsmith. Tough litigator. IMHO he quit SA office on principle. Home for Christmas. Come by the house if you can. Carson.

Chapter 32

illy waited on the porch until Zelda came downstairs after saying goodbye to her aunt. She went to the kitchen for her purse but then couldn't find her keys. She and Odette tore up the kitchen looking for them, when in fact he'd slipped them inside a large book on the hall table for his own reasons. They finally gave up, assuming one of the guests had picked up the keys by mistake.

When Zelda said she was due back in the evening to teach a tap class at the Y, he offered her a ride and suggested that Blue might be coming to Memphis in the morning. If she had a second set of keys, Blue could bring her back for her car. She said she thought that was a wonderful idea.

Out front of the house, he held the car door for Zelda. She tucked her skirts inside and gave him a coy little smile. *Great.* From the looks of it, she thought this was a date. That wasn't at all what he had in mind.

As they turned out of the driveway, she pulled two sticks of gum from her purse. "Doublemint. Want some?"

He shook his head. "Thanks."

She folded a stick of gum in her mouth and started chewing. "Perfect setting for the celebration. Amazing food. Odette should've opened a catering business instead of staying with the Lees all this time."

She bent forward to arrange her skirt over her knees. "Uncle Saunders's tribute was sweet. Aunt Gracie Ella and I stood at the window so we could hear. I'm sure Caroline would've been touched. She loved her daddy."

"Mr. Lee will need time to work through his grief."

She popped her gum. "Losing Caroline is going to be hard on him."

Billy looked over. This person was not going to step into Caroline's role. At least the Lees could afford a platoon of caregivers, and Blue actually cared about the old guy.

He sympathized with Saunders, but he also knew the other side of aging and illness. A different class of the elderly was trapped in their inner city homes, living with fear, the phone their lifeline, and 911 their only backup. He'd hammered into the heads of rookies who rode with him on patrol that the welfare of those people was a big part of their duty.

He had a duty in front of him now. How to begin?

"Would you say Caroline and Robert Highsmith were friends?" he asked.

"I don't know about that. The only time I heard her mention Robert was when she talked about the protective order." She cocked her head. "You're suspicious of him?"

He shrugged. "I'm suspicious by nature."

"Hmm. Well, I read the article in this morning's paper. A big chunk was about your personal life. Where did the reporter get her information?"

He ducked his head. "We dated a while back."

Zelda snorted. "You're too old to date."

"I was being tactful. We lived together. I made the mistake of trusting her. We talked about our childhoods one night. She used what I said in the article."

"Trust isn't a bad thing."

"It is in my business. She's a snake in the grass, but she's also a good reporter."

Zelda crossed her arms. "With all this, I'm beginning to think my family is cursed. Finn's gone, Saunders is ill, and now Caroline's been murdered. Aunt Gracie Ella has gone over the edge. I took her some cake. She thought I was Caroline."

There was his opening. "Your aunt blames Rosalyn for Caroline's death."

"I've heard it before. Finn disappeared and Aunt Gracie Ella started accusing Aunt Rosalyn of having him murdered. She blabbed it to anyone in town who'd listen. Swear to God Rosalyn approved those shock treatments just to shut her up."

He'd wondered the same thing. "What's behind that?"

Zelda slipped on her Ray-Bans. "My opinion . . . it's because Finn was gay. He wasn't open about it, but I think Aunt Rosalyn knew. She's a major homophobe. The thought of him becoming a lawyer and wanting to work at the firm right under her nose probably drove her nuts.

"She must have thought the problem was solved when Harvard Law came into the picture. She started pushing Finn to find a summer internship in DC or with a New York firm hoping he'd be hired. Then at Thanksgiving Finn announced he planned to come home and work at the Lee Law Firm. I thought she was going to stab him with the carving knife. Rosalyn and Gracie Ella excused themselves and went to the kitchen for dessert plates. They started shouting. Uncle Saunders said we should all leave. No pumpkin pie that year."

"So what if Finn was gay?"

She shook her head, hair bouncing. "It wasn't just that he was gay. As a family member, he had the opportunity to make partner. Finn was this tenacious guy. When he got hold of something he wouldn't let go. I think Rosalyn was afraid he would challenge her control."

A flatbed truck stacked with hay bales passed on the opposite side of the road. An ancient yellow Lincoln stuffed with teenagers followed close behind.

Zelda frowned. "I just thought of something. Monday when I was asking Caroline about the ring, another issue came up. That morning Robert Highsmith had asked for sequestered files I'm not supposed to release. He got really upset about it. I said he should talk to Caroline. Well, honey . . . when I told her that, she let me have it. She came out from behind her desk and started shouting about office procedures. She said I should keep my damned ideas to myself. I was humiliated, so I yelled back. We were pretty loud. I opened the door to leave and her assistant was standing there listening. Later in the day Caroline's assistant came to the file room to sign out every file Robert had asked for. Twenty-three of them."

"What was that about?"

"I don't know." She pressed the heel of her hand to her forehead. "It's so depressing. The last time I saw Caroline we were screaming at each other."

She reached over and turned on the radio. A swing version of "Blue Skies" came on. "Oh, God. That's Caroline's favorite song."

"I know."

She snuck a glance at him.

He turned onto the state road that would carry them past the diner. His next question was going to set her off. If he had any sense, he would wait until they were closer to Memphis to get into it.

"Saunders talked about giving every woman in the family a .32 derringer," he said.

Zelda's mouth curved down. "So?"

"The bullet that killed Caroline was a .32."

She stared at him. "You're accusing me again of murdering Caroline?"

"Where's your derringer?"

"I don't know."

"That's not a serious answer," he said.

"Oh, really." She flashed him an angry look. "You got a cigarette?"

"You don't smoke."

She flipped down her sun visor. "You keep insulting me and I'll be willing to start."

He decided not to push it. Riding in a car didn't make this any less of an official interview. If she said the word "attorney" the conversation would be over. He decided to hold his peace and let silence do the work.

A couple of miles passed before she spoke again. "You know I've moved three times in the last five years. The gun is packed away. Swear to God, I don't remember where."

"You know how to use it," he said.

"I'm a hell of a good shot, but you know I hate guns."

"Then why not give it back to Mr. Lee?"

She stared ahead, glassy-eyed. "Uncle Saunders gave me that gun. *Me*. Same as Rosalyn and Gracie Ella. Same as Caroline. Grandmother Taylor and Grandmother Lee carried derringers everywhere, even to church. That pistol means I'm a Lee."

Chapter 33

They rode in uncomfortable silence past rows of tarpaper shacks. He had a lot on his mind, but was still aware that the people living inside those houses couldn't afford an electric bill, so they cooked with butane that blackened the walls and left half an inch of soot clinging to the ceiling. These were families left behind with no education and no hope. They lived with sagging sofas on their porches, rusted cars put up on blocks, and yards full of weeds and snakes. The systemic poverty in the region made his heart ache.

As they drove, the fields became pine forests. Soon they approached the gravel apron of Kane's Kanteen parking lot.

"I'd like to say goodbye to the place," Zelda said. He parked. She left the car to pick her way through mounds of leaves and clumps of brown spiky gumballs that had fallen beneath the row of sweetgum trees. She wandered over to where the picnic table once stood and stopped there to look around.

Billy sat in the quiet and watched her, aware that lights now burned in the diner. Someone had wiped off the Kane's Kanteen sign and propped it against the side of the building, possibly the new owner. He pulled out his mobile to check for messages. No bars. No service. He got out and stood between the car and open door.

"Let's go," he called.

Zelda shook her head and waved him over. He wanted to get back to the city but knew the best way to get his hands on that derringer was to humor her. He closed the door and walked over.

She inhaled and grinned. "Smell the pine? It's like Christmas. I have such great memories of this place. How about you?"

"Not exactly like Christmas," he said.

He'd grown up cleaning out the diner's grease trap and washing dishes. Long days ran into nights, which meant he'd be up until one in the morning getting his homework done. He hadn't minded the work as much as the loneliness. His uncle had provided a roof over his head, but besides sharing chores and watching major league baseball on TV, they had little in common.

His best memories were those two summers with Caroline.

She had called him one night, whispering to meet her at the felled tree in the pasture behind the barn. She was waiting for him, perched on the fallen trunk with a bottle of red wine she'd pinched from her father's liquor cabinet. They drank the wine and watched the July moon roll across the sky. She brushed her bare thigh against his, slipped her hand inside his cutoffs and crooned a love song in his ear. He'd never forgotten the warmth of her lips against his.

Zelda put her hand on his arm, bringing him back. "Do you know who bought the diner?"

"No, but the utilities are on. They must've closed the sale."

She kicked a soggy gumball. "I used to stop here on my way to Airlee. I'd sit at the picnic table reading a book and eating pie in your honor."

"You knew I baked the pies?"

"Oh, sure. I'd watch through the pass-through window, the way you'd crimp the piecrust between your thumb and fingers to trim the edges. You were so serious. I thought, 'Now there's a guy with passion.' I was pretty passionate myself at the time. I wanted to be a choreographer like Helen Tamiris. We have the same crazy hair. Aunt Gracie Ella was the only one who understood me."

She rose on her toes and lifted her arms, danced across the parking lot and did a pirouette at the border of undergrowth. "Remember the raccoon?" she called.

"Of course."

"You came off the porch swinging that mop. You were going to rescue Caroline and me."

Truth was, he hardly remembered Zelda being there. His attention had been on Caroline, always on Caroline.

Zelda walked back to him. "I was hoping when this is over—" she plucked at a strand of yarn on her sweater "—you and I could get together."

The image of Zelda standing in Caroline's driveway came to him—the lime green coat and pink nightgown. Her angry tears had seemed heartfelt that day, but finding out about her resentment toward Caroline was disturbing. Getting together with Zelda was the last thing on his mind.

He took too long answering.

She looked down. "Geez. I guess not."

A late model Saab with a ten-foot ladder strapped to the roof swung into the parking lot and pulled next to Billy's car. Robert Highsmith climbed out of the car wearing the same Cubs jacket he had on the night before. He went to the trunk and fetched a bucket and paint brushes.

What the hell was he doing in Nowhere, Mississippi?

Highsmith walked over. "What's up?"

"Hi, Robert," Zelda said. "We've just come from Airlee. I wanted to say goodbye to the place. Caroline and I loved the diner."

"What about you?" Billy asked.

Highsmith held up the bucket. "I bought the place."

Zelda's mouth fell open. "No way."

After their conversation last night, Billy could come to only one conclusion. "You bought it for Caroline."

Highsmith's face reddened. "We need to talk. I have notes in the car."

Billy thought of two options—Highsmith wanted to get to his car and make a run for it, or he was ready to give up some answers.

"Zelda, please wait in my car," he said.

"Are you kidding? This is getting interesting."

"Then go for a walk."

"It's too cold." She put her hands on her hips, stared at him, then huffed. "Okay. Robert, may I look around the diner?"

"If you want." He handed her a ring of keys. "But it's a mess."

A panel van rattled by as he and Highsmith started toward the Saab. The driver honked and waved. Highsmith had done a proper job of cinching the ladder onto the roof rack, not something Billy would've expected. The guy didn't seem like the handy type. There were four gallons of paint on the floor in the back. A laptop case lay on the passenger seat.

Highsmith retrieved the laptop. "What you're about to see is not a formal statement, but you'll find the timeline accurate." He set up the computer on the trunk, pulled up a document, and invited Billy to scroll through.

The gist of it was Highsmith and Caroline had started an

affair not long after he joined the firm. She wanted to keep the relationship secret until she made up her mind about marrying Sharma. Highsmith had gone along, trying to swing her vote his way.

After she'd called off the wedding, he wanted to make their relationship public thinking the revelation would derail Sharma's harassment. Caroline didn't see it that way and wanted to wait.

The situation had changed eight days ago when Caroline told him she was expecting his child. He was ecstatic. She wanted a quick ceremony held at Airlee so her father could be there. They would fly to Chicago to introduce her to his family and return to Memphis to announce their marriage.

"Why didn't you tell me that last night?" Billy asked.

"Because you assumed the man she was planning to marry was the one who'd killed her. I wasn't willing to be arrested."

"What you've written here is your version of events. You say you were in love with Caroline, you believed she was carrying your child, so you wouldn't have killed her. But she's dead. How do you explain that?"

Highsmith took off his glasses and rubbed his eyes. "Last night I told you I had another angle to consider. I've discovered what I believe is malfeasance inside the Lee Law Firm. It could be the reason for Caroline's murder."

Billy wasn't surprised that Highsmith was laying a false trail to divert suspicion. "Before we get off in the weeds, let's stay with your step-by-step movements on Monday night."

"Maybe you didn't hear me," Highsmith said.

"No, I get the picture. Go ahead."

Highsmith shrugged. "All right. I was working from home on Monday afternoon to pull as much information as I could on the malfeasance. I was desperate for answers, but I needed more time. I called Caroline and asked her to go ahead to Airlee, but to delay the ceremony until ten o'clock that evening.

"By the time I started for Airlee, I was convinced Martin was going to prison and possibly even Saunders and Rosalyn. Caroline's name appeared on several files where there were suspicious discrepancies. I couldn't tell her what I'd found, because if she was involved she might destroy evidence."

"What type of discrepancies?"

"Money siphoned out of trust accounts, hundreds of thousands, probably millions embezzled over the years. I was faced with the probability that my future in-laws were crooks and my bride might be one too. I started driving. My head was really messed up. I felt trapped. I stopped at the Hollywood Cafe in Robinsonville to call Caroline. Her mobile was off, so I assumed she was driving."

Billy was holding back his temper but listening. "What time was that?"

"I don't know. Sometime before nine." Highsmith shook his head. "I went inside for a beer and to think about what to do next. The place was packed with people from the casinos. I ordered a beer and stood against the wall. A woman was banging out honky-tonk on the piano. I finished the beer and tried to reach Caroline again. Finally, I texted her that I was calling off the marriage. Then I drove here. I had a bottle of scotch in the car, so I went inside and got very angry and very drunk."

"You were angry with Caroline?"

"Of course I was. And at my own bad judgment. I have a talent for trusting the wrong people. The State's Attorney in Chicago wanted me to throw a case brought against a local politician. He assumed I would go along. I walked. He tried to make it appear as if I'd been the one planning to throw the case."

Highsmith blew air through his nostrils and tromped away, his back turned to the car while he stared at the road. Then he came back.

"I need to back up and explain. I'd met Caroline at an American Bar conference in Miami. I fell for her on the spot, but she was engaged. After the conference we stayed in touch, networking and all that. At one point she mentioned that her firm was planning to add a litigation department. By then I wanted out of Chicago. I'd been sending resumés around, so I sent one to Rosalyn. She made me an extremely generous offer." He shrugged. "Look what it got me."

Heat crawled up the back of Billy's neck. Caroline was dead and this guy was feeling sorry for himself. "You tried to call her Tuesday morning, didn't you?"

Highsmith's head dropped. "I woke up with a hell of a hangover and feeling guilty. Caroline was the last person I wanted to talk to. This is a dead zone so I couldn't call out anyway. My life had been jerked out from under me. I decided I didn't want to talk to anyone."

Billy slammed his fist on the trunk, his anger boiling over. "Bullshit. Nobody jerked anything. You said you would marry Caroline then had second thoughts. The baby could've been Sharma's, but she tagged you. You decided she'd lied about it to get you to commit. You felt trapped all right. You shot her in the face and left her to die, you son of a bitch."

Chapter 34

S he was shot in the face?" Highsmith asked.

He had that catatonic stare rookies get at their first exposure to unspeakable violence. It's a pure expression. It can't be faked. A cold gust of wind swept grit off the road and circled the Saab. Billy wasn't moved by Highsmith's reaction. Neither did he dismiss it.

Highsmith struggled for words. "Did she suffer?"

"I can't say. But she knew her baby would die. That's suffering."

Highsmith looked like he was going into shock. His gaze wandered from the road to the diner and stayed there. "She told me she came here on Saturdays with her dad and cousins. She loved it. I bought the place as a wedding present. We were going to fix up the house and use it on weekends. A friend in Chicago wants to leave his law practice and move here to open a restaurant for the casino trade. I told him I would give him the diner."

He took a breath. "Even if it turned out I was wrong about the embezzlement, I figured Caroline would never forgive me for thinking the worst of her family. Then I left her at the altar. My life with her was over. My job in Memphis was gone. My future in Chicago was pretty well screwed. I spent a day and a half doing chores around here trying to decide what to do.

"I decided to go back to Memphis and figure things out from there. I was almost to the highway when my mobile started to light up with texts. I pulled off the road expecting a blast from Caroline, but the first was Rosalyn's statement to the attorneys about Caroline's death. I assumed she'd been in an accident on the way to Airlee until I brought up a news article about her murder. I sat there unable to breathe. I read more texts. One was your request for Sharma's harassment file. That made me check the Shelby County 'Who's In Jail' site to see if you'd had him arrested. When he wasn't on the list I called his answering service. They indicated he was still taking appointments. The son of a bitch was free. Walking around."

He brushed his fingers over his forehead. "I wanted to get my hands on him and make him confess. Not my best thinking. I drove to town instead. Went straight to your place. You made it clear there was nothing I could do about Sharma. I thought about the embezzlement scheme and wondered if that was somehow connected to Caroline's murder."

"Is that the angle you mentioned last night?"

Highsmith nodded. "First I had to prove the embezzlement had taken place. The firm's database showed the files I needed were in Caroline's office. There were twenty-three of them. I searched her office, but the files were gone."

Billy knew why. Rosalyn had removed them. He noticed Zelda watching them through the diner's front window. He waved for her to join them. She picked her way through clumps of wet leaves, her arms hugging her chest as if she was cold.

"All done?" she asked.

"Almost. Those twenty-three files you mentioned. Is there something unusual about them?"

"Can you be more specific?"

"Are they different from other client files?"

"Sure. The attorneys can go into the database and look at the preliminary documents within the files, but you need a password for access to the entire file. That's why when Robert asked to see the physical files and I mentioned it to—"

Billy interrupted her. "Who has that password?" He didn't want Highsmith to know Caroline had been upset he'd asked for the files.

"Saunders, Rosalyn, Caroline, and Martin have their own passwords."

"Why Martin?"

"He personally supervises those trust accounts."

"Do you have a password?" Highsmith asked.

She hooted. "They don't trust me to turn off the lights." She rubbed her hands briskly up and down her arms. "Let's talk about this someplace warm."

Billy gave her the car keys. "Turn on the heat. I'll buy you dinner later, but for now I need you to wait in the car. We won't be long."

"If we don't leave in fifteen minutes, I'll miss the tap dance class I teach at the Y," she said.

"I'll tell the manager you were assisting me in a murder investigation. This is important."

She took the keys.

Shadows lengthened as he walked with Highsmith through the pine trees to the tiny house where he and his uncle had once lived. The white clapboard siding needed to be scraped and painted. Plywood had been fitted into the bathroom window frame to replace broken glass. The porch sagged in the middle. Other than that the place looked in pretty good shape.

The shotgun house consisted of a front room with the only bedroom directly behind that, a walk-through bathroom, and then the kitchen where he and his uncle brewed coffee before opening the diner at 5:30 am. Uncle Kane had added a lean-to mudroom on the back of the house that they'd converted into his bedroom. He kept his clothes and a few of his mother's keepsakes stored in a footlocker beside the bed. For company, he tacked up a poster of his hero, home run king Hank Aaron at his induction into the Baseball Hall of Fame in 1982. The mudroom was where he'd slept until he left for his freshman year at Ole Miss.

Highsmith unlocked the front door and flipped the light switch. He'd moved the furniture around. The sofa was pushed against the wall opposite the wood stove, and the chair had been turned toward an old General Electric TV that was set on top of three wood onion crates. Billy could smell pine cleaner in the bathroom and the paint cans sitting on newspaper in the bedroom. On the table beside the chair sat a bottle of eighteen-year-old Laphroaig Scotch.

He'd forgotten the silence of this house. On the barge he was surrounded by horn blasts from the *Memphis Queen II* as she leaves the dock, the clack-clack of semis rolling over the new bridge's expansion joints, and the drumming sound of trains on the track fifty yards away. It felt odd to be in the settling quiet of this place, a house where he hadn't been welcome since the day he'd told his uncle that he had quit law school.

He crossed his arms and leaned his back against the wall next to the door. "Tell me about this embezzlement scheme."

Highsmith regarded him. "You want all the details?"

He nodded. *Enough to catch you lying.*

Highsmith sat on the arm of the sofa. "The first client Rosalyn assigned me was a teenager named Tarek Merkle. A hotel balcony railing gave way and dumped the kid two stories onto concrete. That put him in a wheelchair for life. Rosalyn got him a four-million-dollar settlement and put it in a trust for his benefit with Martin Lee serving as trustee. Tarek's parents bought a wheelchair van so he wouldn't feel limited by his impairment. Last spring he lost control of the van and rear-ended a car stopped in a turn lane. The driver died, a mother of four.

"The computer chip the cops removed from the van indicated he'd been doing sixty-eight in a forty zone. Tarek was charged with vehicular homicide. However, the case hinged on that computer chip, which might not be admissible as evidence. At least that would be my contention. The dead woman's husband couldn't sue the trust directly because Rosalyn had included a spendthrift clause. With four kids, the husband desperately needed money. Tarek was terrified he'd go to prison. Not a good outcome on either side.

"When I took the case, I checked the balance of Tarek's trust. It was almost two and a half million. I suggested to the ADA that if they dropped the charges because of reasonable doubt, Tarek's trust would pay the family a million dollars. That got everyone's attention. The ADA and the family's attorney wanted the balance in the trust verified before he would take it to the judge. I checked the account again on Friday. There was a little over seven hundred thousand. Over 1.7 million was missing."

Billy whistled. "Computer error?"

"You'd hope so, but I've seen this before. I asked the family a few discreet questions. They weren't aware of the loss, which isn't unusual. Discrepancies in the balance can go undetected because the trustee doesn't report to the court. The transactions can be made so complicated most beneficiaries can't tell they're being screwed. A lot of them don't even look at the statements.

"I figured Martin was behind this. I gave Rosalyn and Saunders a temporary pass because they wouldn't question information on annual reports coming from their own son or check the balance of the account. But my assumption changed."

"Why?"

"Before I went to Rosalyn with the numbers, I did some digging. It's an old firm so it has hundreds of clients with trusts. I wrote queries for all trusts in the firm's database that specified the bank as trustee. Two kinds of beneficiaries are the easiest sheep to shear. The first are those who have no relatives to monitor the reports. Second are those with no beneficiary to receive a windfall.

"I spent the weekend sorting the list I had created with my queries of relatives of the trust beneficiary. For the majority of those trusts, the field came up empty. Then I looked for a check box called 'final distribution made' and found trusts that showed no distribution. *No distribution.* All those trusts had minimal balances, just enough to keep the trusts from being cleared and keeping the absence of distribution from being challenged."

"What did that tell you?"

"Something happened to the remaining assets of those trusts. As trustee, Martin could easily have stolen them. I also searched for trusts where Saunders or Rosalyn had drafted the trust instrument. There were twenty-three of those files on site. What shocked me was that Caroline had been named as a backup attorney on seven of the most recent ones, meaning she could represent the trust in court. That made me suspicious she'd known what was going on.

"On Monday morning I asked Zelda to pull those files and send them to my office. She said they were sequestered and unavailable even to me as a partner. That sent red flags flying.

Caroline could be part of the scheme, and I was to marry her that night."

Billy didn't want to believe any of this, certainly not that Caroline might have been involved. "So far I hear more speculation than fact. How is this connected to Caroline's murder?"

"I wanted to believe she had moved the files to her office because she had her own suspicions. If she'd confronted Martin on Monday and threatened to expose him, I'm sure he would've done anything to prevent it, including kill her."

"That's a leap."

"Not when you consider that this morning my ability to remotely access the firm's database was revoked. Martin is in charge of the firm's IT. Only he could have done that. I went to the office. Rosalyn called me in and said she had decided to eliminate my litigation department. She wrote me a $50,000 severance check, asked for my key, and told me to clear out my desk immediately."

Billy came off the wall and went to the window to think. "I'm sure you've prosecuted similar cases in Chicago. You know what evidence you need to persuade a DA."

"I can't go in with a hunch. I need those files, but Martin has probably destroyed them by now."

"What about the funds missing from the Merkle account? That's the foundation for your case."

"The balance is back to 2.5 million. I'm sure Martin has altered the records to cover the earlier withdrawal. My best chance to pursue this is if he's forgotten to delete the backup on those sequestered files."

"Would the DA act on the information you have?" Billy asked.

"Not a chance. I understand the ramifications of going after a family like the Lees. He wants to keep his job."

"That's quite a story." Billy noted the clean floors, fresh paint on the walls, and the empty bottle of scotch, everything the way Highsmith had described it. He'd spent time here and left tracks down to the paint smear on the sleeve of his jacket. There was no cell service and no landline, so that part of his story worked.

They heard Zelda's footsteps on the porch. Bad timing.

Highsmith scowled. "Detective, this isn't over by a long shot."

"It sure isn't."

"Hey, guys, I have to use the bathroom," Zelda called. Billy opened the door. She joined them, glancing around the front room. "I've always been curious about this place. It'll be great when it's fixed up."

She looked at Highsmith. "Has he accused you of murder yet? He pinned me with it on the drive over."

Shut up, Zelda, he thought.

"The bathroom's through there," Highsmith said.

She looked from Highsmith to him. "It feels pretty grim in here. Is everything all right?"

"We're good except for one thing," Billy said. He took out his mobile. "Stand up straight for the camera, Mr. Highsmith." He took the photo. The flash went off.

Chapter 35

Billy drove away from the diner thinking detective work was fairly basic: ask smart questions, take good notes, and follow the trail to the end. The tricky part was hearing what wasn't being said.

Highsmith had given him well-organized and persuasive information. No surprise. He expected a former prosecutor to know how to throw up a smoke screen in a murder investigation. Highsmith had directed attention away from himself by pointing a finger at Martin with enough detail in his story to make his claim plausible. What Highsmith didn't know was that Martin's girlfriend had provided him with an alibi for the night of the murder early in the investigation. He could ask Frankie to test the girlfriend's statement with a second interview. If that held up, Highsmith's belief that Martin had murdered Caroline was hot air. Highsmith's other mistake was including Caroline and her folks in the scenario. Martin a thief? He could believe that. The rest of the Lees? Never. That left Highsmith on the hot seat.

Billy glanced over at Zelda riding quietly beside him. Saunders had, without intending to, further implicated Zelda by mentioning the gun. Billy wanted to get his hands on her derringer, preferably tonight, so he could rule her in or out.

Twenty minutes later, they pulled off of old Highway 61 and parked in front of The Hollywood Cafe's painted brick buildings.

"Hold on," Zelda said. "I pictured a nice piece of grilled fish and a glass of Cabernet at one of the casino restaurants, not deep-fried frog legs."

"Ever had The Hollywood's fried dill pickles?"

"Of course not."

"Let's give it a try."

Most of the authentic Delta blues greats had played within the walls of the Hollywood Cafe at one time or another. The original building had been a commissary on a Delta plantation that sold food and supplies to the workers. The building was moved in the sixties to a street in tiny Robinsonville near Tunica, a second building was added, and the place became a bar and restaurant. The old walls still echo with the blues licks of Son House, Howlin' Wolf, and B.B. King. In the nineties, sweet Muriel Wilkins played her upright piano to packed houses on Friday and Saturday nights.

Zelda dug in her purse for her mobile. "I tried to cancel my tap class while you were talking to Robert, but I couldn't get through."

"You should have service here." He stepped out of the car for some privacy. "I'll check my messages then we'll go inside for a bite to eat." He'd parked between a pickup truck stacked with Sheetrock and two-by-fours and a new Jaguar F-Type convertible with Connecticut plates. Typical of the Hollywood, tonight's patrons were a mix of beer-drinking locals and tourists who'd pulled off of Blues Highway 61 in search of a taste of the Delta.

The bar had been Billy's favorite hangout during summer breaks in his Ole Miss undergrad days. He and his buddies would

come in for draft beer, chicken wings, and world-class blues per-
formed on the tiny stage. Tonight he was a cop coming to verify
a piece of Highsmith's story.

Depending on traffic from Memphis to the casinos, the drive
would've taken Highsmith over an hour. The medical examiner
had estimated Caroline's time of death between nine and eleven
o'clock. Highsmith said he'd been here before nine. If that was
true, it would've been difficult for him to commit the murder
before leaving Memphis.

He checked his texts. Frankie was in the office. He texted
back:

> On the road. Can you do a face-to-face with
> girlfriend to confirm Martin's alibi?

He paced behind the cars and trucks. She responded:

> Will do.

That out of the way, he noticed Zelda waiting for him under
the porch's corrugated metal awning. Inside, the place hadn't
changed much since his college days. Muriel Wilkins's old piano
stood by the door, unplayable now because of its busted keys.
To the left, ten wood tables lined the brick and plaster wall that
had been decorated with tree branches and twinkle lights after a
wedding party. The patrons enjoyed the lights so much they were
never taken down. To the right a cypress bar ran the length of
the room. An electric piano, a small drum kit, and a Peavey Bass
amp stood on the small stage at the back.

They took the last table against the wall. The server brought a basket of Lance Saltines wrapped in cellophane and a saucer with pats of butter softened to room temperature. Billy opened a pack, spread butter on the crackers, and placed them on a paper napkin in front of Zelda. She stared at the crackers and wrinkled her nose.

Behind the bar a guy in his thirties was busy pouring wine and filling glasses with whiskey and ice. "I need a word with the bartender," Billy said.

He stepped to the corner of the bar near the door and caught the man's eye by flashing his shield. The bartender came over, wiping his hands on a towel.

"How can I help you?" His gaze ran down the line of customers seated at the bar.

"Detective Able, Memphis Homicide. You work on Mondays?"

"Every Monday."

He held up his mobile with Highsmith's photo. "Do you remember this man from last Monday night?"

The bartender took the phone and studied the screen. "What time was he in?"

"Middle of the evening. He ordered a beer."

"One beer?" The bartender handed back the mobile. "Not the kind of customer I'd remember."

"What about the servers?"

"A different crew's here tonight. Lilly and Paula will be in tomorrow. You can check back."

"Thanks for your time." Billy pulled out a ten and handed it to the bartender. "Would you send over a glass of your best Cabernet?"

Returning to the table, he saw the buttered crackers he'd put in front of Zelda were gone. She'd ordered for both of them—blackened catfish and fried pickles for her, grilled shrimp, fried green tomatoes, and a side of hush puppies for him.

She tilted her head toward the bartender. "Did you get what you came for?"

"Not exactly."

She opened a pack of crackers, buttered one of them edge to edge, and handed it to him. "You and Robert talked a long time."

Her style of fishing for information had become more sophisticated. "If you're wondering why he bought the diner, he has a friend in Chicago who wants to open a restaurant for the casino trade."

She brightened. "Wouldn't that be great?"

"It's a terrible idea. A pipe dream."

"Yeah, well. Some of us survive on pipe dreams." Her eyes wandered the room. "I'm going to believe Caroline and Robert were secretly, madly in love and were about to be married."

He watched her face, wondering if she was still fishing or if she'd known about their relationship all along.

Her wine arrived. She raised her glass. "To Caroline and Robert." She took a sip. "This is nice. Thank you."

The food came. They split the pickles and fried green tomatoes. The background music was Muddy Waters's "Rock Me All Night Long." Watching Zelda take a bite of pickle, he wondered if he kissed her whether she would taste like pickles. Then he wondered why he'd thought about kissing her. She wasn't the type of woman who attracted him.

While he ate, a middle-aged woman with dark skin and corkscrew curls mounted the stage and took a seat at the piano. She played a series of chords, her fingers moving down the keyboard to test the lower range. She bent to adjust a foot pedal.

He had an idea.

"Save a pickle for me, will you?" He left the table and signaled the bartender. "Was the piano player in the house last Monday night?"

"Sure. That's Nell Ray Tate."

He walked to the stage. "Sorry to disturb you, Mz. Tate. I understand you were performing last Monday night."

She looked him up and down, her lips pursed. "Is this police business?"

"Why do you ask?"

"I know that cop swagger." She grinned. "I got to say, it looks mighty fine on a man like you."

"Yes, ma'am." He cleared his throat. "Did you happen to see this man Monday night?" He held up his mobile with Highsmith's photo.

She slipped on a pair of readers and pointed her index finger to the screen. "I do remember the gentleman. He was leaning against the wall, looking like he'd lost his best friend. I broke my usual set for him and played 'I Got Peace Like a River' instead of 'Two-Fisted Mama.'" She nodded. "Yes, sir. That was one troubled man."

"You remember what time that was?"

"My daddy was a railroad man. I run my show like he ran his trains—on time. I play 'Two-Fisted Mama' at half past eight."

He set a ten on the end of the keyboard.

She frowned at him. "Young man, you don't want to haul me into some courtroom to testify 'cause my memory comes and goes. Talking to you, I say the man was here. If I'm in some courtroom, I might not be so sure."

"No ma'am, it won't come to that."

He walked back to the table thinking that Highsmith had said he texted Caroline from the parking lot. A tower dump would give him the exact time Highsmith had been at The Hollywood, but it would require a subpoena and several days of waiting to get the information. Nell Ray Tate sounded like she was just as accurate. Problem was, the timing cleared Highsmith of the murder before coming to The Hollywood, but not after. It would've been tight, but he had time to drive back to Memphis, kill Caroline, and drive to the house. And he didn't have witnesses to say otherwise.

"The piano player is smiling at you," Zelda said as he sat down. "You certainly have a way with the ladies."

I hope so. He put on a smile for Zelda. "What exactly do you do at the firm?"

"Hmm," she said, "I'll need another glass of wine for that, because what you're really asking about are those sequestered files."

He signaled the server for another Cabernet. "What's so special about them?"

"I don't have a clue. Like I said, only the Lees are allowed access."

"Are they locked up?"

"No. I'm sure they think I'm too stupid to go poking around."

"Who has access to the file room?"

The wine came. Zelda took a big swallow. "Rosalyn, her assistant, and me. Attorneys request a file, I check it out of the system, and their assistant picks it up. When it's returned, I check the file back in. That way I know the location of a file at all times."

"Why do you think Caroline pulled that set of files into her office?"

"We had that fight about them, so I assumed she thought I would give them to Robert out of spite."

"You sound angry."

"Of course. She talked to me like I was an idiot then insulted my integrity by pulling the files. Aunt Rosalyn gave me today off because they're reviewing the filing procedures. I'm the file clerk, and they're doing it without me. I'm sure any changes they make will be about those sequestered files. They're moving them or locking them up." She drained her glass. "Whatever. But I can tell you it's pissing me off."

Chapter 36

After Frankie dropped Judd at his house, she went straight to her desk at the CJC to access the National Crime Information Center, NCIC. Within minutes she had the details of Atwood's arrest and incarceration at California's Avenal State prison. He'd been caught selling a dime bag to a college student in a liquor store parking lot. A search of his car had revealed a half pound of marijuana. He was charged with possession with intent to sell, but because he had no record, his attorney worked out a plea that reduced the felony to the misdemeanor charge of simple possession. He was sentenced to nine months and was out after serving 120 days.

Walker lost Atwood's trail after he'd left prison. At the time Walker didn't have access to law enforcement's current databases, which have vastly increased in scope in the last few years. Frankie wasn't persuaded that Atwood was Caroline's killer, but thought an attempt to locate him would be worthwhile.

She accessed multiple FBI databases using the Data Integration and Visualization System, DIVS. Atwood wasn't currently incarcerated, paying taxes, or collecting benefits. He'd never been issued a passport. That didn't mean he couldn't have slipped into Canada or Mexico. She switched to a commercial database. Atwood hadn't bought a car or house or taken out a loan since leaving prison. He could be anywhere, living invisibly, especially if he was leaching off another wealthy mark. He could even be in Memphis.

Detective Kloss came by her desk to say he was leaving to check a promising lead from the tip line. She texted Billy she was in the office. He responded asking her to do a second interview with Elena Lucchesi, Martin's girlfriend, to confirm the alibi. She called. Elena was home. She texted Billy:

Will do.

She looked up from her mobile to see Harrison Pete standing in front of her desk with a grin on his face. He held up a piece of paper. "I found the marriage license application."

Frankie parked beside the lake in Chickasaw Gardens half a block from Martin's Tudor-style home. Coming up the walk to the house, she saw a young woman with long dark hair standing at the kitchen window, eyes downcast while she worked at the sink. Elena Lucchesi appeared to be serenely removed from the world, unaware she was being observed.

After a rough day in the field, Frankie sometimes wondered what it would be like to have a normal life—making love with a husband, cooking dinner for him and the kids. No dead bodies. No bad guys. She'd chosen her job and wanted to excel. She liked living alone, but if the right man came along and offered her the moon, she might change her mind.

She knocked on a side door sheltered by a porte-cochere,

holding a bunch of sunflowers that she counted on making the young woman feel this was a friendly visit and put her in the mood to answer questions.

Elena opened the door, drying her hands on a tea towel. She eyed the sunflowers.

"I'm Detective Malone. We spoke on the phone."

"Yes. Come in."

Frankie extended the bouquet. "These remind me of Italy. I hope you like them."

Elena took them with a shy smile. "You're very kind."

While the young woman put the flowers in a vase, Frankie glanced around the most amazing kitchen she'd seen other than in the pages of *Architectural Digest*. Elena looked tiny, as small as a child, working in this large space.

"May I ask where your home is in Italy?" she asked.

"My family lives in Rome." Elena moved down the granite-topped island to a large chopping board where she'd laid out an untrimmed tenderloin of beef. "I must continue my work. We have a guest tonight. Martin is . . ." She looked at the ceiling, searching for words. "He likes time."

"He's punctual?"

"Yes."

Elena trimmed the tenderloin and began to remove the silver skin. Frankie joined her to watch. No engagement ring, she noticed.

"Martin's lucky to have a girlfriend who can cook," she said.

Elena looked up, startled. "I only cook and keep his house."

"He's your boss then."

"Well, yes." She patted the meat dry, appearing uneasy.

"That means your presence in the States is up to Martin. Your future depends on him."

Elena shook her head, her silky hair tracing back and forth across her shoulders. "It's not that way. Martin is a family friend. Excuse me." She turned her back, seasoning the tenderloin with salt, pepper, and minced garlic. She began to hum, a subtle way to shut Frankie out.

"May I have a glass of water?" Frankie asked. "I'll get it."

Elena inclined her head toward a cabinet next to the sink.

"I'm sure you've met Caroline," she said, filling a glass.

Elena stopped her work. "She showed me where to buy groceries and the best stores for wine and cheese. We had lunch at the Peabody Hotel. You know ducks swim in the fountain there." Her eyes glistened. "Caroline was very nice to me."

"It's my job to make sure the person who killed Caroline is punished."

"I know," she said in a small voice.

"You told us Martin was here the night his sister died. Was that true?"

"I don't understand. Why do you ask me a second time?"

"Because if you've been asked to lie it's very serious. You may not know that if you did lie you become a part of the crime. I'm here in case there's something you weren't able to say before." Frankie was only guessing, but it sounded good.

Elena put down the knife, her gaze casting about the kitchen. *There was more.*

"I've told the truth. Martin asked me to come from Rome, so I thought . . . But we are not together. I live in the guesthouse."

This beautiful woman was sleeping in the guesthouse. What was the deal with Martin? "You can talk to me," Frankie said.

"No, please. There's nothing to say. My mother takes care of Martin's apartment in Rome. My brother looks after his cars. They depend on him."

"Then let me guess. Martin doesn't go with women."

Elena stepped back, bumping into the island. "You should go. I'm busy with dinner."

"Let me remind you, if you don't tell me the whole truth, you could be in trouble."

Elena's lower lip trembled. "You're asking me to ruin my family."

"That's not true. Think about this. Do you have proof Martin was home the night Caroline was killed?"

She watched the word "proof" swim around in Elena's mind. An idea must have surfaced, because Elena washed her hands and left the kitchen. She returned with a four by six snapshot of Martin and a young man, both bare-chested and standing on a beach with mountains in the background. The young man had his arm draped over Martin's shoulder. Martin was kissing the guy's cheek.

"I made *tagliatelle e pesce* for them on Monday night," she said. "I watched them go upstairs to the bedroom."

"What time?"

"Nine o'clock. From the guesthouse I could see their cars. I watched the BBC news at eleven o'clock. Both cars were still there."

Frankie took out a business card. "Thank you, Elena. That's what I needed. I have a feeling you may require my help sometime. If you do, call me at this number."

On the drive from The Hollywood Cafe to Memphis, Billy and Zelda passed trailer parks and It's All Good Auto Sales, Jumpin Jimmy's Liquor, and a huge black and red billboard that declared WORSHIP AT OUR CHURCH OR BURN FOREVER. His mind went to the problem of putting his hands on Zelda's derringer. He didn't have cause for a warrant, and he would need her permission to do a search.

Quarter after six he pulled up in front of her brick home in an older east Memphis neighborhood. The house was dark except for a single light burning on the screened-in porch. He turned off the engine and let his hands drop from the steering wheel. They sat in the dark listening to the engine tick.

She took the hint. "You can come in if you want. We'll look for the gun."

Half an hour later Zelda was standing on a stepladder and handing boxes down from the top shelf of a coat closet, the fifth space they'd searched. Each time she lifted her arms a band of pale skin showed between the bottom of her sweater and the top of her skirt. She kept telling him she couldn't imagine where the gun could be.

"It's just not here." She extended her hand for him to take as she stepped off the ladder. "The attic is a mess. My mom's stuff is mixed in with mine." She started down the hallway then turned back with an excited look.

"I remember now. I lived in an apartment complex where a neighbor had a break-in. I moved my good things to Airlee for safekeeping. There's a walk-in attic on the third floor. I moved boxes, and papers, and my mother's sterling flatware. The gun must be in one of the boxes."

"You're sure?"

"Has to be. Everybody in the family has things stored there—Christmas decorations, Caroline's things from college. Blue carried the boxes upstairs for me."

That sounded a hell of a lot more promising than rummaging through her attic.

"Are your boxes labeled?"

She laughed. "That would've been a good idea."

"I'll give Blue a call."

Blue picked up immediately. "Whatcha you need, man?"

"I'm with Zelda. Do you remember helping her unload some boxes she stored at Airlee?"

"I do. We put them in the third floor attic."

"We're looking for a derringer Saunders gave her." Zelda's mouth twitched when he mentioned the gun. He gave her a reassuring nod. "Could you go to the big house tonight and check those boxes?"

"That's a problem. My dad's having a bout of sundowners. Mom can't handle him on her own."

"I understand." Billy had responded to calls where dementia patients became confused and even violent when the sun went down.

"I'll look for it first thing in the morning," Blue said. "I heard about Zelda's car keys. Tell her I'll be in Memphis tomorrow. I can bring her back here."

He looked at Zelda. "You need a ride to pick up your car?" She nodded.

Blue lowered his voice. "You're thinking Zelda shot Caroline?"

"We'll talk about that later."

"Because a woman like that . . . she's a good soul, but she needs to be protected from herself, you know what I mean."

He knew. "Thanks. Hope your dad gets better."

He hung up. Zelda was beside him, touching her hair and smoothing the flat of her hands down her skirt. He put on a charming smile. "Which way to the attic?"

"I don't want to do that now." She clasped her hands behind her back. "It's Friday night. I have a bottle of good Jamaican rum and my mom's old record collection. She had a thing for the Beatles and Pink Floyd." She raised her brows. "So do I." She moved in close, letting her breast brush his arm.

Oh, hell. He couldn't let himself think about an evening with an attractive, willing woman. A woman who was a suspect.

Her mouth softened to a pout. "Are you going to drink rum with me tonight, Billy?"

"I'd love to, Zelda. I really would. But I'll have to get a rain check."

S itting in his car outside of Zelda's house, he called Frankie.
"Are you still on the road?" she asked.

"Zelda Taylor rode back with me from Airlee. I dropped her off at her house."

"Did you drop her on her head?"

He laughed. "Swear to God, you've got something personal against that woman."

"She's playing you. And she's after your body."

You got that right, he thought. He ran through the details of confronting Zelda about the derringer, the search, and the call to Blue. He left out the part about the rum.

"Did she get on a stepladder and wave her fanny in your face?"

"Of course. That's required during a closet search."

Frankie scoffed. "The gun makes her a prime suspect. What are you going to do about locating it?"

"Nothing I can do but wait for Blue's call." He started the engine but didn't turn on the headlights. "What about you?"

"Big news. Harrison found the marriage application at the Benton County Clerk's office. Guess who."

"Highsmith. He told me."

"What? When?"

"Long story. I'm on my way in. Any results from the tip line?"

"Kloss has a lead, a retired cop from the old east precinct."

"I'll be there in fifteen."

Chaos reigns at the Shelby County Jail on Fridays. Between four o'clock Friday afternoon and midnight Saturday, more people are arrested than any other period during the week. More people are shot. More murdered.

To get away from the ringing phones in the squad room, Billy and Frankie went to the break room to work despite the overwhelming odor of microwave popcorn. She listened while he ran through his conversations with Saunders and Zelda. He then went over Highsmith's revelation about his relationship with Caroline.

"Why didn't he tell you last night?" she asked.

"He thought I would take him into custody. He had another angle he wanted to investigate."

Billy went step by step through Highsmith's embezzlement story. "He said he didn't show up to marry Caroline because he believes Martin, Saunders, Rosalyn, and even Caroline have been stealing from clients. He wasn't willing to marry her and then have to blow the whistle on her family."

"I don't believe that. He thought she was pregnant with his child. Why didn't he confront her and give her a chance to explain?"

"She would've denied it and had the opportunity to destroy evidence. Highsmith asked Zelda for twenty-three trust files on Monday. He was looking for proof of embezzlement. When Caroline found out he'd requested them, she had the files moved to her office.

"After Highsmith left my place last night, he went to Caroline's office to get the files. They weren't there because Rosalyn had removed them. He says they're no longer listed in the database. They're gone. I asked Zelda about the files. She's suspicious, too. Highsmith doesn't know if Caroline was stealing, or if she caught her brother stealing and he killed her for it."

Frankie sat back and ran her hands through her hair. "Do you believe he's right about the embezzlement?"

"He says he's found something incriminating with one client. Beyond that he has no proof. All I have is his story. We're talking about a respected law firm, and I don't believe for one second that any of the Lees would do such a thing. Except for Martin. That's why I asked you to check his alibi."

"That theory has one problem. Martin's girlfriend stands by her statement, except she isn't his girlfriend. He's gay. She's his housekeeper. He had a boyfriend over Monday evening who stayed the night."

Billy hooted. "I'll bet Momma Rosalyn doesn't know that."

"Where does that leave Highsmith? You think he's our killer?"

"A witness puts him at The Hollywood Cafe at 8:30 on Monday night. I believe Sharma is our guy. Highsmith is a contender and then Zelda. If Blue finds the gun we can run a ballistics comparison and rule her out."

"We have a possible fourth." She handed him the psychiatrist's report on Atwood.

He skimmed the pages and frowned. "We can't chase this."

"I'm certain Atwood has the capacity to commit murder, and we don't have to chase him. I'm using the FBI's Data Integration and Visualization System to look for him. It's a single-source search capable of pulling from hundreds of databases and datasets. The search is broad and fast. I'll locate him. Then we'll know."

"I realize you have a second agenda. Judd Phillips wants to get his hands on that dirtbag."

"There's that," she said, shrugging.

"How much time do you need?"

"Another hour or two and I'll be satisfied."

"Do it then close it down," he said.

The break room door swung open. Detective Kloss strode in smiling. "Hey, kiddies. Daddy's brought home a treat." He opened his memo book. "Sixty-three year-old Sergeant Munford Hale, retired, has twenty-two years with the MPD as a uniformed patrol officer. Monday evening, November 14th, he arrived at the Shelby Farms jogging track at 9:05 pm for his nightly walk. He noticed a familiar black Escalade with a specialty Tennessee plate for the Elvis Presley Memorial Trauma Center at the Med. Mr. Hall could not tell if the vehicle was occupied at the time. It began to rain, so he returned home." Kloss turned the page. "He was certain about the day and time."

"Why was the vehicle so familiar?" Frankie asked.

"He sees it on a regular basis. He identified the owner as a tall male, mid-thirties to mid-forties. He jogs on the track, some-times in surgical scrubs."

Billy grinned. "We got the bastard."

Chapter 37

Middlebrook gave Billy the go-ahead for search and arrest warrants for Dr. Raj Sharma. The affidavits would spell out probable-cause evidence: Dr. Sharma's harassment of the victim, two .32 caliber revolvers, and Sergeant Munford Hale's statement. The search warrant would include all footwear, clothing, and weapons along with electronic devices and any other probable evidence or contraband. Billy asked Frankie to trace Sharma's mobile to his home address. They had to move quickly.

A world-weary female patrol officer had nicknamed him "Detective Cool" because she said he never let the bad guys see him sweat. The name didn't apply tonight. He was bouncing off the walls.

At 9:32 pm the magistrate issued the warrants. The charge against Dr. Sharma was first degree murder.

The night was cold and moonless. A vanload of tactical officers and three cruisers followed Billy's and Frankie's cars to Sharma's two-story Georgian home at the end of a cul-de-sac. Lights burned in the back of the house. They were close now.

They posted a cruiser at the opening of the street then quickly rolled into the cove. Another cruiser angled into Sharma's driveway to block the garage bays. Two tactical officers slipped to the back of the house in case the doctor tried to run.

He and Frankie assembled the rest of the team at the double front doors. Billy spoke quietly. "The suspect owns handguns. Assume he's armed." He glanced at Frankie. "Ready?"

"Ready."

He rang the bell and rapped several times with the metal knocker. "Police, Dr. Sharma," he shouted. "It's Detective Able. Open the door."

Frankie looked at her watch, timing one minute. She nodded.

He pounded the door with his fist. "*Police.* Open up or we're coming in." He bent forward, listening. No movement on the other side. He felt pressure building behind him, the men's anticipation. They were ready to breach the doors. He counted down slowly from twenty-five still listening. Then he stepped aside.

A burly officer came forward with a thirty-pound metal battering ram. He took a side stance and swung it in an arc at the door. The wood cracked and splintered. A second swing and the doors crashed open. Three officers in tactical gear hustled in with their weapons drawn, their boots squeaking on marble tiles. He and Frankie followed with their SIGs drawn. She moved with the officers through the downstairs, clearing room by room, the burglar alarm beeping its countdown. The alarm converted to a whooping siren upping the tension. Billy directed one officer to the garage and another to the kitchen to answer the security company's call on the landline.

Frankie came running back. "Not down here."

"Upstairs," he said. They pounded up the steps with officers close behind them. Billy took the master, the place Sharma would most likely be hiding. Frankie and an officer hurried down the hall to clear the other rooms.

Billy stopped short of the bedroom's open door, all juiced up, his heart slamming in his chest. "Dr. Sharma," he called. "It's Detective Able. Step into the open with your hands up."

He peered around the casing and scanned the room then eased inside, the barrel of his SIG pointed skyward. One bedside lamp burned dimly in the corner. The bed was made, pillows propped against a bolster and a tall gilded headboard. A closet door stood open on the wall to his left. On the far side of the room, the bathroom door stood partially open with its light on.

He waved to the officer to look under the bed and in the closet. He crossed to the bathroom. "Sharma," he barked, and kicked open the door, moving into the spa-like bathroom with its shiny tile surfaces and gleaming fixtures. He checked the shower and water closet, and then turned to see one of the officers from downstairs standing in the doorway.

"Detective, the Escalade is gone. I found this on a charger in the kitchen." The officer held up a mobile phone.

Damn it. Sharma didn't forget his mobile. He left it so he couldn't be tracked. An old trick. Cops think they have a crook pinpointed. They race to some remote location only to find a phone sitting on a stump.

He came out of the bathroom to find Frankie pacing the Tibetan carpet at the foot of the king-sized bed. The glance she threw him said she knew about the mobile and was just as disappointed. Too frustrated to speak, he passed her and went to the nightstand. Inside the drawer lay a revolver on top of a stack of pharmaceutical pamphlets. He reached for it then decided to leave it for CSU.

Frankie peered around his shoulder at the gun. "I'll have Sharma paged at the MED, and I'll drive by the Baptist Hospital and Shelby Farms parking lots. He may not carry his phone when he's jogging."

Billy gritted his teeth. "That doesn't make sense. The son of a bitch skipped on us."

"I'm going anyway," she said.

He walked her to her car. Neighbors stood in groups on the sidewalk wearing coats over their pajamas. Officers waved them back and encouraged them to go inside. The CSU van arrived. Billy went back in the house.

The living room had the sleek opulence of Italian contemporary furniture mixed with jewel-toned fabrics from India. Billy searched the downstairs for a gun safe then went to Sharma's study.

A young detective seated at the desk stood when he entered. "I've found a weapon, sir."

Billy went around the side of the desk to see the stainless steel barrel of a Beretta 92F in the bottom left hand drawer. "We're missing a .45 Colt, a 9mm Glock, and a .32 revolver. Could be more guns around. Keep your eyes open," he said to the detective.

He picked up an envelope on the desk addressed in an elaborate hand. The return address was New Delhi. Sharma's sister had written to say their mother was suffering from depression because of the wedding cancellation and wouldn't leave the house. The sister admonished him as a bad son and said he should've come home after heaping so much humiliation upon them. Family was paramount in Sharma's culture. His feelings for Caroline must have suffered after receiving that letter.

Across the room stood a wall of bookcases filled with medical books and framed diplomas from Cambridge University, Oxford Medical School, and Johns Hopkins. There were also commendations from two international charities and appreciative letters from patients. A brass box on a top shelf contained the Glock. A detective had found the Colt in a kitchen drawer next to the back door. That left one missing .32 revolver.

"Detective Able," a woman's voice called from the entrance hall.

He stepped out to see a Rubenesque tech with wavy auburn hair on the second floor landing, leaning over the railing. "Could you come up, please?" He took the stairs and found her in the master bedroom.

"I've bagged the revolver for the ballistic comparison," she said. "We're almost through the walk-in closet. Two pairs of slacks have minuscule spots of blood on them, which isn't unusual for a surgeon who does rounds. I've reviewed the shoe impressions taken at the scene. None of his shoes are even close, but we'll bring everything in. There might be more in the garage."

"He doesn't strike me as the type to leave a pair of shoes in the garage," he said.

"No. Everything in the closet is expensive and kept in perfect order."

She held up a plastic evidence bag containing a prescription bottle. "I found this in the bathroom. It was caught between the trashcan and its liner."

The bag contained an empty prescription bottle with no pharmacy or doctor's name, only a string of chemical symbols on the label.

"I've never seen anything like it, and I've seen just about everything," the tech said. "These docs are geniuses at hiding their prescription drug habits."

He went downstairs, mulling over Sharma's possible drug abuse. Cold air poured through the broken doors as he monitored the evidence bags going out. The temperature had dropped to just above freezing. Frankie, wrapped in a trench coat, hurried up the front walk toward him.

"I've spoken to Security on duty at the MED and the Baptist," she said. "They haven't seen Sharma or his car. And I drove by Shelby Farms. That guy Munford Hale was sitting in the parking lot with his car's engine running. We had an odd conversation."

"Meaning?"

"He said he was on a stakeout, waiting for Sharma. He told me to leave."

"The old war horse. Good for him," he said.

"He thinks he's on the job."

"He's just bored with sitting at home. Can't blame him."

She shrugged and watched a CSU tech come down the stairs with a bag of clothes. "How's it going?"

"We've found every weapon except the second revolver."

"Better let Middlebrook know what's happening."

"I want to talk to Vanderman first." He dialed, waited five rings. It was late.

Vanderman answered. "Yes, Detective."

He told the attorney about the arrest and search warrants and that Sharma had left his mobile on the charger.

Vanderman was silent. "Hold on." Billy put the phone on speaker so Frankie could hear. Vanderman came back two minutes later. "I'll have Dr. Sharma at your office tomorrow morning. Does nine o'clock work?"

"You've spoken with him?"

"Yes."

"Where's the doctor sleeping tonight?"

"I don't ask my clients those questions."

"Tomorrow then, Counselor."

"Have a good night." Vanderman hung up.

"Well that was civil," she said.

"Vanderman isn't burning any bridges. He may want me to cut his next client a break. You noticed he got in touch with Sharma immediately. The doctor must have bought a burner phone and given the number to Vanderman."

"You think they'll come in tomorrow?" she asked.

"I don't know, but Vanderman is staking his reputation on it."

Chapter 38

Billy left Sharma's house, winding through back streets to get to Poplar Ave. Little traffic. No moon. The search had been a misfire. It was like bringing a SIG up smooth and balanced. Pull the trigger. All you get is a *click*.

Frankie had agreed to stop by the Baptist Hospital and ask the pharmacist to try and decode the compounds listed on Sharma's prescription. Even though Frankie and the tech thought the bottle was evidence of drug addiction, they couldn't be certain until the compounds were identified. However, addiction would explain some of Sharma's recent behavior.

Frankie would go home and get some sleep. In the morning they would work up an interrogation strategy in case Sharma and Vanderman did show up.

Billy passed a darkened Chick-fil-A and the bright lights of a 24-hour Walgreens. Sitting at the cross street on his right was a yellow 1970 Boss 302 Mustang. It tore out in front of him, the kid in the passenger seat whooping out the window as they whipped around the next corner. Billy reached to light up the Charger's LEDs and give chase, but then stopped. Not his job tonight. He had a lot to think about. Plus, there was something pulling at the back of his mind.

He slowed at a red light and watched the cross traffic. Thoughts churned to the surface. Back at his uncle's house, Highsmith had said, *This isn't over by a long shot.* At the time he'd thought Highsmith meant their conversation wasn't over, but that wasn't right. The look on his face had said a lot more.

Billy had once witnessed a pit bull dangling five feet off the ground from a rope tied to a barn rafter. The dog had jumped up and grabbed the swinging rope in its jaws. It refused to let go. Highsmith didn't appear to be the pit bull type, but it's a mistake to make assumptions about people. Highsmith had failed to get the information he needed and was now locked out of the law firm. He could still be planning to go in after those files.

A car behind Billy honked. The light had turned green. He hit the gas. Okay, damn it. He'd closed a lot of cases trusting his instincts. Right now his instincts said to cruise by the law firm and make sure Highsmith's judgment hadn't been knocked off the rails.

He drove the mile and a half to the firm. Slowing, he approached seeing no lights on in the building except for the downstairs foyer. He decided to go ahead and check for the Saab in the back parking lot. As he was changing lanes to make the turn, headlights filled his rear view mirror. A black Ram ProMaster cargo van shot past him and made the turn into the firm's driveway, hitting the upslope so hard the vehicle went airborne. It then disappeared behind the darkened building.

He and every other cop in the city knew who traveled in that van and several others like it. They were the KODA Group, an elite security service hired to protect wealthy individuals and their property. What made the service so effective were the 24/7 mobile units able to respond to a security breach within minutes.

No reason for the Lee Law Firm to have that kind of protection unless they were expecting an intruder.

Billy turned into the driveway, cut his lights, and rolled quietly into the illuminated back parking lot. The van was angled at the rear entrance with its cargo door open, the crew already inside the building. His tension eased when he realized Highsmith's Saab wasn't in the lot, only the van.

The KODA Group protects what is irreplaceable—works of art, extravagant jewelry, vintage automobiles, and the lives of people who fear retaliation or abduction. KODA's job was to show up fast and stop an intruder before he could do damage or make off with the goods. To do that, a KODA client's security system feed was routed to the vans and monitored there. Break-ins were never reported to law enforcement. That meant no cruisers would show up at the Lee Law Firm tonight. Just him. Unmonitored responses meant KODA was free to take intruders to what's known as "back alley court" and apply their own form of justice. The intruder is then dumped at the ER if he's lucky. Rumor had it that some intruders disappeared altogether.

He rolled down his window and listened. No commotion inside. Must've been a false alarm. He put the car in reverse and was backing around the van when he saw Highsmith's Saab parked in the shadows behind the building next door.

Oh, hell. If Highsmith was inside, he was in trouble. Now what, call for backup? If he did that and KODA had proof that Highsmith had broken in, he'd be locked up for sure. He flung open his car door and ran to the rear entrance. He could handle this, he hoped.

The back entrance was unlocked. He slipped through a porch area and peered around the corner into a hallway. A darkened stairwell on the right led to the offices upstairs. Male voices coming from above sounded like KODA. The voices grew louder.

"Back off!"

That was Highsmith's voice, pitched higher than usual. Billy took the stairs two at a time. More voices. A scream of pain.

Billy rushed across the second floor landing and was reaching for his weapon when fingers dug into his shoulder from behind. He ducked and twisted out from under then swung a round-house right. His fist connected with a nose. The bone cracked. The man grunted, his hand coming up to protect his face. Billy drove his knee into the guy's nuts. The man doubled over. He took him down with a hard left to the side of the throat. The guy dropped, out cold.

Billy bound his hands and feet with flex cuffs, pulled his SIG, and ran down the long hallway, hearing another familiar voice coming from Caroline's office.

"Tase the son of a bitch and get him out of here," Martin yelled.

"I'm about to light you up, son," said a heavier voice.

At the doorway he saw two KODA operatives with their backs turned, one pointing a Taser at Highsmith. Highsmith was behind the desk holding a metal column lamp crossways in front of him. Martin lurked in the corner, his face eager with excitement.

A man lay on the carpet with one hand at his side. Blood oozed from between his fingers. Apparently, Highsmith had stabbed him with the finial on top of the lamp.

By damn. Highsmith had some grit after all.

"Police!" Billy trained his weapon between the shoulder blades of the man holding the Taser. "Drop it! Hit the floor."

The operatives knew the drill. They dropped to their stomachs, hands behind their heads. Highsmith looked relieved but didn't lower the lamp. Martin came out of the corner. This was his building. He was the key holder of the property.

"We caught him in the act of stealing proprietary information," Martin said. "And he attacked this man." He pointed to the wounded guy who was coming to his feet.

"These people—" Highsmith started.

"Not a word out of you," Billy said. "And put down that lamp."

Highsmith set the lamp on the desk, his face flushed with anger. This was probably one of the few times in his life he'd been powerless.

"I want him charged with breaking and entering and aggravated assault," Martin said, knowing he was well within his rights.

What a foul-up. Billy had to get Highsmith out and fast. "On your feet, gentlemen," he said to the other men on the floor. They stood. "Keep your hands where I can see them. Who's in charge?"

The man who'd been wielding the Taser spoke up. "O.W. Chase, Sergeant USMC retired."

"Sergeant," Billy said. "Are we done here?"

Chase nodded. "I'm good with calling it even."

"That's not your decision," Martin hollered at Chase.

"Shut up," Billy barked at Martin, "or I'll arrest you for interfering with an officer."

"We're out of here," Chase said, hustling the wounded man along.

Billy turned to Highsmith. "Now you. Hands behind your back. I'm hooking you up."

Highsmith froze.

"Do it!"

He came from behind the desk and placed his hands at the small of his back. Billy cuffed him and took him by his elbow intentionally jostling Martin hard as he passed. When they reached the parking lot, the KODA van was gone.

"How did you know I was here?" Highsmith asked.

"Keep walking. Do *not* tell me if you got what you came for."

Billy helped him into the back seat, certain Martin was watching from an upstairs window. *The little shit.* Billy got behind the wheel and heard Highsmith squirming against the cuffs.

"What do you think he'll do?" Highsmith asked, using a strong voice to cover how shaken he was.

"He'll try to figure out what you saw in there and report it to Rosalyn. She'll worry about what you know. I'll bet she'll stay up all night forming a strategy."

He heard Highsmith breathing, adrenaline burning up his oxygen. Billy felt the same. He pulled out onto Poplar and headed west. They passed stately homes set far back from the street insulated by brick walls, iron gates, and century-old trees overhanging the sidewalks. He'd like to be in on the KODA debriefing tonight when Sergeant Chase explained how a nerd with a desk lamp had held off his team.

In the rearview mirror he checked Highsmith and saw his cheek puffing at the bone where a punch had landed before he'd gotten his hands on the lamp. Billy could almost hear the wheels turning in the man's mind, thinking how close he'd come to being tased and dragged into a van.

How had Martin connected with the KODA Group in the first place? Ah. They must protect the warehouse where he stores his car collection. So why call in the big guns for the firm? There can't be anything of tangible value so it must be secrets that would destroy the firm if they were stolen. Information in those files.

"How long were you in Caroline's office before they showed?" he asked.

"Long enough."

"What about Martin?"

"I don't know how or when he got there. He may have been at the bank and they called him."

"You know those guys could've chopped you up and fed you to the hogs. Boom. Gone. That's probably what Martin had in mind."

"I handled myself okay."

Oh, right. "You said Rosalyn took your key. How did you get past the lock?"

"I learned the tricks of B&E men when I worked at the prosecutor's office. Locks aren't a problem."

"What about the alarm?"

"I figured Martin was too lazy to change the code and he hadn't." Highsmith shifted in the seat. "Pull over. Get me out of these cuffs."

"I'm taking you in."

"Seriously?"

"KODA has a security video that proves you broke in."

"I worked in that building until yesterday. I'll say I forgot something, so I went back."

"Except that you just confessed to me you went in that building unlawfully. It's my duty to take you in."

"Bastard," Highsmith muttered.

He checked the rearview mirror. Highsmith was staring vacantly out the window. Another mile to the Poplar viaduct then a fifteen-minute drive to the Shelby County Jail. If he went through with this arrest, Highsmith would lose his license to practice law. There'd be no justice in that. Apparently, the guy did a bad thing for a good reason. Billy had done the same thing more than once. He'd just never gotten caught. Besides, with

KODA's involvement he was beginning to believe Highsmith's claim about the embezzlement.

But if he let Highsmith go and Rosalyn pressed charges, the chief would come down on his head. Director Davis had warned him to play it straight. If it came to light that he'd turned Highsmith loose, his own job would be at risk.

He took a right into the deserted Poplar Plaza Shopping Center and parked in front of Spin Street Music. The iconic thirty-foot tall image of Elvis in his gold lamé suit glowed in the showcase above the store's entrance.

"Why are we stopping?" Highsmith asked.

"To make a call." He hit Frankie's number on his mobile. She answered.

"You still at the hospital?" he asked.

"I'm at Walnut Grove and Yates."

"I need you to swing by the Lee Law Firm and see if the place looks buttoned up."

"Sure. Why?"

"I'll explain later."

"You always say that," she said.

"I know. Did the pharmacist decode Sharma's script?"

She made him wait. "It's definitely not cold medicine." He could hear the click of her turn signal. "I'll do a drive-by and text in a couple of minutes."

He sat back. Street sounds bled through the closed window. In the back Highsmith was looking up at the towering image of Elvis outlined in strips of blue neon and lighted by spotlights. It had been a close call with KODA. Both of them could've been injured. It wasn't over yet. Martin was obviously so pissed off he'd be willing to walk through fire to put Highsmith behind bars.

Billy twisted around in his seat. "What in the *hell* were you thinking? You went in to steal evidence that you know can't be used to get an indictment."

"I had my reasons."

"Reasons ain't worth shit when you're sitting in lockup."

Highsmith drew a deep breath and exhaled.

"What is it?" Billy asked.

"You said Caroline might have sent a letter to Sharma admitting she'd left him for another man. I was that man. So if Sharma killed her, I was the reason. I couldn't handle that. I was desperate to find some other killer. Some other reason she'd been murdered. That was Martin. I wanted it to be that way."

Billy almost felt guilty. The man had made him suspicious at the barge, so he'd exaggerated what was in the letter to make him react. As a prosecutor, Highsmith had played the same kind of games, but it was still dirty pool.

A cruiser running code whipped through the light at Poplar and Highland, the sound of the siren deepening in the distance. "Tell me why you broke into the firm when you didn't have the computer passwords you needed," he said.

"I took a chance. I guessed at Caroline's password and hit it on the first try. BlueSkies. It was her favorite song."

"I know that."

Highsmith gave him a sharp look. "Caroline told me the two of you had an intimate relationship. She said she was a mixed-up teenager back then."

Billy looked away, not wanting Highsmith to see how upset he was. Jesus. Caroline must have told him everything.

"She said she regretted the way she'd treated you. And I knew our relationship would make you angry," Highsmith said. "Like now."

"You've got a bigger problem than that. I don't believe your reason for jilting Caroline."

Highsmith's head hung down, the blue neon coloring his face. "It was a lousy excuse. I didn't believe it either. I wanted Caroline to love me the way she loved you during your high school romance. Instead, I was the guy she didn't want anyone to know she was sleeping with. She made that quite clear. She left Sharma and then realized she was pregnant. I think she was terrified he would find out and come after her again, so she told me the baby was mine. I thought I didn't care whose baby it was, but I guess I did.

"She insisted on a quick wedding. I was already having doubts when I stumbled onto Martin's embezzlement. You know how it went from there. That night at The Hollywood I felt justified walking away from her."

"Then you hid out at the diner and licked your wounds."

Highsmith's face stiffened. "I'm not proud of it. I was heartbroken. Disillusioned. I was going to have to blow the whistle on her and her family."

Billy got out of the car and went around to open Highsmith's door. "Come on. Get out." He unlocked the cuffs.

Highsmith shook out his arms. "What now?"

Billy's phone pinged with Frankie's text:

Lee Law Firm closed up. See you AM. Bring donuts.

"Get in front," Billy said. "I'm taking you to your car."

Chapter 39

B illy gave up on sleep at 5:35 am. He showered then went to the sofa to work on a strategy for the coming confrontation with Sharma.

Five days gone since the murder. If Sharma had an alibi, Vanderman should have produced it by now unless the doctor was preventing him from revealing it. Or Sharma was innocent but had no alibi, or he was guilty as a bucket of sin.

Looking at the evidence, they had a solid case. Sharma's harassment set the tone. Munford Hale had placed Sharma's car near the crime scene. The .32 revolver in his nightstand could be the murder weapon. If not, the second .32 might be under the driver's seat of the Escalade. The prescription bottle could be an indication of drug addiction, the kind that makes a hotheaded man more violent. That would add an interesting slant to the interrogation.

In a perfect world Sharma would walk into the squad room and confess. With Vanderman there, that wasn't going to happen.

Finished with his notes, he made a breakfast of eggs over medium, bacon, grits, toast, and orange juice. Plenty of coffee. He pulled into the CJC lot at 7:35 am. The overweight officer Frankie had nicknamed Snackbar was standing outside the rear entrance door smoking a cigarette. As soon as Billy got out of the car, Snackbar was on him.

"Got a minute, Detective?"

He took a breath of cold air. "Sure. What's up?"

"I heard Munford Hale placed your perp near the Lee crime scene."

"You know Hale?" Billy asked.

"He's a fishing buddy." Snackbar flicked the cigarette against the wall. "Good officer in his day. Committed." He rubbed the side of his nose with his forefinger and looked down the street. "You know how it is with us old farts. His mind started playing tricks a few years back. He took early retirement because he knew he was slipping."

Oh, shit.

"What are you telling me?"

"He gets his days confused. Can't remember his grandkids' names. The wife lets him drive to Shelby Farms at night. He says he walks the track, but he sits in the car and listens to the radio." Snackbar shrugged. "His testimony won't hold up in court, but there's no reason you can't use his statement to pressure your suspect."

In the squad room, Billy found Frankie at her desk unpacking her satchel. Her complexion looked dull from a hard week and lack of sleep. He would like to take her out for a hot breakfast instead of her eating those stupid PowerBars. He'd want to tell her about his takedown of the KODA operative on the landing, Highsmith wielding the lamp, and the consternation on Martin's face when he'd walked Highsmith out of the building in cuffs. But he couldn't do that, because he would also have to tell her he'd caught Highsmith red-handed committing a felony and then let him go. That could lead to all kinds of hassles for both of them.

All he could give her this morning was the news that Snackbar had just blown a hole in their case.

She waved to him and covered a yawn. "Sorry. Not awake yet. And I'm afraid there's not much positive news. The ballistic comparison on Sharma's revolver is negative, and the lab is having trouble analyzing the specks of blood on the slacks. One good thing. The pharmacist at the hospital traced Sharma's prescription bottle to a hospital in Houston."

"We've lost our witness," he said.

She squinted. "What? What's the problem?"

"You picked up on it last night. Munford Hale has dementia." He recounted Snackbar's parking lot revelation.

She dropped her head in her hands and groaned.

"Hold on," he said. "Hale may have a memory problem, but that doesn't mean Sharma's Escalade wasn't in the parking lot on Monday night."

She lowered her hands and looked at him as if he was nuts. "We can't use it. Vanderman will discredit his testimony on cross."

"We can use it today as leverage. Vanderman doesn't know Hale has dementia. And if Sharma has a drug addiction, I want to use it. You think you can identify the drug before they get here?"

She sat back. "I put a call into the Houston hospital, but I don't hold much hope they'll talk to me. I've given the list of compounds to Dr. Ramos and asked him to try and identify them as a backup."

"Ramos? You're still seeing the witchdoctor?"

She gave me a grim look. "He's a highly regarded psychologist who happens to be a Santeriá priest. He has the same access to medical research sites as any M.D., and he's willing to help."

She started typing. "And who I see is none of your business."

Billy was still thrown by the bond between straightlaced Frankie and the mysterious Cuban psychologist. Her ties with the Santeriá religion, which started during her Key West upbringing, had been a surprise. Still, Ramos was a smart guy and had played a role in breaking their last big case. He might come through again.

At nine o'clock, the secretary at Reception buzzed the intercom. "Detective Able, Mr. Vanderman is here."

"Is his client with him?"

"Not unless he's the Invisible Man."

"I knew it," Frankie said, ease dropping.

"On my way," he said.

Vanderman was standing next to the reception desk in his thousand-dollar suit. When he saw Billy he thrust out his hand. "Dr. Sharma's flight from Houston was delayed. He'll be here in twenty minutes."

"I have a warrant for his arrest. How do you know he's not on a plane to Fiji?"

"He'll be here," Vanderman said, but he looked uncomfortable.

"I'll give him the twenty minutes. After that I'll have him arrested in the parking lot."

He left the attorney pacing among Reception's plastic chairs and returned to his desk.

"And?" Frankie asked.

"Sharma's flight was delayed. Houston."

"Houston means he made a drug run, or he's AWOL. Vanderman showed up to protect his own credibility."

"You may be right," he said, his fallback response when he wanted to shut down a conversation. He'd been in this position before, a tight case unraveling. He went to the break room and returned with a cup of scorched coffee. He checked his mobile. It was after nine and still nothing from Blue. Maybe his dad had gotten sick during the night. Billy texted his concern and paced around the squad room, ending up at the window where the Pyramid gleamed above the mighty Mississippi. A pigeon landed on the ledge and eyed him.

He looked at the clock. "Six minutes," he told the bird.

Detective Kloss waved him over to his desk. "I heard you say Munford Hale has dementia. I don't understand. He was right as rain yesterday when I interviewed him."

A fried chicken biscuit sat in front of Kloss in its greasy wrapper. Kloss picked it up. "You've got Sharma on the ropes even without Hale's ID, right?" He took a bite.

They both knew the murder charge depended on Hale's testimony.

"Not exactly," Billy said, watching biscuit crumbs fall in Kloss's lap.

Kloss took another bite and chewed. "A female cab driver is coming in. Cabbies see a lot of shit on the road, you know. Maybe she's got something."

Billy nodded, only half listening. As he was walking back to his desk, the secretary buzzed in.

"Detective. Tall, dark, and agitated just showed up."

Frankie looked up from her keyboard. "I'll send uniforms downstairs to look for the Escalade. If it's not there, we'll check the house."

In Reception, Vanderman shook Billy's hand like they hadn't done it a few minutes earlier. Sharma loomed behind his attorney. Billy hadn't seen him dressed in anything but scrubs. Today he wore tan slacks, a red sweater, and a brown leather jacket. He had his hair slicked back, his brow an ashen color. He looked thin, almost skeletal.

Sharma stepped around his attorney and stabbed a finger at Billy. "You broke my front doors. You violated my home." His voice sounded rough as if he'd been huffing sand.

"Settle down, Doctor," Vanderman cautioned.

"You weren't home so we let ourselves in," Billy said. "I hear you've been in Houston."

Sharma threw Vanderman a nasty look, obviously furious his attorney had disclosed the trip.

"Detective, I need a moment with my client," Vanderman said.

"This way." Billy ushered them down the hall, an acrid odor trailing Sharma. In the squad room, Vanderman ignored Frankie as he passed her desk. That was a mistake. One day she would be the lead detective on a case he was defending.

He showed them into the interview room with four chairs around a table. Sharma stalked past him, and Vanderman closed the door behind him.

Billy turned to Frankie and shook his head.

"A hospital attorney called while you were in Reception," she said. "They wouldn't tell me a thing. I'm counting on Ramos to come through." She cocked her head toward the interview room. "Sharma looks awful."

He went to his desk and picked up the arrest warrant and a case file that he'd bulked up with enough extra material to put a scare into Sharma. Billy liked his reputation as a closer, but this time he had very little ammunition. He noticed Vanderman had opened the door.

"Put your phone on vibrate," Frankie whispered. "I'll buzz you if Ramos comes through with intel on the drugs."

He walked in, noting that Vanderman had seated Sharma at the table and positioned himself behind the chair for control. Billy would've preferred to put Sharma in a chair with his back to the corner and go after him, but that wasn't about to happen with Vanderman there. The doctor had his head down and was flipping a burner phone from hand to hand as Billy took the chair across from him. He laid the arrest warrant on the table. Sharma pocketed the phone, deliberately avoiding eye contact.

"Dr. Sharma," Billy said. "You have an opportunity to help yourself by explaining what happened between you and your former fiancé on Monday night."

Vanderman peered over the top of his glasses. "Talk to me, Detective. Not my client."

Billy tapped his finger on the warrant. "He's going to be charged with first degree murder. If he cooperates, the DA may consider reducing the charge to second degree."

Sharma picked up the warrant and handed it over his shoulder to Vanderman. "Get on with this. I have a surgery scheduled in two hours."

Vanderman read the warrant and tossed it on the table. "If your witness swears to this identification he'll perjure himself. Put him on the stand, and you'll be in trouble."

Vanderman sounded confident, but then he was a professional bluffer. "Our witness is a former police officer, a trained observer," Billy said.

Vanderman pulled an envelope from his inside suit pocket and withdrew two rectangular pieces of paper. "That may be, but he's wrong in this instance. My client flew out of Memphis on Monday three hours before Miss Lee was murdered. Here are his boarding passes." He dropped the cards on top of the warrant.

Billy picked them up and studied them. They looked authentic. "He could've ducked out on the flight."

"The airline will verify that I boarded the aircraft." Sharma waved his hand in disgust. "This is ridiculous."

The boarding passes were a blow, but Billy refused to give up. There had to be some explanation, but damned if he could see it. If he could fire up Sharma's temper, the doctor might blurt out something incriminating. And he knew the man's weak spot.

"I don't accept these passes as an alibi. Someone could've flown in your place. What I *do* know from evidence we seized at your home is that Caroline humiliated you and your family. Your mother is sick with shame. Your friends are laughing behind your back.

"You were worried Caroline had another man. I can assure you she did. And I've met him."

Sharma lunged to his feet. Billy expected an explosion, but Vanderman gripped his client's shoulder and pushed him down into his chair.

"You're lying to make me angry," Sharma said. A twitch had begun at the corner of his mouth, but he took a breath, put his elbows on the table, and eased forward. "I'm a doctor. I save lives. You save no one. You mop up after the mongrels who shoot each other down in the street. You're nothing but a garbage man."

"That's enough, Doctor." Vanderman pulled out his mobile. "I have more proof right here."

"No!" Sharma said, straightening in his chair. "We've given sufficient proof of my innocence."

"Innocent men go to jail all the time," Vanderman said. He tapped the screen and slid his mobile across the table to Billy.

Billy picked it up. The screen showed a letter from Dr. Wallace Trane in Houston. It stated that Mr. Raj Sharma had been with him until eight o'clock on Monday. And Dr. Trane had seen Mr. Sharma the following morning on rounds.

"Dr. Trane is your personal physician?" he asked.

"None of your business," Sharma snapped.

Vanderman reached across the table for his mobile. "This proves Dr. Sharma was not in Memphis at the time Miss Lee was murdered. Dr. Trane will FedEx a signed and notarized affidavit later today."

Vanderman pocketed his mobile. Sharma crossed his arms and bared his teeth in a hostile smile.

Game over. Billy's mobile vibrated in his pocket, thank God. He stood. "Excuse me."

Frankie was waiting outside the door with a note pad in one hand and Sharma's prescription bottle in the other. "You look like you've been hit by a bus."

"We're done," Billy said. "Sharma has a boarding pass for a flight he took Monday evening. Dr. Trane in Houston sent a letter stating *Mr.* Sharma was with him at the time of the murder."

"Trane in Houston," she said. "That fits. Ramos tracked down the compounds in the prescription. Dr. Wallace Trane is the principle investigator for a phase III clinical drug trial for Huntington's Disease. Sharma must be a participant."

"Huntington's. Jesus. That's a living hell and then it kills you." Billy turned back to look through the one way mirror and saw that the tick at the side of Sharma's mouth had worsened.

"That explains his outbursts and weight loss," she said. "Even worse is the impaired cognitive ability and uncontrolled movements. Ramos said that if Sharma isn't exhibiting full-blown symptoms of the disease, the compounds he's taking are powerful enough to make him very sick. You think Trane knows Sharma is a neurosurgeon?"

"I'm sure Sharma did everything possible to hide his profession from Trane and his illness from the medical community here. He had an ironclad alibi for the night of the murder, but he didn't want his trips to Houston and his connection to Dr. Trane exposed. He waited until he was charged to produce his alibi."

"He's still operating on patients," she said. "We should find out if Vanderman knows about the Huntington's."

"I'll do that now." He took the prescription bottle and wagged it at Frankie. "Thanks, partner."

"Light him up," she said.

Through the one-way mirror he saw Sharma on his feet and waving his hands at Vanderman, probably berating him for revealing his connection to Trane in Houston. Billy opened the door.

"That bitch," Sharma snarled to Vanderman. "Caroline deserved what she got. My father warned me she would bring shame on our family."

The attorney's gaze flicked to Billy. He leaned in and spoke to Sharma.

"Do *not* tell me to shut up," Sharma said. He swatted the air in Billy's direction. "I don't care what he hears."

Billy held up the script bottle. "Maybe you'll care about this. CSU found it during our search. My partner traced it to Dr. Trane in Houston." He glanced at Vanderman, who looked alarmed.

He put the bottle on the table. "You said Caroline deserved what she got. What about your patients? Do they deserve a surgeon so loaded up on drugs he can't think straight? How many have you killed?"

"That's slander," Vanderman said.

"No, it's a question. Your client is participating in a drug trial for Huntington's Disease. Our next call will be to Dr. Trane to find out if he knows Sharma is a practicing neurosurgeon."

"What Dr. Trane knows isn't my responsibility," Vanderman said. "We came to prove Dr. Sharma did not kill Miss Lee. We've accomplished our goal. End of story."

"Counselor, if you knew about the Huntington's and didn't report it to the state licensing board and hospitals where Dr. Sharma operates you're in deep trouble yourself."

Vanderman drew himself up. "Dr. Sharma has the right to attorney-client privilege. That prevents me from revealing to outsiders anything I know about him."

"Bullshit. There's no privilege when an attorney knows his client intends to commit a crime. That's crim law 101, the crime-fraud exception. Sharma stated he plans to operate in two hours. Stop him or I'll make damn sure your own license gets jerked."

Billy glanced over at Sharma. The guy should look pretty beat up by now. Instead, a wild kind of energy was pouring off of him. Definitely not the person he'd want to see leaning over him with a scalpel in his hand.

Sharma's lips drew back in an ugly snarl. "You can't stop me from practicing medicine."

"Vanderman will do that," Billy said. "And afterward, you'll need an army of lawyers when the malpractice suits start piling up. Now both of you, get out."

Chapter 40

Billy called the chief and caught him at the grocery store shopping for his granddaughter's birthday party. Middlebrook put him on hold while he walked to the kosher section where he said it would be quieter.

"Go ahead," the chief said. "And speak up."

He gave him a rundown on Sharma's alibi, his medical condition, and the warning he'd given Vanderman about notifying the licensing board. "The son of a bitch is scheduled to operate today," he said. "If Vanderman doesn't act, he'll cut open someone's head in less than two hours."

The line went quiet. He heard the store's public address system echoing over the phone. "Chief?"

"Yes, I'm thinking. If you're wrong we're risking a slander suit. I'll have to notify General Counsel first."

"Sharma's patient is the one who's at risk."

"All right, you've put me on notice. I'll make the call and get action. My son can take the grandkids to Chuck E. Cheese's for the party. For your part, if Dr. Sharma didn't kill the Lee woman, who did?"

He looked at Frankie seated next to his desk. "We have another person of interest," he said into the phone.

She nodded in agreement.

"Then get to it," the chief said. He hung up.

Frankie pulled over a yellow pad and wrote Robert High-smith's name in block letters. "The groom," she said. "No alibi and a strong motive."

Seemed like nothing fazed her. They were starting to communicate in glances and shifts of the shoulder, a raised eyebrow. He had wondered if that kind of partnership was possible with a woman. Now he knew.

Next she wrote Zelda Taylor. "Again, no alibi. She had a fight with the victim the day of the murder. She owns a .32."

"I haven't heard from Blue about the gun."

"He knows the significance?"

"Absolutely," he said. "His dad must be sick. We'll come back to that."

She wrote the name Clive Atwood then drew a line through it. "I completed the search while you were in with Sharma. He died eight months ago of AIDS."

He thought about that. "Have you called Phillips?"

"I'm putting it off."

He stared at the two names on the pad. Last night he had Highsmith in cuffs and he'd let him go. He still couldn't see the man as the killer. Zelda was an outside possibility.

What had they missed?

Across the room, Detective Kloss had the receiver cradled under his chin. Kloss had worked homicide for five years. He hummed movie theme songs all day long, highly irritating, but he closed cases, and carried his share of the load. Billy waved at Kloss. Kloss grinned and flipped him the bird.

"I'll talk to Kloss, see if there's anything from the tip line," he said to Frankie.

"I need fuel. I'm going for a breakfast burrito from the cart on the corner," she said. "And we need some decent coffee. I think you could use a double espresso."

He walked over to stand in front of Kloss, who was doodling and saying uh-huh into the receiver. He gave Billy an eye roll, scribbled on a pad, and tore off the sheet.

Cab driver in Reception.

What the hell. He walked down the hall to where a bulky middle-aged woman in men's gray work trousers and a short beige jacket was leaning against the wall and picking at a cuticle.

She straightened at the sight of him. "Hi. You're Detective Able. Your picture was in the paper." She stepped forward and shook hands, one strong downward stroke. "Opal Cook." She glanced around, smacked her lips. "Home to the homicide squad. Can I get a tour of the forensics lab?"

Great. Kloss had stuck him with an NCIS fan.

She must have read the dismay on his face. "I'm not a badge bunny looking to get thumped. If you don't have time to hear what I've got, I'll head for the barn."

He gestured toward the hallway. "No, no. We appreciate you coming in, Ms. Cook. I'll bet you could use a cup of coffee."

In the interview room, he began with a few innocuous questions for the cabbie then started in. "Tell me about Monday night."

"Sure thing. I picked up a flag at the airport. The drop was the Walnut Bend subdivision, so I took I-240 and headed east through Shelby Farms. The rain started. I noticed a person walking the shoulder on the far side of the divide."

"Which direction?"

"West. Near the light at Farm Road."

"What time?"

"The airport pickup was at 8:27." She squinted at the ceiling. "No traffic, so I made Shelby Farms around 8:45."

The timing worked.

"I figured the person I'd seen walking had car trouble and cut through from Sycamore View. I dropped off my fare and was planning a turnaround to make the pickup. I never flag a stranded person. It's bad karma."

She patted the flat of her hand on the table. "You said this is an interview room, but it's interrogation, right?"

"It's both. Let's stay with Monday night," he said.

"Sure thing. It's just that I wanted to be in law enforcement, but I've got this heart murmur."

"Sorry to hear that. Bet you would've made a good cop."

"Thanks. Now let's see." She looked up again, searching her memory. "It started raining harder. And dark . . . *man*, was it ever dark. I figured someone had already picked her up, and then I spotted her near the curve at the overpass. The shoulder's good and wide there."

He stopped writing. "You said 'her.' Was there something that made you believe the person was female?"

"I don't know." She blinked, thinking. "Tall. Could've been a man, but that wasn't my impression."

"How was the person dressed?"

"A square-cut jacket, hit about mid-thigh. Head covered but not with a hat."

He nodded and kept writing.

"Coming up from behind I tapped my horn. She had to know I was there. My headlights were on. She was carrying something she used to wave me on. I pulled up so I was even with her and rolled down the window."

"You keep saying 'she.' There must be a reason."

She thought about it. "Nowadays women don't accept rides from strangers. I guess that made me assume it was a woman."

"Did you see her face?"

"No. She never looked over. Traffic was coming up from behind, so I drove on."

"What age would you guess?" he asked.

"Not a kid. I could tell by the walk. I've got an eye for detail. Have to stay sharp in my business."

"Do you remember the color of the item she waved at you?"

"Blue."

"How big was it?"

"Bigger than a washcloth. Not as big as a beach towel."

He put down his pen and stood, trying to appear calm. "Wait here, please." He left the room and asked Kloss to step in and complete the driver's contact information.

His pulse was up. Here was a possible break coming out of left field.

Frankie was eating her breakfast burrito in the break room. She pushed his cup of coffee forward. "I see you caught an interview."

"The sweater from Caroline's house. Is it in the property room?" he asked.

She put down the burrito. "Should be. Why?"

He gave her a rundown of his conversation with the cab driver. She went to the doorway and watched Kloss showing the woman around the squad room, stopping at the dry erase board to explain how they tracked solved and unsolved cases.

Frankie turned around. "Is she for real?"

"I think she saw something. Finish your burrito. I'll be back."

"You sound hopeful," she said.

"Too soon for that." But she'd read him right. Hope was exactly what he was feeling.

He took the elevator to the basement and returned fifteen minutes later with a paper bag folded over at the top. Kloss had taken the cab driver to the interview room and left her with a stack of PR pamphlets for the department. Frankie joined him in the interview room. He took the sweater from the sack and spread it on the table.

The driver leaned over it. "The color is in the ballpark." She straightened and gave Frankie a once-over. "You're a detective?"

"I am. What do you mean by ballpark?"

"If I didn't have this bad knee, I'd have your job," the driver said.

"I thought it was a bum ticker," Billy said.

"It's both." She gestured at the sweater. "The color fits what I remember. How about you stand over there and wave it," she said to him.

He went to the far end of the room, turned his back, and waved the sweater at his side. He turned around to see a puzzled look on the driver's face.

"It's the right size and color. There's something else. She was wearing boots."

"Short or tall boots?" Frankie asked.

"I can't say." She looked from Frankie to him. "Tell me something. Did I almost pick up a killer?"

The cab driver gone, Frankie joined him at his desk. He picked up the sweater. "Zelda has one exactly like this," he said. "She was wearing it yesterday."

Frankie took it and inspected the neckline. "Hand knitted. No manufacturer's label. I've seen sweaters like this at craft fairs. Or it could've been knitted as a gift."

"Let's walk it through," he said. "The cab driver described what she believed was a tall woman wearing a square-cut coat and boots. She waved something the size and color of this sweater. Zelda fits her description and owns a blue sweater like it."

"What would put Zelda in Caroline's car on Monday night?"

"How about this: Saunders couldn't be at the wedding so at the last minute Caroline asked Zelda to go with her. Caroline went to pick up Zelda. She said she was cold. Zelda loaned her the sweater for the drive down. She shot Caroline and took the sweater so there'd be nothing to tie her to the scene. She waved the cab driver on, so she wouldn't be identified."

"How did she get home?"

"The hospital is an easy walk from the crime scene. City buses run past there every half hour."

"It works," she said. "We need that derringer. Can someone else at Airlee look for it?"

"Odette could, but there are a lot of boxes in the attic and Zelda's aren't marked. The real risk is Odette telling Mr. Lee what she's up to. We'll lose our confidentiality."

Frankie nodded, thinking.

"What's on your mind?" he asked.

"I want to reread the physical evidence reports. There's something about the fibers I'd like to check."

"Do that and then locate Zelda's mobile to see if she's home. We need a search warrant for her house for the clothing and the car for the gun in case I can't get hold of Blue. I'll write the affidavit and pull together a team to go to the house."

He made the calls and wrote the affidavits. Frankie came back carrying a report.

"I knew it," she said. "Most of the fibers were trapped in the lace on the back of the dress. We didn't pay attention to the ones snagged on the shoulders and the front. That indicates that Caroline put one of the sweaters over her shoulders. I say it was Zelda's sweater. I checked her mobile. It's at her house."

He stood with the affidavits in hand. "I'll call you from the magistrate's office as soon as I have the warrant. Meet me downstairs."

Chapter 41

We have a search warrant," Billy said.

Zelda stood in her doorway holding a cup of coffee. She had on an emerald green wrapper and nothing underneath. Even barefoot she was five foot seven or eight, a tall woman, same as the cab driver had described.

"You didn't need a search warrant last night, did you, Officer Billy?" she said, and smirked.

A detective behind him cleared his throat. Frankie, standing beside him, produced the warrant. Zelda reached out for it, scanned it, and frowned.

"What's this about clothing? And you know the derringer and my car are at Airlee."

"You've been served," he said. "Please step aside."

Her chin lifted. She threw open the door, her robe parting as the door crashed into the wall. A flash of breast showed before she could snatch her robe closed. She stepped back. "Come in, you son of a bitch. Search the goddamned house. Have a party."

"Calm down or we'll put you in the back of a squad car," Frankie said.

"You and who else?" Zelda's cloud of hair moved about her head as if it was electrified.

Billy eased in front of Frankie. "Ms. Taylor can wait on the sofa while we do the search." He raised his brows at Zelda.

"I want to get dressed first," she said.

A woman officer followed Zelda into the bedroom. They returned in minutes, Zelda with her hair held back in a clip, without makeup, her lips and cheeks pale.

A detective had begun digging through boxes in the front hall closet—Christmas tree lights, umbrellas, hats, and gloves. Another detective went to the back hall to lower the attic's fold-down stairs. The rest of the team searched from a list—a field coat, a blue sweater, shoes and boots, and firearms, specifically a .32 derringer.

Billy and Frankie entered Zelda's bedroom and saw the blue sweater draped over the back of a chair. Frankie checked the neckline for a label. "It's the same except for the buttons. These are wooden. The ones on Caroline's are mother of pearl." She bagged the sweater and took it to the tech to be labeled.

Perfume wafted off the dresses and blouses in Zelda's closet as he sorted through them. He squatted on his heels to poke through a row of high-heeled leather boots, sandals, and running shoes. Four shoeboxes marked Christian Louboutin contained expensive-looking heels with red soles. He reached into the back of the closet and brought out a pair of short leather boots, lace-up, flat-heeled, and covered in mud.

His heart sank.

Frankie came up behind him. "Paddock boots. They look like Dehners."

He found the small cloth tab on the side with that name. "How did you know?"

"My father thought he could make up for ignoring me with riding lessons and a show horse. If you ride English, you wear paddock boots. Dehners last forever. Have you checked the heel pattern?"

He turned the boot over. Mud caked the heel and sole. He went to the bathroom and used a pocketknife to scrape mud into the toilet. The footwear examiner would compare the boot heel to the impression taken at the site. The lab would compare the mud to the bison field.

"Billy, look at this."

Frankie was standing in the doorway, an officer behind her. He held up a coat with brass snaps, a corduroy collar, and blue tartan lining. Billy had seen a hundred coats like it on city folks coming in the diner after quail hunts and dove shoots. It's a classic style made of cotton and rubbed with wax to make it waterproof.

She took it from the officer. "We found this in the laundry room closet. There's mud on the front." She gestured toward the boot. "You think the heel impression is a match?"

He studied the ridges on the heel. "We have a winner."

They went to the living room. Zelda was seated on the sofa holding a book she wasn't reading. She came to her feet when she saw them.

"All done?" she asked.

"We have a few questions," he said. "How did these boots and coat get muddy?"

She looked puzzled. "I wear those to the barn when I'm at Airlee. The coat I wear on dove shoots. I guess I should've cleaned them up."

Frankie held up the sweater. "Caroline has one like this."

"Aunt Gracie Ella knitted them as Christmas gifts. So what?"

"Zelda, we're taking you into custody until we sort some things out," he said.

She looked from Frankie to him. "Sort *what* out? How about my gun?"

"I haven't been able to reach Blue," he said.

She gave him a remote look. It was dawning on her how much trouble she was in. "Can't you get someone else to look for it?"

He shook his head.

"Please, Billy. I didn't do this." She sounded frightened.

He recited her rights. Even though he was holding possible proof that she'd killed Caroline, the words stuck in his throat. He cuffed her, not wanting anyone else to do it, and walked her down the steps with his hand on her elbow to support her. An officer assisted her into the back of his cruiser. As the cruiser pulled away, she turned to stare at him through the rear window.

They left Zelda's house for the CJC at half past one, Frankie driving. He thought about the tears Zelda had cried over her murdered cousin. He'd believed her tears were genuine.

His phone buzzed. It was Blue.

"My dad had a stroke at four this morning. Hemorrhagic."

"God, I'm sorry."

"He's out of surgery and in ICU. I'm on my way to line up a room for my mom at the Super 8 near the hospital. I apologize about Zelda's gun. I know it's important."

"Least of your worries, my friend."

"If a Tunica County deputy shows up at Airlee with a search warrant, it will upset the hell out of Mr. Lee."

"I'll take care of it. You look after your folks."

"Something else," Blue said. "Odette came to the hospital. She said Mz. Gracie Ella ate breakfast with Mr. Lee this morning. In case you want to talk to her, she's acting like her old self again."

"What brought her out of it?"

"No idea. She's come around like that before."

"Thanks for letting me know about your dad. Keep me informed if you can."

They hung up. "Is his dad going to be all right?" Frankie asked.

"He's a strong man. A lot of fight left in him. By the way, Gracie Ella Adams seems to have regained her senses."

Chapter 42

Back at the CJC, Frankie peered around her computer monitor at Billy. He was sitting across the aisle with his head down over the notes he was preparing to interrogate Zelda. Since his conversation in the car with Blue he'd been quiet. Reading Zelda her rights had been hard on him, but the real crusher had come when she'd given him that pitiful look as the cruiser pulled away.

Damn, that woman was good.

Frankie understood that the Lee family had played an influential role in his childhood, particularly Saunders Lee and Caroline. His shock and anger at the crime scene made it clear he'd been close to the victim, even in love with her. Probably his first love.

Then Zelda had gotten under his skin with her tears and tantrums, her crazy hair and her long dancer's legs. Looking past her as a suspect and focusing on Sharma had made sense at the time. Now, after recovering so much evidence from Zelda's house, they were clearly on track. That's how she saw it.

Judd came to mind. She had news about Atwood and Zelda. She considered waiting to call until she knew how things would shake out with his cousin, but that could take hours. She rubbed her forehead and stared at the phone. She would give him the information on Atwood and hold off telling him Zelda was in custody until some evidence reports came back.

She dialed the number. "Judd, it's Detective Malone. Are you in town?"

"Hi! Yes, I'm sticking around until this case is resolved. Our visit to Arkansas yesterday was a wakeup call."

"In what way?"

"I really needed to hear your advice. I'm moving on. There's an A.A. meeting in my neighborhood. My first visit is tonight."

"That's great, Judd." She hesitated, wondering if the news about Atwood would break his resolve.

He picked up on her hesitation. "Something's come up?"

"I've completed the search for Clive Atwood."

"And?"

She heard the tension in his voice. Nothing she could do but press ahead. "He died in an AIDS hospice eight months ago."

"Dead. From AIDS. Oh, my God."

He had to be wondering if Atwood had been infected in prison or before. "He's been living in California under a pseudonym he used when he wrote for Princeton's daily newspaper."

He sighed. "I wanted to bring the bastard to justice and give my aunt some peace. Well . . . At least we know."

She let out a breath. "I have some good news. Your aunt appears to be better. The cook at Airlee reported she's eating and acting like her old self again."

"That's wonderful news. She's a grand lady, always so generous. She treated Caroline and Zelda like they were her daughters."

The sweaters came to Frankie's mind. Zelda had said they were Christmas gifts. Judd might know more.

"Listen, Judd. Mrs. Adams knitted blue sweaters for Zelda and Caroline. Do you know anything about that?"

"Oh, my God, those sweaters." He laughed. "Aunt Gracie Ella knitted them for the girls and one for herself, but she didn't knit one for Aunt Rosalyn. She was staking her claim on the girls. The three of them wore their sweaters to family gatherings. Rosalyn ignored the whole thing. She probably didn't care."

"Mrs. Adams has a sweater? Is it like Caroline's and Zelda's?"

"That was the point. They're identical."

"You're a good man, Judd Phillips. I have to go now."

Working through his notes, Billy realized he'd made the mistake of putting critical thinking on hold when it came to Zelda. She'd lied to him, she withheld information, and in the end she'd admitted her lifelong envy of Caroline. Given a healthy push, envy can turn to hatred. Finding the derringer would seal the case against her, but with so much physical evidence piling up, he figured the murder weapon wouldn't be necessary to get her confession.

He was thinking through his strategy when his mobile rang. It was Blue.

"How's your dad?" he asked.

"The docs are hopeful. I'm almost at the hospital now. I went by Airlee earlier to feed the dogs and turn out the horses. I went through Zelda's boxes. I didn't find the gun."

"You're sure."

"Hey, buddy, I'm on the same side as you. I was very thorough. I searched the car's interior, but I couldn't get into the trunk without the keys."

The keys were hidden on the hallway table. He considered asking Blue to go back, but he was already close to the hospital.

"Thanks, Blue. Remember me to your mom and dad."

He hung up. Frankie was standing in front of him.

"The gun?" she asked.

"No gun. The only place Blue couldn't search was the car's trunk."

"Never a dull moment around here. I just spoke with Judd. Guess what. There's a third sweater."

The interview room was claustrophobic gray: gray walls, gray floors, gray metal furniture, oppressive lighting, no windows, a tiny desk shoved against the back wall. All those gray tones worked together to create a sense of powerlessness in a suspect. The atmosphere had been specifically designed to elicit a confession. It often worked.

A sallow-faced officer brought Zelda into the room with her hands cuffed in front of her. Billy instructed him to remove the cuffs and indicated she should take the rigid aluminum chair beside the desk. In jeans and a T-shirt, and without makeup she looked younger. She rubbed her wrists and took a seat. No need for him to establish rapport. There'd been too much of that already.

"You've been well-treated?" he asked.

"I guess so." She spoke quietly without looking at him.

He made her wait while he thumbed through a file full of papers, pretending to scan page by page. He'd memorized the important information earlier.

She shifted in the chair. He glanced up. "I advised you of your rights. Did you understand them?"

"Of course I did."

He scribbled on a legal pad and closed the file, confident Frankie was observing through the one-way mirror in the door.

"We're here to talk about items we seized from your home that connect you to the murder of Caroline Lee. You've told me about your relationship with your cousin, your long-term resentment, even hatred. Just prior to her murder, you believed she'd lost your mother's ring and that she'd lied to cover it up. Is that true?"

"I guess so."

"She belittled you over your handling of some trust files. You said she made you angry."

Zelda stared at him, crossed her arms.

"Caroline was a successful attorney. Set to get everything she wanted. You were getting nothing . . . like always."

"I don't think—"

"You claim she called you early in the evening on Monday and asked you to feed her cat. I want to throw out a different scenario. Caroline's call was actually a last-minute request for you to drive with her to Airlee and be a witness at her wedding."

"Not true," Zelda said. "I don't even know who she was marrying."

"Don't interrupt. Caroline was deliriously happy. It was too much for you. You put your gun in your purse. On the way to Airlee, you forced her to pull over."

Zelda wetted her lips. "That didn't happen. Has Blue found my gun?"

"Stay with me. When did you last wear your paddock boots?"

"I don't understand. What's with the boots? I forgot to clean them. Is that a crime?"

He gave her a cool stare, pen poised over the pad.

She shrugged. "I don't know. Probably in September. I went trail riding a few times."

"And the coat?"

"Last spring. Turkey hunting season. The guys never shot anything. They sat around and drank. So did I."

He pulled a physical evidence report from the file. "Fibers from your sweater are the same as the ones found at the crime scene."

Her eyes narrowed. "Billy, whatever you're up to, it won't work. Just tell me if Blue found—"

He held up his hand. "You have no alibi, you've lied about your relationship with the victim, and I had to learn from your uncle that a gun you own is the same caliber as the murder weapon. We have your motive, opportunity, and your means."

"My gun didn't kill anyone. And of course my sweater is the same as Caroline's. They're made from the same wool. You don't need a test to prove that."

"We're checking it for blood spatter."

Her lips parted, incredulous. "You saw me in that sweater yesterday. You think I'd wear it with Caroline's blood on it?"

He pulled two photocopies from the file and handed them to her. "This is a close-up of the heel of your paddock boots. The second is an impression of a footprint from the crime scene. They're identical. That's because you were wearing those boots when you killed Caroline."

She let the pages flutter to the desktop, having gone pale behind a spray of freckles he had not noticed before.

"None of this makes sense," she said.

Three days ago he probably would've believed her.

"I understand your situation more than you realize," he said. "I've seen how the family treats you. You're a Taylor not a Lee. You've always been second in line behind your cousin. They protected her when she got in trouble with the law. They left you sitting in jail for two days. Caroline was given every opportunity, a partnership in the law firm, a beautiful house. You're a talented choreographer, but all they did for you was give you a job as a file clerk."

He glanced at Frankie through the one-way mirror. "Caroline didn't tell you she was pregnant or that she was getting married. Not until she needed something from you."

Tears sprang in Zelda's eyes. "Pregnant? Caroline was *pregnant*? Oh, my God."

He gave her a moment, gauging her reaction. "She was about to start a whole new life. I understand why you might hate her, what drove you to kill her." He leaned in. "I can make a difference if you tell me the truth. Once we leave this room it's going to be a different story."

She swallowed, her face wet with tears. "You didn't tell me about the baby." She shook her head. "And now you're trying to trick me into saying I killed her. I'm done here. I want a lawyer. I want Aunt Rosalyn. She'll take care of me." She sniffed, looked away, and looked back. "And you. You can go to hell."

He left Zelda in the interview room until the officer returned to escort her to holding. Relying on her aunt for representation was a bad idea. Rosalyn would hire an attorney who would serve the firm's and Rosalyn's interests, not Zelda's. They would bully Zelda into a plea bargain to avoid the media circus of a trial, which was good. If she was guilty.

Frankie came over. "What do you think?"

"I hoped she would trust me enough to confess."

"She held up better than I expected," Frankie said. "She seemed genuinely surprised about the pregnancy."

"That's how I saw it." Cornered like that, there'd been something brave about the way Zelda had fought back. Her parting shot that he was trying to trick her into confessing stung. That type of manipulative comment had influenced him from the start.

"The Luminol test on the sweater came back positive but for only trace amounts of blood," Frankie said.

"We'll need a match to Caroline's blood type and a match from the soil sample before we can charge her." He checked his watch. "I want to speak with Gracie Ella Adams one more time. I'd like to put my hands on her sweater."

"Why? I thought you were sold on Zelda."

"Gracie Ella knew about the pregnancy," he said. "She knew Caroline was cold that night. I want to know how."

"That's easy. Caroline called her on the way to Zelda's house and told her. Or she stopped by Gracie Ella's house to show her the dress then went to pick up Zelda."

"Mrs. Adams lives within walking distance of Shelby Farms. She owns a .32, and she's nuts."

Frankie brushed her hair from her forehead, irritated. "You really are having second thoughts about Zelda's guilt."

He didn't want to admit that doubt had crept up on him while interrogating Zelda. He had no basis for it, only a feeling. "I want to search Zelda's trunk for the derringer and talk to Mrs. Adams one more time. Just to cover all the bases."

"Talking to Mrs. Adams will be a problem," Frankie said. "While you were with Zelda, I called Airlee. I spoke with the nurse. Mrs. Adams stormed out of the house this morning after breakfast. She was so upset she backed her car into the porch. Did a lot of damage to the house, but she drove off anyway. They alerted the highway patrol to watch for her."

"What triggered that?"

"The nurse didn't know. Apparently she was fine until she picked up the local paper. Then she started ranting."

"What was on the front page?"

"Agricultural reports and a story about a chicken farmer. The nurse said Judd called after Mrs. Adams left. He's going to try and find her."

Chapter 43

Rosalyn searched her desk drawer for a bottle of aspirin. Her head was pounding. Too little sleep last night and too much worry. At least the office was quiet. She'd given the staff season tickets to the Memphis Tigers basketball games. There was a big Saturday game today, which meant she had the place to herself.

She found the bottle, took two aspirin, and breathed in deep. Bands of warm sunlight lay across her desk. She closed her eyes and tried to relax. The private phone line buzzed, startling her. She opened her eyes almost afraid to check the caller ID. She'd spoken to Robert Highsmith thirty minutes earlier and urged him to come to the office for an important talk. She hadn't given him specifics. If he was calling now to cancel, they were in trouble.

The ID read Phillips J. She picked it up.

"Aunt Rosalyn, it's Judd. Your housekeeper gave me this number."

"Yes, Judd." She ground her teeth in irritation. Two days ago he'd wasted an hour of her time by dropping in to offer his condolences. What could he want now?

"Aunt Gracie Ella left Airlee this morning very worked-up," he said. "Have you seen or heard from her?"

"Why, no. I'm sorry to hear that. If she calls, I'll get in touch immediately." She hung up and pressed her fingers to her temples. Why couldn't anyone in this family be normal? Judd drank. Martin was greedy and narcissistic. Gracie Ella was crazy. Even Caroline was . . . whatever it was that got her killed.

Martin had called last night yelling that Robert Highsmith had broken into the firm's offices and possibly downloaded sequestered files in the backup database. The security firm that worked for Martin caught him. In the midst of the confrontation, Billy Able arrived and arrested Highsmith. Martin had been so angry he wanted to press charges. She'd said no, the last thing they wanted was Robert Highsmith standing before a judge explaining what he'd been after. She was also worried about the reason Able had showed up. Hardly a coincidence. She'd spent the rest of the night deciding what to do.

This morning she was relieved to learn that Able had not booked Robert after all. But that might not be the end of it. Martin hadn't been able to tell if Highsmith completed the download, but if he had, he could be preparing to go to the DA to take down the Lee Law Firm. The only way to find out where things stood had been to call him.

She left her desk for a chair in front of the fireplace. Flames leapt around the gas logs. She had to prepare for the meeting, get in the mood. She'd worn red, the color of strength.

She intended to remind Robert that she could be an adversary or an ally, depending on whether they reached an agreement. She'd tell him she made an emotional decision to close the litigation department too quickly. It was a mistake. She wanted him to rejoin the firm as a full partner and receive Caroline's percentage of the profits, worth at least a million dollars a year. If he took the bait, she would control him until she could dispose of him.

She had another advantage because he was living in a strange city, had a pricey mortgage, no job, and no friends. If he decided to stay in Memphis without her help, she could put a black spot on him. He wouldn't find work with any other firm in town.

Still, his agreement to meet with her today could be a trap. If he started asking questions that might incriminate her, she would toss him out with a show of indignation in the event he was recording the conversation.

If that happened, what would she do? Shift the blame was her usual tactic. It would be Robert's word against Martin's that over a million dollars had bounced out of the Merkle Trust Fund and back. But if the DA decided to pursue it, an audit would provide proof. She wasn't involved in the bank's business, so she could pretend ignorance and point at Martin. However, if she did that he'd go berserk and reveal everything about her, Saunders, Caroline—everybody. No, the best strategy with Martin was to do nothing. The DA wouldn't be able to tie her to that specific embezzlement. If Martin was arrested, he would need her money and influence so badly he'd be crazy to try and take her down.

If an investigation of the firm moved forward, Caroline and Gracie Ella were easy targets. Neither could defend herself. She could tell the DA that Gracie Ella had played a major role at the bank supervising those trust accounts before she went around the bend. She'd explain that her sister-in-law had never been right in the head.

If she had to, she could imply that Caroline had joined Gracie Ella and Martin in the embezzlement scheme. She and Saunders had trusted their family so completely they'd never considered checking up on them. They were shocked and saddened.

As a last resort, she could point out that her husband had

run the firm for many years with an iron hand. If the DA went after Saunders, she would defend him by throwing up dilatory roadblocks until the inevitable happened. The Parkinson's was advancing rapidly. Her husband wasn't going to live forever.

The room grew warm. She clicked off the gas logs and went back to her desk. After this meeting she would drive to Airlee and spend the rest of the weekend with Saunders. Blue's father was in the hospital, so they were shorthanded. Times like this she missed her daughter. Caroline had taken care of the boring parts of the business and looked after her father. She would've fielded condolence calls and handled the drop-in visits from these people they barely knew.

Rosalyn sighed. Her headache was back. Two more aspirin and some fresh lipstick would put her right. As she stood she heard Robert's knock at the door. She checked her watch. Fifteen minutes early. Better early than to not show up at all.

Chapter 44

F rankie crossed the narrow street to the public lot behind the CJC. Judd waved from his BMW and pushed open the passenger door for her to get in.

"Thanks for coming," he said.

"What couldn't you say over the phone?"

"I have a problem that I can't handle. Aunt Gracie Ella left Airlee a couple of hours ago. I'm told she crashed her car into the porch and drove off."

"I know. Mr. Lee's nurse told me you've been trying to find her."

He put a hand on the steering wheel. "I've driven by her house a couple of times. Aunt Rosalyn hasn't heard from her. Martin won't respond to my texts, the bastard. I'm sorry to bother you, but I realized it's November 17th. Finn went missing five years ago today. The nurse told me Aunt Gracie Ella took one look at the front page of the newspaper and stormed out. She must've seen the date. She's lost Finn and Caroline, the two people she loved the most. I'm worried she might commit suicide at the rice field. I started to drive over then realized I'm not equipped to handle the situation."

"You were right to call," Frankie said. He didn't know she and

Billy had their own reasons to find his aunt. "Have you talked to the Crittenden County Sheriff's Office?"

"First thing. The duty officer said an oil tanker truck flipped on I-40 just west of the new bridge. Cars are on fire. No one's available to chase down an old lady in a rice field."

"Excuse me. I have to make a call." Frankie slipped out and walked two cars away before dialing Billy.

"Where did you go?" he asked.

"I'm in public parking with Judd Phillips. It's the anniversary of Finn's disappearance. He thinks Mrs. Adams has gone to the rice fields, possibly to commit suicide."

Billy whistled.

She told him about the tanker spill and that no deputies were available. "I'm going to drive Judd over there. I think you should follow in your car in case we need to do a search."

"I'll meet you in the side parking lot," he said.

Billy checked his weapon and pulled on his black leather jacket as he walked to the elevators. He and Frankie were about to cross the state line to intervene in a possible suicide attempt. If things went south, it would be a hell of a bureaucratic mess. But if Gracie Ella was okay, he intended to bring her back to the CJC. That third sweater was weighing on his mind.

He was exiting the elevator when his mobile rang. It was Highsmith. "Sorry," Billy said. "Can't talk. We've got a situation."

"You need to hear this *now*."

Highsmith's tone brought him up short. He stepped into an alcove. "Go ahead."

"I've been through the files I downloaded—"

"Jesus, Highsmith."

"Listen to me. I was right. Saunders started embezzling years ago. Mrs. Adams was the bank's senior trust officer at the time. Every illegal transfer I've seen has her signature on it."

Billy slumped against the wall. He'd suspected this but still. It felt like he'd stepped in a sinkhole. For him, Saunders had been the soul of Southern honor and gentility. Gracie Ella, a capable and nurturing human being. He'd thought of the Lees as people of principle. Turned out they were common thieves.

"The amounts Saunders embezzled were comparatively small," Highsmith said. "Rosalyn and Martin have been stripping whole accounts."

"What about Caroline?" he asked, but knew the answer.

"She was in on it." Highsmith cleared his throat. "For what it's worth, the day we went for the marriage license she talked about starting a small firm in Holly Springs. I have to believe she wanted out."

"If this has been going on for years, why did no one at the bank catch on?"

"The Lees ran a slick operation dependent on the senior trust officer being a family member. First Gracie Ella Adams and now Martin. If I hadn't caught him looting the Merkle Trust, I doubt they would've ever been exposed."

Billy started for the exit, his attitude toward Gracie Ella having done a one-eighty. Were they going after a suicidal woman or a criminal making one last stop before fleeing?

"Thanks," he said. "Gotta go."

"No, wait. This is important. Rosalyn called and asked me to come to her office for a talk. I assume she knows I have the files and wants to negotiate her way out."

Billy stopped at the door. "Are you going?"

"I'm in the parking lot now. Her car is here. I've knocked, practically beaten down the door. She hasn't answered her phone. I've got a bad feeling about this."

Billy followed Frankie into West Memphis by way of the old bridge. He could see the drivers on the new bridge standing outside their cars to watch the black smoke from the tanker fire drift over the soybean fields on the Arkansas side.

On Broadway Avenue in West Memphis, they hit stop-and-go traffic. Once that let up, he called Frankie's mobile and gave her the rundown of his conversation with Highsmith including last night's break in.

"Why didn't you tell me this morning?" she asked.

"I didn't know if Rosalyn would press charges against Highsmith. If she had, the director was going to come after me for not arresting him. You had no knowledge of the break in, so you were in the clear. None of that matters now. We have to take care of what's in front of us. What's your experience with suicide calls?"

"I handled my share in Key West, but you're the one to talk this woman down. Hold on."

He heard Judd speaking in the background.

She came back. "Judd wants to know the plan."

"He stays out of the way. I'll approach Mrs. Adams. She may be armed, so you'll cover me. If we can't shut this down quickly, Judd is to call the Sheriff's Office and tell them what we're into."

They drove Highway 147 past vinyl-sided houses perched at the edge of the worn-out asphalt road. Four-wheelers and pickups crowded the driveways, clothes on the line, kids and spotted tick hounds on the porches. After thirty minutes, she turned onto a gravel strip running across the top of a man-made levee built to service the rice fields. The day was bright and cold. Sunlight bounced off water that stretched over hundreds of acres on either side.

She slowed as they came to the terminus. His mobile rang. "Judd sees her station wagon parked in front of that row of storage sheds to your left. The memorial marker for Finn is through the undergrowth on your right."

They pulled up on either side of the station wagon. The right taillight was busted and the rear bumper had detached after Gracie Ella's collision with the porch. Judd got out and inspected the damage while they reviewed their plan.

"The marker is twenty feet beyond those scrub trees," Frankie said. "Past that, the land slopes to a drop-off into the rice field." She stepped in and lowered her voice. "I'm counting on you to not play the damned hero."

He nodded, feeling the weight of his weapon on his hip. After hearing from Highsmith about Gracie Ella's past, the confrontation about to take place was far more complex.

Judd led them through the patch of scrub trees. Ahead, clumps of dense undergrowth obscured the view of the rice fields. They stopped at the perimeter of the trees, all of them relieved to see Gracie Ella pacing the edge of the slope. Her left hand hung at her side, clutching the end of a blue sweater that trailed behind her on the ground.

Judd shook their hands. "Thanks for this," he whispered. "Good luck."

He and Frankie moved toward the two-foot-tall marker. Gracie Ella ignored their presence. She had on the same clothes as in the guesthouse—a field coat, a long print dress, and short leather boots.

"What's that pile of red beside the marker?" he whispered to Frankie.

"I don't know. It's the spot where they found Finn's clothes."

He listened. "She's talking to herself."

"No, to Finn." Frankie squinted. "I don't see a gun, do you?"

"Hard to tell."

Gracie Ella stopped, her gaze locked on the rice field, transfixed by something in the water. Bushes blocked their view, so he couldn't tell what she was staring at. They had to move closer.

"Ready?" he asked.

Frankie nodded.

He approached from the right, moving across the stretch of damp packed earth. Frankie slipped in behind to his left. He scanned Gracie Ella again for a weapon. Some suicides don't want to die; they want to be talked out of killing themselves. Some want to take other people with them.

"Mrs. Adams," he called. "It's Billy Able, Memphis Police Department. We spoke at Airlee. I'm that kid from the diner."

Her gaze went to him then back to the water. She cocked her head as if listening to something. He edged toward the water, seeing first the tops of brown grass then . . . *holy shit*. Rosalyn Lee was standing thirty feet out in water up to the tops of her thighs, stark naked, hunched over with her arms crossed to cover her breasts. Her wet hair was plastered to the side of her face.

Shivering, she saw him and called out. "Help me."

She sounded weak. How long had she been in the water?

Gracie Ella inclined her head toward him, eyes glittering. "Finn was cold. Now Rosalyn knows how he felt."

He moved closer. Fifteen feet from Gracie Ella, he was able to see the dull gleam of a derringer tucked in her palm. He got it. Rosalyn was a stand-in for Finn. This was a reenactment. This was about revenge.

"Mrs. Adams, we can't help you as long as you're armed," he said. "Drop the gun."

"I don't think I will," she said through parched lips.

Frankie heard the word "gun" and pulled her SIG. She moved into her shooting stance, elbows bent to allow the recoil to ride back. A derringer is deadly across a poker table, but the range is limited to around thirty feet. Hitting Rosalyn at that distance would be a miracle. If she did, a baseball bat would do more damage. He was closer and in a lot more danger of being shot than Rosalyn.

But Gracie Ella was talking, not shooting. He caught Frankie's eye. *Wait*, he mouthed. She nodded.

"Can you tell me what this is about, Mrs. Adams?"

"You know. Everyone knows because I've told them. She had my son killed so he wouldn't find out she was stealing."

"You self-righteous bitch," Rosalyn yelled. "You stole money for years, you and your brother. Did Finn know that?" She looked imploringly at Billy. "Get me out of here. I'm freezing."

"You don't understand, dear." Gracie Ella smiled. "You're no longer in charge."

He glanced at Frankie. They both knew the situation was going sour.

"You wanted Rosalyn to suffer. You've accomplished that," he said. "Now put the gun on the ground."

Gracie Ella's eyes stayed on Rosalyn. "She has to confess."

"Confess!" Rosalyn screamed. "I did not harm your son. He was my family." She began to sob.

Gracie Ella shook her head. "You don't care about family. Your own daughter was pregnant and you didn't know it. You weren't invited to her wedding. She wanted me there. *Me*."

Rosalyn's mouth fell open. Her eyes cut to Billy.

It fit. Gracie Ella had given him clues in the guesthouse. She said Caroline was cold. She knew about the baby, and she had that pile of blue wool in her lap, the sweater.

Some things you don't want to see. Some answers you don't want to know.

Gracie Ella killed Caroline.

He was afraid his voice was gone, but it came out soft and reassuring. "You didn't mean to hurt Caroline."

She met his eyes. "Hurt her? Not that beautiful child. We all loved her. Spoiled her terribly. She knew I would come with her even on a cold rainy night."

"You mean Monday night?" he asked.

"She didn't want her coat to crush the lace on her sleeves, but she was cold, so I gave her my sweater for her shoulders. We were driving. I told her Finn would've loved to see her in the dress. He appreciated beautiful things. She turned on the radio so I wouldn't talk about Finn, but I didn't stop. I asked if she knew what her mother had done to him. She said, 'This is my wedding night. Please stop talking about Finn.'"

Gracie Ella gestured at Rosalyn. "Her daughter was happy and alive. My son was gone. Dead."

She looked down at the derringer. "Somehow this was in my hand. I remember Caroline grabbing for it." Her expression darkened. "I walked home in the rain and sat at my kitchen table for I don't know how long. I came here to be with Finn." She raised the sweater and stared at it. "This follows me everywhere I go." She dropped it.

"You stupid bitch," Rosalyn screamed. "Your son was screwing a drug dealer. That's what got him killed. You murdered Caroline for nothing."

A gust of wind ruffled the water. Gracie Ella swayed. She

spoke so softly Billy could barely hear her. "Finn told me the light on the water is beautiful this time of day." She dropped the derringer and pulled a Smith & Wesson .357 Magnum revolver from her coat pocket.

"Drop it!" he shouted, his SIG clearing the holster.

"Shoot her," Rosalyn shrieked.

He glanced at Frankie and shook his head. This was his call, his duty.

His finger wrapped the trigger. "Last warning. Drop the gun or I'll shoot."

The revolver came up slowly, aimed at Rosalyn. "She has to be punished."

"No," he yelled, but he had already squeezed the trigger.

The SIG's recoil rode up his arm, the report echoing off the water. The bullet spun Gracie Ella away from him. She folded in a heap. His training kicked in. He moved to her side and knelt to quickly check for more weapons. He drew back a palm smeared with blood.

He rolled her over. Her eyes opened. "Finn," she panted. "Finn."

"It's going to be all right," he whispered.

You say those kind of words no matter what, but his heart wasn't in it. He was angry. Angry for Caroline, angry for everyone. The whole damned thing was a heartbreaker.

Frankie scooped up the derringer and revolver and ran to Rosalyn who'd begun sloshing through the water toward them. She collapsed in the shallows on her hands and knees, gasping and sobbing. Judd was there with his jacket off to wrap around Rosalyn. Frankie and Judd pulled her up the slippery incline together.

"Help's on the way," Judd called over his shoulder to Billy.

Billy moved Gracie Ella's coat aside to check the wound. No arterial bleeding. He took her hand. She squeezed it.

"So ashamed," she mumbled. Her eyes closed.

Frankie raced toward the trees. "I'll get a blanket and the kit," she yelled.

Judd had his arm around Rosalyn's shoulder supporting her and guiding her toward the pile of clothes. She stumbled, weeping, and kicked a bare foot at Gracie Ella as she passed by.

"Murderer," she spat. Judd bundled her away.

Frankie came back with the first aid kit and knelt to tuck the blanket around Gracie Ella. "I heard sirens," she said, breathing hard. "They're minutes away."

Chapter 45

**AUNT OF MURDER VICTIM SHOT
DURING HOSTAGE TAKING
Anniversary of son's disappearance
triggers violence**

The investigation of murdered attorney Caroline
Lee took a tragic turn on Saturday when a Memphis
police detective shot and wounded the victim's aunt,
Mrs. Gracie Ella Adams of Memphis. Mrs. Adams
had allegedly kidnapped Mrs. Rosalyn Lee, mother
of the murder victim, and held her at gunpoint in
frigid waters. The shooting took place at a flooded
rice field in Crittenden Co., Arkansas, the spot
where Mrs. Adams's son disappeared five years ago
to the day.

Sources say Memphis Detective Billy Able
wounded Mrs. Adams after she threatened to shoot
Mrs. Lee. Mrs. Adams is currently in serious condition at the MED.

Family member Judd Phillips, concerned about

Mrs. Adams's mental stability, contacted Detectives Able and Malone and requested assistance after Crittenden Co. Sherriff's deputies had been unable to respond due to the oil tanker truck spill on I-40.

Detective Able has been placed on administrative leave pending investigations to be conducted by the Crittenden County Sherriff's Office and Memphis City Police Department.

The hours following the shooting weren't as difficult as Frankie had expected. A helicopter airlifted Gracie Ella and Rosalyn to the MED. She and Billy spent the rest of Saturday and all day Sunday giving statements to the Sherriff's Office and the Memphis Police Department's internal investigators. As senior officer on the scene, the shooting had been Billy's call. Because he'd discharged his weapon, he'd been placed on administrative leave until cleared by the "shooting board."

On Monday Frankie returned to duty as lead detective for the Lee investigation. The evidence needed to bring charges of voluntary manslaughter against Mrs. Adams for the murder of Caroline Lee had been collected at the Arkansas crime scene— blood on the sweater, mud on the boots from the bison field, the heel impression, and a positive ballistic comparison from her derringer.

The MED's surgeon reported to Frankie that the .40 caliber bullet had entered below Mrs. Adams's rib cage, sliced her anterior/superior liver, and narrowly missed her lung before exiting. She came out of ICU and into a private room under 24-hour guard and suicide watch.

On Tuesday, Frankie was back at the MED, waiting for an

elevator in the lobby. The doors slid open. Judd and Jerry Vanderman stepped out.

Vanderman frowned when he recognized her then cranked it
up to a smile. "Good afternoon, Detective Malone. Are you here
to see Mrs. Adams?"

"I'm checking her progress." She glanced at Judd, who was
clear-eyed and appeared to be steady on his feet.

"You should know I'm serving as counsel to Mrs. Adams,"
Vanderman said.

"So Mr. Phillips has told me."

Judd nodded. "Hello, Detective." He'd texted her on Monday
concerning his plans to hire Vanderman to represent his aunt.
He added:

> Your actions saved both my aunts' lives. May I take you
> for dinner at Itta Bena as a special thank you?

She'd responded:

> Perfect.

Gracie Ella would need a skilled attorney like Vanderman.
She faced not only charges of voluntary manslaughter but also
aggravated kidnapping. Because she'd crossed the state line
with Rosalyn, both state and federal charges could be filed
concurrently; however, the ADA said he doubted the U.S. attorney would bother. Down the road, she would likely face
class B felony embezzlement charges. Frankie had a feeling
Judd would be the one on the hook for the staggering amount
of legal bills.

She paced the MED's parking lot to get a little air and called Billy to tell him about her encounter with Vanderman.

"Was he rude?" he asked.

"No, but it was a stretch for him."

"You're now lead on a case he's defending. Are you looking for payback for his earlier dickhead behavior?"

"Not right away. I'll make him wonder when the hammer will drop." She smiled to herself, enjoying the thought.

The sound of a tugboat tooting its horn came over the phone. She pictured Billy at home, grounded like a kid who'd thrown a baseball through a window or dented his dad's car. Only this was different. He'd shot a woman and nearly taken her life. A lot of good officers have been knocked out of commission by the effects of the use of deadly force.

"I've been thinking," he said. "Mrs. Adams claimed she didn't remember shooting Caroline yet she removed her sweater, the only thing that tied her to the murder."

"I thought about that. She wasn't as disoriented as she pretended to be."

"She's definitely nuts," he said, "so she'll get a reduced sentence in return for a guilty plea for the manslaughter. The aggravated kidnapping charge will be harder to defend. She forced Rosalyn to drive to the rice field with intent to do harm. It's clear premeditation."

Frankie stopped beside her car. "Somewhere along the way I'm expecting a pat on the back from the chief or the director."

"That won't happen until I'm cleared and maybe not even then."

"I don't see why. In one week we've gone from nothing, to conjecture, to knowing who committed the murder." She heard the tugboat horn again and checked the time. "Well, that's it for me. All I've got. What are your plans?"

"I'm going to hang my new flat screen."

F rankie drove to the CJC with Billy's welfare on her mind. Between Caroline's murder and the coming embezzlement charges, the list of collateral damage was growing. Zelda and the employees at the Lee Law Firm and Airlee Bank would lose their jobs. Robert Highsmith had suffered a terrific loss; however, he might find some comfort in working with the Economic Crimes investigators who would soon issue an arrest warrant for Martin. Taking Martin down would be the first step in bringing the Lees to justice for betraying their clients.

Her mobile rang. The name on the screen read Lee, M. She pulled over. What was that sleaze up to now?

"Malone," she answered, brusquely.

"It's Elena Lucchesi calling. You gave me this number."

"Of course, Elena. How may I help you?"

"I'm not having trouble. I wanted to call . . . Martin is very upset about his aunt. We are leaving for Rome this afternoon for a break. I don't think I'll return to Memphis. I wanted to say goodbye."

Frankie almost dropped the phone. The investigators in Economic Crimes probably hadn't considered Martin as a flight risk. "Is Martin there now?"

"He's driving here from his office. Our bags are downstairs."

"I'm glad you called, Elena. Best of luck in Rome."

She hung up and immediately phoned the investigators. The chase was on.

Leo sat in a patch of sunlight on the floor and watched Billy as he struggled to hang the flat screen TV on the straps he'd attached to the wall. He'd made a list of several chores around the barge, knowing his reinstatement could take up to three weeks. He was okay with that. Yesterday he'd set in motion a big project, something he'd mulled over the past week. If it came through, he would need those three weeks to make the deal work.

Monday night he'd called Blue to check on his dad and to go over Saturday's events in the rice field. He then gave Blue the disturbing news that Gracie Ella Adams had been the one who'd killed Caroline.

The line had stayed quiet a long time. "Why did she do it?" Blue asked.

"A broken heart. A twisted mind. A long-standing feud between two women. Really, it came down to revenge."

At the end of the conversation, he told Blue where to find Zelda's car keys. Fifteen minutes later Blue called back.

"The gun was in her trunk in a box under a bunch of shopping bags. I hear she's really upset about you taking her in for questioning. I'll be in Memphis in the morning. If you want, I'll call her about the keys and offer to pick her up."

"No, I'll call."

Blue chuckled. "Good luck, my friend."

Billy left a message for Zelda saying he had information about the gun. She called right back.

"Where was it?" she demanded.

"In the trunk of your car. Blue has your keys. He'll be in Memphis tomorrow if you want a ride to Airlee."

He could hear her breathing into the receiver. "I'm so mad at you I don't know what to say."

"I was doing my job, Zelda. I won't apologize for it."

"I wanted to be important to you. You made it clear I was just another criminal."

He started to defend himself, but then didn't feel he had the right. He let it go.

She drew in a breath. "Judd has spoken to a choreographer in Las Vegas. There's an opening for an assistant. I'm going to move whether I get the job or not. I want out of this town."

He pictured her hip-deep in showgirls dressed in sequins and ostrich feathers. Somehow that made sense.

"Best of luck, Zelda."

"Goodbye." She slammed down the phone.

He went to the kitchen to stow his toolbox under the sink. The cabinet door banged shut. The sound set off the image of Gracie Ella's body spinning away from him with the force of the bullet. His heart jumped in his throat. The same thing had happened yesterday when he knocked a book off the table. Last night he'd dreamed about blood on his hands. He couldn't go back to sleep until he got up and washed them.

He was angry with Gracie Ella for forcing him to use his gun. Was she going to shoot Rosalyn or had she set him up for suicide by cop? And what about Caroline? He would never know if Gracie Ella planned the murder or if uncontrollable rage had taken over.

Revenge is like a downed power line seeking a path to ground. It can grab any innocent bystander. This time it took Caroline.

Policy required him to attend meetings with a shrink before he resumed his duties. He wasn't sure if he would talk about the flashbacks and dreams. He damn sure didn't want to be sidelined as emotionally unfit. Taking the shot had been the right decision, but pretty much everything you do in this job has its cost.

His mobile pinged a text from Frankie saying she wanted him to meet her at the Shelby County Jail, the last place he wanted to be. He texted back:

Why?

She responded:

Chicken soup for your soul.

Frankie met him in the jail's law enforcement lobby.

"You need to see this," she said as a deputy ushered them through the bolted door to the Intake Center.

Tuesday afternoons are quiet in Intake, mostly DUIs, participants in domestic squabbles, and bond skips—all of them seated in the rows of high-backed, plastic chairs waiting to be processed. Across the room, handcuffed to a green wire bench, sat Martin Lee. He already wore a standard inmate's blue jumpsuit, which meant at this point in the process he'd been searched twice by the arresting officers, fingerprinted and possibly strip-searched for contraband.

"Mr. Highchair Tyrant is on his way to the slammer," Frankie said, a note of satisfaction in her voice. "What do you think?"

"I think the universe is finally spinning in the right direction," he said. "I'm surprised Economic Crimes served the warrant. They usually take their time."

"He was about to skip town." She ran through her conversation with Elena. "They stopped the limousine on the way to the airport and had to forcibly remove him. He punched an officer."

"Resisting arrest." Billy grinned and walked around the bench. Martin had a dazed look, his face bloodless as a peeled grape. He grimaced when he realized Billy was standing ten feet away and began to yank at the cuffs securing him to the bench.

Billy crossed his arms. "You should stop that. You're not going to get much of a result."

"Get away from me," Martin said, continuing to clank metal against metal. "I've called the mayor. You and your bitch partner will be gone by tonight."

"Your beef is with Economic Crimes, not us. We just stopped by to say welcome to our world."

Martin bared his teeth in an ugly smile. "This isn't over. You have no idea who I am or what I can do."

Billy gave a short, sharp laugh. "I had your number the first day we met at the diner. That call you made to the mayor? It should've been to a lawyer."

Martin spat a clot of mucous that landed short of Billy's boots. He stepped back. He almost felt sorry for the guy. Martin's ancestors had passed down their wealth along with an outrageous sense of entitlement. Eventually that kind of society collapses. It appeared the walls of Jericho South were about to come tumbling down.

Two deputies walked over, one with keys. Martin stopped yanking on the cuffs and hunched his shoulders.

"You done talking, Detective?" a deputy asked. "Because this ol' boy's been unruly ever since he came in. He's going into a holding tank."

"Good idea," Billy said. "Otherwise, the inmates are going to beat the hell out of him."

Martin's face went slack. The deputies hauled him to his feet, hooked him up, and turned him around.

"Martin," Billy said. "You're about to enter the most disagreeable phase of your entire life."

Chapter 46

The rain began an hour before Blue came through the mud-room door carrying a load of household cleaners and a deep dish pie.

"Temperature's dropping," he said to Billy, and kicked off his wet shoes.

"They're calling for ice later on," Billy said. "Thanks for coming out." He took Blue's coat, noting how his friend moved as if his bones were aching. Taking care of a plantation and two old, ailing men was a wearing job.

Blue presented the pie. "A gift from Odette. It's bourbon pecan. Still warm. She asked me to say, 'Welcome home.'"

He took the pie, the aroma of toasted pecans and good whiskey filling his nose. It smelled like love to him.

Blue pointed to the Hank Aaron poster still tacked to the mudroom wall. "Now there're some memories. You and me were headed for the major leagues back then. Here we are pushing thirty-five, and we're all broke down."

"Speak for yourself, Gramps," he said. "I still have my glove ready to go to work."

They went into the kitchen where he'd spent the last half

hour scrubbing his uncle's electric stove. Leo stuck his head out from under the kitchen table and meowed.

Blue bent down to look at him. "You keeping this tomcat?"

"You don't keep a cat. The cat keeps you."

Blue grunted and straightened.

"You want coffee with your pie?" he asked.

"Sure." Blue looked around. "The place ain't in bad shape for having stood empty five years."

"The mice left. Nothing to eat. I'm having a phone line put in. The closing is set for the end of the week. Go ahead, have a seat."

Blue took one of the rickety chairs, and they talked while Billy started the coffee. He put slices of pie on the plates and took them to the table.

"Tell me about your folks," he said.

Blue took a bite of pie. "Mmmm. That's good." He wiped his mouth with a napkin. "Dad's coming along. Mr. Lee suggested my folks stay at the big house while my dad recovers. They talk about campaigning Hawk on the national bird dog circuit. Then they go and take their naps. My mom's getting some rest. I'm about caught up on work."

Billy ate his pie, listening. "It's good your dad is there. He'll keep Mr. Lee from missing Caroline so much."

"I imagine so."

Rain slid down the windowpanes like chilled glycerin. Billy poured the coffee.

Two Saturdays had passed since the shooting at the rice field. Blue was up to date on Gracie Ella's condition, so Billy told him the story of Martin's arrest. What he couldn't talk about was the bigger issue, the embezzlement scheme. The indictment could be weeks or even months coming. When that happened, Saunders would be arrested along with Rosalyn. Life would change at Airlee. Blue's job would be at risk.

Blue took a swallow of coffee. His eyes shifted and he frowned. Billy knew that look from when they were kids. "You got something on your mind?"

"Did you buy this place to get out of the city or was there another reason?"

Billy took a bite of pie. It'd been a long time since he'd sat across the table from an old friend. Only Blue knew him well enough to ask that question.

"You remember when I quit law school and Uncle Kane got so mad?"

Blue nodded. "Sure do. He kicked you out."

"He said I was like my father. I would never amount to anything. I gave it a few months and called him. He hung up on me. I sent birthday cards and Christmas cards. Never heard from him."

"Shooo. Your uncle was a tough man."

"Seeing Airlee and the diner again brought all of that back. I decided it was time to claim my home. I asked Highsmith if he wanted to sell the place." He looked around at the cracked linoleum, the rusted refrigerator, and his uncle's Ole Miss coffee mug still hanging on a hook over the stove. Billy's Memphis PD mug now hung on a hook beside it.

Blue surprised him with a grin. "Now you're talking. And you need a good woman. How's that partner of yours?"

His mind went to Frankie as it had done several times in the last few days. He'd imagined her coming down for the weekend to fish, eat barbeque, and hear some blues at The Hollywood. He pictured her sitting on the sofa in front of the wood stove, the house so quiet they could hear each other's heartbeat. The place had one big bed. He'd imagined her in it.

"Frankie's good." He felt his cheeks flush. "She's fine."

He offered Blue more pie. They finished up while the rain pelted the roof.

"I'd better get on the road before it starts freezing," Blue said. He was getting his coat when they heard a car door slam. "You expecting company?"

"That's Highsmith," Billy said on his way to the front room.

Highsmith came in with his glasses fogged and splotches of rain darkening the shoulders of his coat. First thing, he handed a brown sack to Billy. "Here's a thank-you for saving my bacon from the KODA gang."

Billy unwrapped a bottle of Jack Daniel's No. 27 Gold limited edition. "This is mighty fine Tennessee whiskey. Hard to come by. Thank you, Counselor."

Blue came in from the kitchen buttoning his coat. Billy introduced them.

"Chicago's a great town. Good ball club." Blue looked at Billy. "If the weather clears, are you up for working the bird dogs sometime this week?"

"Sure, unless I'm called back for duty. I've been told the shooting board is about to wrap up the investigation."

"I'll be in touch." Blue gave both of them a casual salute before running for his car in the rain.

Highsmith hung his coat on the hook by the door and looked around. "The house is taking shape."

"Still a ways to go. I'll shore up the porch and paint in the spring. You want some pecan pie?"

Highsmith settled in the chair while Billy cut the pie. While he was at it he poured himself two fingers of the good Jack. He knew Highsmith was interested in the house, but his real reason for driving down was to go over the DA's case against the Lee Law Firm.

"During discovery Rosalyn's attorney will request the files I downloaded," Highsmith said. "They would love to get that stolen evidence in front of a judge and have the case thrown out. I withheld the files from the DA. I didn't even talk about them." He took a bite of pie and pointed to it with his fork. "What makes this so good?"

"Browned butter and plenty of bourbon," Billy said. "Go ahead."

"Once Martin has been indicted, certain Lee Law Firm clients will receive an anonymous letter that recommends they have their trusts audited. The letter will also suggest they present any irregularities to the DA."

Billy realized this guy was a hell of a good strategist, the kind who lands on his feet no matter what's in front of him. He would've been the right man for Caroline, a steady husband like Saunders had wanted.

Highsmith set his plate on the table. "I was thinking about what would have happened if I hadn't checked on the Merkle account that Friday. Caroline and I would be married now with a child on the way. Eventually, we would've started a firm in Holly Springs, probably bought an old house to fix up. We would've had jolly babies, big dogs, and extravagant Christmases. I'd be ignorant of the malfeasance taking place at the Lee Law Firm." His eyes reddened. His gaze wandered the room. "I'm sorry. The loss is just now hitting me."

Billy looked over. "I think you were right about Caroline

wanting to leave the firm. You and the baby would've been a fresh start for her."

He was glad to have something to offer this man who'd been through so much, but personally, he didn't believe it. Caroline was raised a Lee. It's almost impossible to walk away from your birthright, especially in the South. He wondered if that was what his uncle had believed about him.

Highsmith nodded and stood. "We'll leave it at that." He went to the door and lifted his coat off the hook. "Seems my fortunes have changed. As soon as I decided to leave Chicago, I sent out a batch of resumes and followed up with several interviews. I got an offer from the Department of Justice in DC, but Rosalyn's offer was better, and I had wanted to give private practice a try.

"Last week I called the DOJ and said I was available. They got right back with an even better offer. I leave for Washington tomorrow. I'll have my power of attorney sent to you right away, so you can close on the house. You'll be good for each other."

They shook hands and said goodbye. Billy stood on the porch and watched through the pine trees as the Saab's taillights pulled out onto the state road. He thought of Caroline. Maybe she would've been happy with Highsmith and her baby. No way to know. He couldn't save her, but he'd found the justice she deserved. Still, in this case he'd lost a part of himself.

The four o'clock Illinois Central rumbled across the back of the property. He remembered how much he liked this life, the translucent haze above the plowed fields at dawn. The distance the eye can take across a pasture that rises and dips and ends in a line of sycamore trees and river birches. He liked mules. He liked their strength and how no one early really owns them. They agree to work until they don't agree then nothing can make them move. The last thing you want in this world is a mule that's mad at you.

Kind of like a homicide cop.

He went inside to stoke the fire just as the rain turned to snow.

Acknowledgments

A difficult novel tests the patience and endurance of the author's mate. Rob Sangster—an excellent novelist in his own right—has fielded endless legal questions, parsed grammar puzzles, and set aside his own tasks to participate in brainstorming sessions at all hours. Thank you, Rob. This book would not exist without you. You're my hero.

Many thanks to extraordinary storytellers Will Heaton, Esq., and Johnnie Walker, retired private investigator, for contributing Southern color, indispensable realism, and sharing years of experience in the legal profession.

Thank you, Lou Putney, Esq., for engaging in "what if" conversations during the early development of the plot. Your knowledge gave the story legs.

To the following friends and acquaintances who so generously provided expertise, early reads, professional opinions, and moral support:

Shaun Bradley; Donnell Ann Bell; Debra Dixon; John Edmunds, Esq.; Kim Fay; Debra Heaton; Phoebe Heckle; VK Holtzendorf; Leslee McKnight, R.N.; Professor Steve Mulroy; Linda Orsburn; Dr. Billy Payonk; Dr. John Ross; Don Sedgwick; Martha Shields; Erica Silverman; Alicia Steeves; and my mother, Doris Turner.

And sincere appreciation to Robert Gottlieb for his support and Tessa Woodward for believing in my stories.

About the Author

Born in Memphis, Lisa Turner is a mystery author who coils the roots of Southern identity around her characters, then pushes them to the edge. She travels between her ancestral home in the Deep South and her writing haven on the wildly beautiful coast of Nova Scotia.

About the Author